Advance Praise

"MacEnulty writes with sympathy, wisdom and—an unexpected blessing—humour."

— *The Guardian*

"MacEnulty shows us the hardships of prison life, the ways of coping, and the compromises in a way no outsider could. We believe what she tells us, as she draws on what were her own experiences on both sides of the system. Switching between the inner vision of each of her characters with skill and ease, she develops the story in spare and immediate prose."

— *Tangled Web*

"MacEnulty's strong writing ability brings it above the emotion to form a full bodied story that leaves a lasting impression. She is able to lead readers into the lives of her characters by slowing revealing their stories, unfolding the details one by one to open a panorama of survival and substance. She draws tears and cheers for her women through deft plotting and in depth character development, a triumph of heart blended with talent. A winning combination."

—Radmore, *Front Street Reviews*

"This multi-dimensional novel explores the characters with insight and compassion."

— Catherine Holden, *Shape Magazine*

"It's terrific ... perfectly paced ... riveting"

—*The Times*

"This is a cracking novel well worth seeking out...first class."

—*Daily Express*

"A spare, disciplined prose that no one will be able to read without thinking of Hemingway. But MacEnulty has made the style her own."

—*The Observer*

The Pink House

The Pink House

Trish MacEnulty

Apprentice House
Loyola University Maryland
Baltimore, Maryland

First Edition

Printed in the United States of America

Paperback ISBN: 978-1-62720-103-2
E-book ISBN: 978-1-62720-104-9

Design: Apprentice House
Editorial Development: Valerie Jean
Editing: Karl Dehmelt

Published by Apprentice House

Apprentice House
Loyola University Maryland
4501 N. Charles Street
Baltimore, MD 21210
410.617.5265 • 410.617.2198 (fax)
www.ApprenticeHouse.com
info@ApprenticeHouse.com

This book is dedicated to
the memory of my beautiful friend,
Kitty Gretsch.

Our share of night to bear,
Our share of morning,
Our blank in bliss to fill,
Our blank in scorning.
Here a star, and there a star,
Some lose their way.
Here a mist, and there a mist,
Afterwards – day!

— Emily Dickinson

From the Journal of Nicole Parks

I promised Lolly that I would write the story of my time in prison. She said I should call it a memoir, so here it is. Some of it is from my journals, and some of it I remember though there is plenty I have forgotten, thank you very much. But what I can't forget is Lolly Johanssen and what she taught us in her classes. Lolly is the person who inspired me to be a writer. Some people go to prison and end up finding God. Lolly helped me to find me.

I was in prison for possession of narcotics and for carrying a concealed weapon—an unregistered firearm at that. But what you need to know about me is that I am not, nor have I ever been, a dope fiend. I have never done any drugs, have never stuck any drug-type substance up my nose or in my arm, and have never even smoked a blunt. To tell you the truth, I pity addicts because their lives do not belong to them. They belong to the drug. I should know because even though I never touched drugs or smoked a nasty cigarette in my life, I had my own addiction: to a man. A smooth as melted chocolate, sweet-between-the-sheets man named Antwan. And that's how I wound up in this place – this prison with its pink buildings up in the middle of Nowhere, North Florida. Sometimes we joke that it's a big old pink palace, and we're all a bunch of ladies in waiting, waiting, waiting.

In some ways prison is just like any place else; there's a game to it.

You can be all cool and rebellious and you can do every single day of your time and then some if they can figure out more charges to put on you. I have seen that happen to many a stupid-ass woman. They sneer at the C.O.s and refuse to do their work and get written up and locked down every day. They know they are the shit. I decided right away that wasn't the way I wanted to play the game, and I got put into a different category. See, even those people who run the prison are willing to cut you a little bit of slack, well not exactly cut you slack. Let's see. How can I say this so that even if it isn't factual, it might be a little bit true? There's a few things, a very few things, that they offer to inmates that aren't so bad. It's mostly for show so they can say they're trying to rehabilitate us. If you can get it in their minds that you are one of those who won't cause any trouble and will make them look good, then you can get in that certain category of inmates who are eligible to take programs. We were a small group, and it wasn't like it looked like a big privilege to the others. I mean, going to a writing class? Most of them would rather slam their heads into a brick wall. But me, I knew that anything a little different from the everyday same ol' same ol' would be good. And I had always liked to write. I kept a journal all through middle school about all the stupid little fights with girls and the crushes I had on various boys. Then in high school my English teacher helped me get a scholarship to the University of Miami, and I was the first one in my family to go to college. Now, I am the first one to wind up in prison.

I come from a respectable family of AME Zion church-going, hard working folks, and I had destroyed their dreams for me. I was their A-student girl, the one who was going to be some kind of professional, a lawyer or something. Unfortunately, I was learning about the law the wrong way. Now, what I wanted more than anything else was to get back on track, to earn the respect of my momma and daddy and somehow regain a portion of all I had thrown away. So when the lady asked if I wanted to take a poetry class, I said, "Yes, ma'am. I'd like that very much." And I somehow felt as if I might get a piece of my life back, a small piece.

So there were twelve of us out of a population of 670 women and the class was on Thursday evenings -- same time as the NA meetings, but you already know that I didn't have to go to that. They didn't have Antwan Anonymous meetings. That first night we stood at the fence of our zone, watching the poetry lady walk up to us. She was a tall skinny white lady with short dark hair and she limped as she carried a satchel case over her shoulder and some kind of box in her hands.

"She walks funny," someone said. "She got a club foot?"

When she got up to us, she smiled this big wide smile as if she knew all of us really well and she was so happy to see us. We forgot about her foot. She handed the box to Lucille and looked around at our faces.

"This is going to be great!" she said.

At first I figured she would be sort of like those professors I'd had in my one year at the university—nice but clueless. I found out pretty quickly that she was different. It was the way she looked at you as if she saw something inside you that you had no idea was there. When she suggested I change a word here or there in my poem, I didn't take offense. I knew she was right. Even the hard cases seemed to like her.

We had class in the library, and for twelve weeks, we couldn't wait till Thursday nights. If our phone privileges fell on that night, we ignored them. She gave us notebooks and colored pens and pencils. Sometimes she'd sneak in some chewing gum. We'd chew all through class and then wrap our spent gum in paper and she'd collect it before she left so no one would know. And for two and a half hours, we'd write about anything we wanted to write about. I wrote poems about my daddy's daddy who was a sharecropper, about my great-great-grandmother who escaped from slavery to live with the Indians in Florida, about growing up near the cane fields, about catching fiddler crabs, about missing Antwan, about the azure waters off Bimini and the funny little man who sold me a straw hat when we were there. I don't know why, but it made me feel free. It took me out of that environment, and it seemed like whatever we wrote, Lolly somehow made us feel that we were on a par with Shakespeare or Langston Hughes. And sometimes she'd bring poems to read to us—poems by Nikki Giovanni or Gwendolyn Brooks or a guy who had been in prison named Ethridge Knight. When we read our own stuff aloud, Lolly would watch us with her big green eyes, and she'd nod or sometimes close her eyes like she was listening to music, some Grover Cleveland type stuff like my dad used to listen to. We thought she was an angel.

One night someone asked her what happened to her foot.

She laughed, took off her shoe and showed it to us. It wasn't real! We were shocked. She rolled up her pants leg and showed us that the whole leg all the way up to her thigh wasn't real.

"This is my Barbie leg," she said. "I had cancer when I was fourteen years old, and they had to amputate my leg just above the knee."

"Oh, my goodness," someone asked. "Do you have those what-do-they-call-em pains where your leg used to be?"

Lolly nodded. "Phantom pains? Yes, sometimes it hurts like hell."

We understood the idea of phantom pains. Some of us had pieces of our hearts amputated, and we hurt where there shouldn't have been anything at all.

Lolly had big thick eyebrows, and when she pretended to be serious, her eyebrows would scrunch up and her freckled face would get crinkly and she made you laugh. Once she showed us that leg, some of us stopped feeling so damn sorry for ourselves. After all, we'd lost our freedom but we would gain that back eventually. She'd never have her leg again. And it made us love her all the more. So, we wrote and wrote, hoping that our abundance of words would make her happy and somehow they did seem to.

Then the program was over and she said she'd try to give us another program that summer. Lolly was true to her word. Only this time instead of writing poetry, we were going to put on a drama production.

Friday, May 20

The door to the Blazer opened. A pair of black stiletto heels landed on the pavement. The feet inside the shoes were nicely arched, the ankles slender, legs shapely. The owner of the legs locked and slammed the door. She looked in the rectangular side mirror at her reflection and noticed a smudge of lipstick outside her lip line, rubbed it off with her index finger, whispered, "what the hell" and turned to go inside the French restaurant where the party was being held. The night was warm as melted candle wax, and there were no stars to be seen in the gray-black sky. As she walked across the parking lot, she ran a finger over the cusp of her right ear, counting the earrings—a nervous habit.

Jen didn't like parties. She usually drank too much, said something wildly inappropriate and wound up going home with someone who was married to someone else. All right, she had only pulled that stunt once, but it had turned into a two-year affair that ended that very day with a phone call from the wife, advising Jen that her attentions would no longer be needed.

"I have forgiven Daniel," she said, "but I promise you, he won't be making any more visits to Tallahassee to see you, and if you show up here in Atlanta, I will eviscerate you." Then she hung up. *Eviscerate was a lovely word*, Jen thought; *equivocate, eliminate, eviscerate*. This all confirmed what a psychic in Cedar Key had told her a few weeks ago: "He will dump you like a load of dirt and never look back."

So, after one failed marriage and an affair that was worse than a failure, here she was at the ripened age of thirty-two without a hell of a lot to show for herself except a ten-year-old Chevy Blazer, a suspended driver's license and a cat with allergies. But she looked great in her little cobalt blue dress, and after a couple of glasses of whatever cheap wine they were serving at this thing, she wouldn't care about the rest.

She was walking along the stepping stones toward the veranda of the rambling wooden house turned fancy restaurant when a voice called, "Dr. J."

She wheeled around. Gary was trotting toward her.

"Doctor?" she asked. "I'm not a doctor yet. I'm still ABD, and when did we get so formal?"

"AB what?"

"All But Dissertation. It means I've done all the course work, passed the tests and now I have to write a damn tome to get the piece of paper."

Gary smiled, and yes, he was disarming, distracting, slightly dismaying. He had been flirting with her relentlessly for the past three months, helping her with the young performers at the Shakespeare Festival, an event which provided the excuse for this "appreciation" party. He was also a student in her theater arts class at the university.

"Sorry . . . Jen. Wow. You look really nice. Great dress."

"Thanks. I've had it forever." Ex-husband Lyle bought it for her. No need to go into that.

"So, you came by yourself?" Gary asked, awkwardly. He was just an inch or two taller than she with a soccer player's physique and soft pink lips that she had never really noticed before.

"Yes. And where's your date?" she asked, gazing at him in the weak light from the restaurant.

"I don't have one." He looked around as if for his invisible playmate.

"Then let's cause a scandal," she smiled and tucked her hand through his arm. "Maybe I'll get fired from my oh-so-high paying adjunct position. I'm sure Amanda Hathaway, my nemesis, will be here, and she's dying for an excuse to make sure I get crossed off the list."

"Why would you get fired? The semester is over, Professor Johanssen. I'm not your student anymore."

"Then why are you calling me professor?" She let her body shift close to his. Together they walked up the steps onto the veranda of the 1920's house that had been converted into the town's showcase restaurant, Chez Pierre.

Sure enough Amanda Hathaway, the grand dame of the theater department, noticed them and said archly when she "accidentally" ran into Jen in the bathroom, "Isn't it past your date's bedtime?"

"I believe it is," Jen had answered and swung out of the bathroom without a backward glance. Amanda Hathaway had been in several Broadway hits in her younger years. She was now a full professor of theater at the university and she had never accepted the idea of someone like Jen actually having a job there, too, even if it was a crappy part-time position. Jen managed to get excellent evaluations from her students, and she'd done the necessary course work. But Jen was a woman. An attractive woman with plenty of talent. And Amanda Hathaway couldn't stand her.

"How old *are* you?" Jen asked Gary as she slid on top of his naked body and ran her tongue along the side of his salty neck.

"I'm twenty-one," he said. Okay, she thought, that's only eleven years difference. She spread her legs and straddled him, not letting him inside her yet, just gently rubbing against him. She wished she hadn't drunk so much, but if she hadn't, certainly she would not be here in her bed with a student. A former student, she reminded herself. She'd already turned in her grades.

He rolled her over and parried like a fencer. Nicely done, she thought and pulled his face toward hers so she could suck his lips. She scraped his back with her nails, she moaned loudly, she thrust back at him. The hell with that bastard in Atlanta and his stupid wife, the hell with her ex-husband, Lyle, and his stupid girlfriend. She was getting royally serviced by a beautiful boy who had made a good solid B. He leaned down and sucked hard on her nipple. Maybe it wasn't too late to change that to an A.

Morning. Her tongue felt thick in her mouth, her body heavy as a camel's. She opened her eyes and saw Gary sitting naked beside her with a cup of coffee.

"Coffee? You made coffee? Who sent you? God?" she asked.

Gary smiled at her.

"My head hurts," she said, pushing herself to a seated position. She was grateful the blinds were closed, and it was dim in the room. At least they'd come to her apartment and she wouldn't have to pee in the bathroom of a 21-year-old male.

"We drank a lot," he said.

"Yes, but you're young and you have a nice, fresh liver," she said, taking the cup from his hands. She knew what she really needed was water to get rehydrated, but caffeine wouldn't hurt right now—open up the capillaries, get the blood flowing. She could hear it whooshing inside her head.

"Are you teaching this summer?" he asked.

"No, I don't know what I'm going to do. But I need to figure out something. The worst thing is . . ." and she stopped to laugh bleakly. "The worst thing is I lost my driver's license. I got a DUI last month and they suspended it. Bastards."

"But you drove your Blazer to the party last night."

"Oops," she said, shrugging.

He lay down on his side and propped his head with his hand. "That was funny what you said last night."

"What did I say?"

"We were talking about that bulimic girl in class, and you said you knew the difference between bulimic and anorexic because the word 'bulimic' had that barfy-bile-burping connotation. And that led you to wondering why 'bucolic' meant something beautiful and peaceful when it sounded like a combination of bubonic and cholera."

"Did I say that? I thought you said it, and it made you seem funny and so fuckable that I had to take you home."

He ran a finger over her thigh in circles. She was sitting up in the bed, looking down at the bristles on his scalp.

"No, you said it, but I'm glad you brought me home anyway," he said, glancing up at her with a question in his eyes. She felt him growing hard, nudging her knee. Oh well, in for a penny, in for a pound, she thought and placed the coffee cup on the end table.

He was easing his way into her, both of them a little tender from the night before when the phone started ringing. Jen closed her eyes tighter. Gary stopped mid-stroke and asked if she had to answer it. She shook her head, and they continued onward. But the rhythm had been broken, and she was unable to have a climax. His orgasm seemed perfunctory, the B student doing his best.

When he rolled off her, he asked if she was feeling all right.

"Oh, fine. Just cut off my head and impale it on a lamp post in front of the bar where we went last night, will you? As a warning to others," she said, turning on to her side. She reached over and picked up her phone to check her voicemail in case the call had been important—someone offering her money or a job. She heard Lolly's voice and deleted the message without listening to it.

"Who was that?" he asked.

"My sister, the biggest pain in the ass who ever lived." She placed the phone back in its cradle.

"I didn't know you had a sister," he said.

"Why should you know that? You're my student for God's sake. Why should you know anything about my personal life?"

"Well, I know that you have a rather large freckle on your ass. That's pretty personal."

Jen laughed and buried her face in her down pillow.

"So tell me about your sister."

"Oh, God. Do I have to?" She rolled over, reached for the coffee cup and drank even though it was no longer hot.

"No," he answered.

"She had cancer."

"Is she okay?"

"It was bone cancer. They wound up cutting off her leg just above the knee." She gazed at the line of light at the bottom of the blinds and remembered being left at home alone during the operation. She had refused to go to the hospital.

"Yikes."

"She was fourteen years old. I was sixteen. I remember thinking, that was so like her to do something like that. Get cancer. I mean, she was already Momma's little darling. Then when she got sick it was like I just disappeared. Everything went to her. We had no money left for anything else. I had to quit my acting classes. I couldn't get new clothes. We sold our car and had to take the bus everywhere."

"But she lost her leg," Gary said hesitantly.

"Exactly. So how could I complain? I mean, I looked like a total and complete asshole. Even now, you're thinking, 'well . . .' but you don't know what it's like. When we were little I always had to take care of her because Mom had to work all the damn time. Our father thought child support was a jock strap for little boys. Then when we finally got a little older, Lolly's cancer turned our lives upside down. And you know what? When Momma died, she left the house to Lolly because she thought I was married and would have my husband to help me. I hadn't told her that I was divorcing him because he was off fucking someone else whenever my back was turned. She figured it out before she died, but she never changed the will."

"You sound bitter." His eyes were narrow, peering curiously at her, but his voice was soft, not judgmental.

"I'm not bitter. I'm hung over. Listen, I'm gonna take a shower. You should probably go home." She kissed him, then stood up, opened her closet door and pulled on a cotton robe.

"Yeah, you're right," he said. He sat up and slid on his jeans. "I'm going back home to Tampa tomorrow. So I guess I won't see you again till the fall."

"Gary, I'm not like one of your little girlfriends. I'm not going to be offended if I don't hear from you again. I mean, it was fun, but let's be real, okay?"

"Okay," he said, awkwardly. "I really enjoyed working with you though. You're really talented and all. I thought the play went great, and you did a great job with those teenagers."

She managed to smile. Anything to get him out of her apartment so she could get cleaned up. She wondered if she'd be able to get anything accomplished at all today.

For one thing she had to figure out how to make some money to keep her rent paid up for the summer. She hadn't gotten any summer classes, but someone had called her from the hippie school nearby and asked if she'd be interested in directing the plays for the summer camp. The pay wasn't much, but if she could scrape up one or two extra odd jobs, maybe act in some instructional videos for the state, she could get by. That was what life was all about, right? Get by. Just survive one day to the next.

The phone rang as Gary was leaving. Jen walked past it and went to take her shower. Her bathroom was small and old-fashioned with little white hexagonal tiles on the floor. The shower faucet had big white porcelain handles. She thought that even if she were rich, she would want a bathroom just like this. She ignored her bleary-eyed reflection in the mirror on the medicine cabinet and turned the water on very hot.

When she got out ten minutes later, she heard a knocking on the door. She slipped on her robe and went to the door in her bare feet and swung it open. In the hallway at the top of the stairs, Lolly stood with light from the window swirling around her, dust motes glittering.

"Jesus, you are persistent, aren't you? I told you, Lolly, I can't come help out with your prison class," Jen said, turning her back and heading into the kitchen for a Diet Pepsi. Lolly followed with that familiar clomping motion. "I've got to earn a living, you know. Some of us don't have free rent."

"I'll pay you," Lolly said.

Jen slowly pivoted on one foot and looked at her sister.

"How much?"

"Is two thousand okay?"

Jen sighed. Two thousand would be perfect.

"How often do we have to go there?"

"Once a week for fourteen weeks. Saturdays. We can ride together. You'll really love it, Jen. I promise you."

Jen opened a package of ginger snaps and ate one.

"How'd you get money?"

"I got a grant," Lolly said.

"How much are you getting paid?"

"Well, my gas is covered," Lolly said.

The martyr, as usual, Jen thought.

"God, you make me feel like such an ogre. I take two grand and you take nothing."

"Look, it's important to me that this program is successful. If it is, there's a possibility of getting some federal grants to do more programs for a lot more people. And you're the only one I know who can help me. I can do poetry and journal writing, but I don't know anything about drama. I need your help, you can teach me, and you need money. Can we do that without a big goddamn fight?"

Lolly had her arms crossed over her flat chest and her head was tilted in an impatient, questioning manner. Jen studied the stance; it signified so much. Could be useful for some future role.

Then she realized what she was agreeing to—one of Lolly's do-gooder projects. Jen didn't want to do it, but what choice did she have?

She sighed, "When does it start?"

"I'm going to meet with the women the first Saturday of June, and we'll officially get underway June 10," Lolly said. "Are you in?"

Jen tried, but couldn't think of a reason to say no.

"You'll have to drive. You know I lost my license," Jen said.

"Deal," Lolly said. Jen held out the bag of ginger snaps, and Lolly took one.

Friday, May 27

Sonya lay face down on the cold tile of the bathroom floor in B dorm of the North Florida Correctional Institution for Women with Magna, a strawberry blond titan, astride her back. Magna's hand, fleshy but powerful, was wrapped around Sonya's neck.

"You see this, Gypsy bitch?" Magna asked, waving a pack of Newports in front of her face. "These are mine. I marked this package 'cause I knew there was a sneaky little thief taking my shit. You better keep your dirty hands to yourself or I'll break each one of your fingers." With the hand that was not wrapped around Sonya's neck, Magna dropped the cigarettes and twisted Sonya's pinky finger out of its socket.

Sonya's eyes bulged. She tried to kick her legs. She'd never been a fighter, but she knew how to take a beating. Then again, no one had ever tried to outright kill her before.

Mercifully, Magna dropped Sonya's finger and unwrapped her other hand from around Sonya's pinched neck. Sonya gasped for air. The big woman pushed herself off Sonya's back, jabbing her ribs with a swift kick as she did so. Sonya grunted. She heard the bathroom door open and close as Magna walked out with the pack of cigarettes. Sonya rolled on her back and tried to breathe.

What had she been thinking, stealing from a gorilla like that? It wasn't like Duke didn't put money into her account. She got the maximum every month. But stealing was so easy; it came naturally. Magna had left that locker door wide open, distracted by a screaming match between two girls in love with the same stud.

Sonya struggled to a sitting position. She noticed a small pool of pee on the floor from where she'd wet herself in fright when Magna first stole up on her and knocked her down. She held her finger gingerly. It felt like it was broken. It had swollen up and was red and throbbing. That night in the hotel – the other time she'd gotten a serious beating – she'd gotten a broken nose and two cracked ribs. But she also had access to plenty of pain killers and plastic surgery that made her nose look better than before. She should probably try to stand up, but the pain and the fear had left her feeling dizzy.

She leaned back and stared at the row of sinks above her, the pipes like chrome arms bent into the wall. She'd been stealing since she was seven years old, letting her hand whip into a cash register while her older sister flirted with the clerk or her uncle pretended to be stealing something from the back of the store or her mother feigned chest pains. In and out, her hand went. Little Flash, they called her. But back then she never got caught.

A pair of black brogans moved into her eyesight. Shit, she thought, instinctively curling in on herself like a snail, but the hand that reached down and touched her shoulder was gentle.

"Hey, Sonya, are you okay?" The voice spoke like someone singing. It was Indian. Sonya looked up gratefully. Something about Indian's presence calmed her. Sonya nodded her head and tried to stand. Indian put her hands under Sonya's arms and helped her up.

"Man, this looks bad," Indian said, taking Sonya's finger in her hand. Sonya wanted to pull away but something about the way Indian held onto it felt so soothing. Indian began slowly massaging the muscles of the hand, her strong fingers working across the ridges of Sonya's hand, and then abruptly she popped the finger back into place. Sonya felt a searing lick of pain, but then almost immediate relief. "Try not to move it for a while. It should be all right."

Sonya was unable to utter her gratitude. Shame lay like a weight on her tongue.

The door opened.

"Alice Jaybird, what is going on in here?" a shrill voice asked. It was that blond officer everyone called C.O. Barbie, sticking her nose as usual where it didn't belong.

Indian turned to the woman with a gentle smile. *She never lets them get to her,* Sonya thought.

"Sonya must have slipped on the floor. There's a wet spot right there. I was just helping her up," Indian said.

C.O. Barbie looked suspiciously at them.

"Are you hurt?"

Sonya shook her head. Her finger throbbed, her ribs ached and her throat felt like it had been set on fire, but she had survived worse than this.

"All right then, one of you clean up that spill and the other needs to get out of here," the C.O. said. "I don't want any funny stuff. If I find out you're up to anything, I'll send both of you to the box."

She turned on her heel and exited the bathroom.

"Are you sure you're okay?" Indian asked.

"I'm all right," Sonya finally rasped.

"Well, try to stay out of trouble," Indian said, patting her back. "It's not worth it. Go get yourself cleaned up. I'll mop this up."

Sonya walked back to her bunk and got some clean underwear, a dress and a towel from her dresser. She wouldn't be allowed to take a shower now, but she could give herself a little birdbath. She wondered how many of these women knew what just happened to her. Were they laughing at her? She hated to be ridiculed more than anything else in the world. It stung like angry wasps. But the Indian, Alice Jaybird, wouldn't laugh at her. And that was somehow a comfort.

After she cleaned herself up, Sonya went to the dayroom where the TV was playing. About fifteen women were passively watching "Law & Order." Daffy, one of the boisterous ones, sat up front and had a running commentary going about how stupid the po-leece on the show were and how the ho's didn't act like any ho's she had ever known. Daffy's comments were more entertaining than the show. Back home Sonya hadn't watched much TV. Duke always had it turned to some sports channel, so she spent her time lounging in her king-size bed reading magazines or playing with the baby. Tomas was the baby's name, named after her grandfather from Warsaw. Little Tomas. Even now she could remember exactly what his chubby little hands felt like in hers. It was so easy to make him smile. He was just beginning to pull himself to a standing position when she had stupidly let herself be taken away from him. Stupid. She had actually wanted to go back to work, had missed it, missed the thrill, that excitement when some chump fell for one of her scams, and it was true that Maria was no good without her. So she had left the baby with Dina, and gone off to do what she did so well, little knowing that she would never hold her baby again. *He won't even know me*, she thought, *next time I see him. He'll be at least four years old, and he won't know his own mommy.*

It was time for the last count before lights off. Sonya stood up with the buzzer but she stayed as close to Daffy and her crowd as she could. She didn't want to see Magna, but there was the big woman scowling at her just outside the door. Sonya turned her head away. She noticed a sign on the bulletin board by the CO's office. "All Inmates Signed up for Drama Class must attend every Saturday through September."

She stared at the sign. Saturdays. That would be good. She needed to be out of this dorm as much as possible. It was probably too late, but she'd go to her classification officer on Monday and see what she could do.

Saturday, June 3

Lolly went outside to inspect her carpet roses in the evening light. She wasn't one for the big fat cultivated roses. She liked lantana, bougainvillea, azaleas, lilies and irises. She liked long, stalky flowers and bunchy flowers like hydrangeas and she loved flowers that came from trees like the voluptuous magnolias and the delicate crepe myrtles. The wisteria were her favorite, but they were mostly faded and gone. She walked through her garden, admiring the blooms. Spring was over, but the summer blossoms were throwing their arms open and letting loose. She stopped to replenish the bird feeder from a sack of seed she carried with her. A couple of cardinals had a nest in the chinaberry tree just outside her bedroom window.

Sometimes she'd see thrushes, finches, sparrows, or blue jays out here. And of course mockingbirds. When she was young, she had loved that book *To Kill a Mockingbird*. But the father character, Atticus Finch (a good bird name), was wrong about mockingbirds. They weren't harmless innocents, those birds. They were as pugilistic a bird as she'd ever seen. She would laugh out loud when she saw a mockingbird chasing down a crow twice its size. She'd even seen one go after a hawk. And they thought nothing, for that matter, about swooping down and dive bombing a dog or a person who came too close to their nests. They were protective, those birds, unlike so many human parents. Oh well, Mama had tried to protect her. But no one can really do it, can they?. Life comes at you in a fury and takes whatever the hell it wants. Just be grateful with whatever it leaves you.

She climbed the steps up to her porch. Her stump was hurting, chafed from wearing her prosthetic all day. She sat down on the swing on the front porch and thought back to her trip to the prison. She had wanted to go the first time without Jen, to meet the new group. Several of them had taken her poetry workshops, but she had some new ones, too. They were so excited they were going to work with a real actress. It looked like a good group. She wondered what Jen would make of them, and what they would make of her.

A tan pickup truck pulled into her driveway. Aunt Jewel got out. With her curly white hair and soft pretty skin, Aunt Jewel looked so much like Lolly's momma had looked before she'd died of a heart attack eight years earlier.

"Hey, darlin'," Aunt Jewel said, coming up the steps of the porch, holding a pie plate. "I brought you some lemon chess pie. I just had an urge to make pie today and thought you might want some."

"Yum, thank you," Lolly said. "Come in and take a load off."

Aunt Jewel plopped down in one of the Adirondack chairs with a heavy sigh.

"It's going to be a long, hot summer when it gets here," she said.

"Mmmm," Lolly said. "I'm sure it will be hot for you."

"Election years tend to be hot." Aunt Jewel sighed again. "Hot and dirty. Where you been today, sugar?"

"Out at the women's prison."

"Oh, you doing that again?" Aunt Jewel asked.

"Yeah, and guess what? Jen's going to come work with me," Lolly said.

"What? Miss High and Mighty is gonna do something for someone else? Well, shut my mouth," Aunt Jewel said. Lolly giggled.

"Oh, I'm paying her or else there's no way in hell she'd come."

"Not out of your own pocket?" Aunt Jewel looked aghast.

"No. The Department of Corrections got a grant, and the woman who wrote the grant really wanted me to try giving a drama program, so I hired Jen."

"I'm surprised they let you in there at all to help those women," Aunt Jewel said, stretching her hands out and examining them. "Especially with a Republican in the governor's mansion."

Lolly stood up and plucked dead leaves off one of the hanging ferns.

"We don't exactly advertise what we're doing. The corrections people love these kinds of programs. It helps with both security and recidivism, and they've got the stats to prove it. But they don't tell the public that they're doing anything that could be construed as coddling."

"That's right," Aunt Jewel said, "'cause we want to make sure those people are just as messed up when they come out as they were when they went in. The mentality of people astonishes me. And they call themselves Christians, which is the funniest part of all. You know I got in a big fight with some of those busybodies at church the other day."

"Why?" Lolly turned toward her Aunt, who now had a mischievous grin on her face.

"Oh, they were going on and on about homosexuals and how they had no business in church. I said, 'Look, Jesus never mentioned homosexuals so therefore he either didn't know about it or didn't care about it. Or he was one.' I think they wanted to burn me at the stake."

"Aunt Jewel, you are so scandalous," Lolly said with a laugh. Aunt Jewel's expression turned peevish.

"Jesus said, 'love thy neighbor as thyself and don't judge others.' What's so damn difficult about that?"

"I don't know, Aunt Jewel. I don't know. People are just scared, I guess."

"Well, I'm going to head home. Come see me soon. I need you to help me put up a new bird feeder. The squirrels tore my last one to pieces."

Aunt Jewel stood up and Lolly kissed her on the cheek.

"Thanks for the pie," Lolly said as Aunt Jewel strode back to her pickup truck.

Lolly picked up the pie from the round metal table where Aunt Jewel had left it and turned to go inside. Sue, a friend from work, had invited her to the movies, but she didn't really feel up to it so she called and canceled. Saturday night and all she wanted to do was to eat some left over Thai food and read a book.

After her dinner she decided to take a bath. Her bathroom was small and covered in green tile. She'd need to redecorate in here, she thought. Maybe make a mosaic. She lit a vanilla-scented candle and undressed, drawing a hot bath. As she eased herself into the water on her one leg, she looked down at her body. How long had it been since a man had touched her? More than a year. *Damn it*, she thought. She used to see a guy named Sean. He was a French horn player, and what he could do with his lips was pretty spectacular. But then he got a symphony job in California and moved away. She missed him. Most men were afraid of her. Was it because of the leg? Or just because she didn't take any crap from them? Being a feminist didn't mean you were dead down there, she wanted to tell them. She leaned her head against the plastic waterproof pillow she'd stuck against the bathtub wall for just this kind of deep, soothing soak.

Her hand drifted toward her breasts. They were small and firm. She'd always been flat-chested even though neither her mother nor her sister were. She thought it had something to do with the radiation they had shot straight at her chest area in order to kill the bone cancer. She closed her eyes and slowly moved her hand over the tissue. She felt something odd. So she squeezed it with her fingers. She opened her eyes and squeezed again. She sat up and looked down at her left breast. It didn't look different, but it definitely felt different. She felt it again. There was a hard pebble inside. The water suddenly felt cold and she got out of the tub, wrapping herself in a terry robe. She refused to touch her breast again. Instead she went into her living room and sat down on the green and black couch and watched television until she fell asleep.

From the Journal of
Nicole Parks

It was here in prison I discovered my gift. The gift of listening. They come to me. White, Black and in-between, young and old, vicious killers and women with no more business in here than your kindergarten teacher. They tell me things. The loudmouths and the quiet ones, too.

I observe all from my throne (my bunk square in the middle of the room). I know every secret. I know that sweet old grandma in the corner is the source of the compound marijuana. I know that mean Magna cries late at night and worries about her sick mother. I know that Viola Carpenter is a little crazy behind her Bible-reading front and that the chubby Jewish American princess from Miami is one generation away from West Virginia hillbillies on her mother's side.

This place is some kind of madhouse. What I do is watch and listen. We got more intrigue in this place than on six Spanish soap operas combined. The girl who bunks across the aisle from me is a gypsy named Sonya. The gypsy has dark brown hair and she looks like she is getting ready to sprout wings and fly away at any given moment. She doesn't say much, that one, but her eyes talk. Her eyes are dark as wells and they peep out through her eyelashes at just one person—Indian.

Now that's funny to me because Indian isn't exactly Big Stud on

Campus. Indian must be in her late twenties and she's done a lot of time. Killed a liquor store clerk when she was fifteen, they say. A robbery gone bad. You got to wonder what someone is doing out robbing people when they are only fifteen years old. But I like Indian. Yesterday she asked me if I was going to take the drama class. I said, no, there was way too much drama around here already. Then Daffy, who was chomping on a bag of Hot & Spicy Pork Skins, said to me, "Your girl Lolly is the one running it," and I said, "For real?" She said, "Yep." So I went to my lazy-ass classification officer and told her she needed to sign me up for Miss Lolly's class.

I am excited. If Lolly is teaching it, then we'll for sure do some writing and I can shine like I always do. I wonder if we'll be writing plays and whatnot. I've never written one before. Speaking of drama, back to the Drama of B Dorm—so Sonya's heart beats for Indian, but Indian treats everyone the same. She stays out of trouble, doesn't get on other people's nerves, and laughs about things that seem to piss off everyone else. I can't help but wish I had her – what's the expression? — savoir faire? That may not be right, but it sounds good. Meanwhile, Panther, that black as midnight, slinky cat with the skinny hips like a boy's, has a thing for Sonya and is always trying to pester her.

"How come you won't go with me, Gypsy girl?" Panther asks her, and Sonya just sort of sneers and says, "Don't call me out of my name."

"Okay, but you are a gypsy, aren't you? One of those t.c.—traveling criminals, right?"

"Not a traveler. They're Irish. My family is from Poland," the gypsy says.

I myself didn't know that any gypsies came from Poland, but I guess they come from all over. Something in the blood makes them wander around cheating old ladies out of their savings. Some life. I tell you what. I have gotten an education in this place, way more than my two semesters at the University of Miami, F-L-A. But, of course, it's not nearly as much fun. The guys at Miami were off the chain. And the dorm was different, too, but in some ways it's not so different. Having to live with white girls. Those were rich white girls, and the ones here are mostly poor. Not all of them, mind you, but you got lots of girls in here who would have been considered nothing but trailer trash by those saddity little rich bitches down there, all driving their SUVs and their Beamers that they got for their 16th birthdays. I didn't really fit in all that good, being on scholarship and all. Maybe I wanted to fit in and that's how I got hooked by Mr. Antwan with all his paper.

There isn't much excitement going on in here for me. C.O. Barbie seems to be looking for something to write me up about. Not just me. But everybody. Yesterday Daffy left a towel on her bunk and bam— write up time! And the other day a dang button popped off my dress. She wouldn't even let me go to work. "Go to the laundry and get a button put on that dress," she says. So I go to the laundry and they don't have any buttons, and then I'm stuck. So finally I was able to talk the laundry C.O. out of another dress. Most time I try to ignore the C.O.s. Instead I think about my man, Antwan. I know it is hard for him to be out there and not messing around with all those women who want him. He is like some kind of Black Cary Grant—women chase him down with a lasso. Or that's how it always seemed. I wonder will he be waiting for me when I get out. It looks like I could go to work release in the fall. That's not that far away.

Wednesday, June 7

Sonya worked in the kitchen. It was hard work. She had never been much of a cook. She and Duke usually went out to eat or got pizza or take out Chinese. Or they went to her parents' apartment and ate the pirogues and sausage that her mother, Dina, made. Dina was a fantastic cook. And still a glamorous woman. She liked to wear a fur stole over her perfectly matched suits. In Florida there wasn't much opportunity to wear fur, but when they traveled north, the minks always came out of the storage closets.

"Dress like a million bucks, babee, and they will never suspect you of nothing," Dina used to say. It was her mother's idea that she should marry Duke who was older by a good ten years. He was not a pretty boy. He was not funny. But he was quick with his hands and with his wits. Not quick enough though. Not quick enough to save her when the old man they were robbing turned out to be a retired Seminole County sheriff. Oh, Florida. What a horrible place to be stuck in. She wanted to be on the road or back up in Montreal where it was cool. Mostly she wanted to be with little Tomas. She knew Duke and her mother were taking good care of him, and soon he would be learning the ways of their kind. Rule number one: "Never talk to strangers." Yes, that meant something different for their children.

It was still dark as she walked to the kitchen, preparing for her workday. The only good thing about being in the kitchen was that your shift ended earlier than the other work shifts and you could sometimes take a shower in peace. She and Curly, a young Jewish girl from Miami, were on duty that morning, making grits and a huge pan of powdered eggs. Most of the other women got fat on this prison food, but the sight of it sickened Sonya to the point that she had lost probably ten pounds. Panther was making biscuits.

"I hate the weekends," Sonya said as she stirred the bright yellow eggs. "Everybody has visitors but me."

"I don't have much in the way of visitors either," Curly said. "They got us all the way up in the damn boondocks here. My people can't come up here all the way from Miami every other weekend for the next twenty years."

"They say they are going to change this into a men's prison soon and then maybe you'll get sent to Broward. That's near Miami, right?"

"A lot closer than this. How come you don't get any visitors?"

"My family," Sonya said, glancing around, "they all have warrants on them. Except for my baby boy and that's only 'cause he's too young."

"Your whole family? Damn, you must have had a helluva upbringing," Curly said with a laugh. "Hey, how's your record here? Got any write ups?"

"No, not yet," she said, thinking of the ambush by Magna and how that could have turned worse than it was if the C.O. had found them. Idiot Magna—willing to go to the box for a pack of smokes.

"You ought to sign up for this drama class. That way you won't be moping around the dorm." Curly poured the grits into the boiling water.

"I asked my classification office if I could take it. She said it's too late to sign up. Who else is in it?"

"Lucille, of course. She's such a smarty pants."

Sonya laughed to hear such a quaint expression come from the Miami girl's mouth.

"And Nicole. Another college girl. But you don't have to be all that smart. I got in, and all I have is a GED. Indian is signed up, too."

Sonya didn't look up. She didn't want to give her feelings away. She had never been in love with anyone before, certainly not with Duke. She wasn't even sure if this was love. How could she be in love with a woman? What did women do together? Well not much, if they were in prison, because opportunities for privacy were rare. At least her ignorance in those matters would not be much of a problem. Then again, as far as she knew, Indian had no girlfriends. But she had been locked up so long. How could she not have given in at some point? Indian was an enigma and that's probably what attracted Sonya.

"You know, there was some girl from A dorm signed up, but she just got transferred to work release. You should go find out if you can take her place."

"Maybe I'll check it out," Sonya said. "What is drama? Acting? I can act. Boy, can I act."

She thought back to the many hits they had made—she and Maria, her cousin. She was always the one to approach the victims. Some blue-haired old lady out clipping her roses. It was so easy to strike up a conversation with them. She never knew what she was going to say until suddenly there she was, looking into the old eyes, smiling and asking about the woman's roses, her grandchildren, her late husband. And then Maria would ask if she could use the bathroom. And the mark would be so caught up in Sonya's spell that she would hardly know what she had said, didn't know she had given Maria permission to go inside her house and riffle through her belongings while Sonya kept her distracted.

Of course, it was even easier with the old men. Such lonely old talkers. Damn, you couldn't get them to shut up. There was one who had cared for Sonya so much that he emptied out his bank account of twenty-seven grand to help her get a kidney operation, which she never needed and never got, but he was so happy when she came back a couple months later and said the surgeons had healed her. Sonya almost felt sorry for him, the old fool. The thing that made her good was that she got caught up in the game. She actually liked these people while she was talking to them, befriending them or whatever. She had enjoyed the old man—Roger, that was his name—she had enjoyed his company, and played checkers with him and imagined that he was her grandfather. Her real grandfather had been one of the toughest gangsters on the streets of Warsaw. Funny, what an accident of birth could do for you. The children of presidents became politicians. The children of movie stars were now movie stars, too. And the children of criminals, well, they became criminals. There was not one single legit person in the whole clan. She was like her mother and her grandmother. She was like her cousin and her sister-in-law. And when they needed somewhere to hide, there was always an aunt or uncle willing to spare a bedroom or a pull-out sofa.

She looked over at Curly. Curly's father was not a criminal. He was a wealthy businessman, just the sort of person she would have loved to swindle, but more often than not the people who lost their money to the Yakowski clan were not wealthy, and they did not know how to keep their money from slipping from their fingers into the pockets of others.

The kitchen crew had to wait to feed the compound before they could eat. Sonya made coffee and Panther and Curly filled the bins. A very fat c.o. named Dawkins was their supervisor. She usually sat on a stool that her enormous buttocks draped over and ordered the women about. One of the male guards came in and strolled past the line, picking up a biscuit for himself. It was finally light outside. The buzzer rang and everyone from the kitchen crew got on the line to serve.

The doors opened and the first ones came in. It was always the same—the younger more aggressive ones race-walking in with the others stacked up behind them. Alice Jaybird was never in a hurry. She came loping in about halfway through the line.

"Hey, watch what you doin'," a dark-eyed woman said to Sonya when a bit of egg fell off her tray.

"Oooh, Mariposa, don't read the poor kitchen girls," her friend said.

"I'm not reading them. Just ol' clumsy fingers here," the one called Mariposa said with an evil glance at Sonya. Sonya was taken aback. She didn't know this woman. Why was she so nasty?

Mariposa had short black hair and a round face. She was muscular, and something about her looked like a little prize fighter. She moved on, shooting Sonya one last hard glance.

"Nevermind," Panther said to her. "She ain't shit, Gypsy."

Sonya shrugged.

On the way back to the dorm, Panther walked beside her.

"You want to watch TV with me tonight in the dayroom?"

"I don't like you like that," Sonya said to Panther.

"Are you some kind of racist?"

Sonya didn't answer her. It was true she had been brought up not to associate with Africans. But she wasn't supposed to associate with Irish or Spanish either. Only Polish. She was getting more close exposure to people in prison than she had in her whole life.

"So that's it, huh?" Panther said.

Sonya turned to her irritably.

"Can't I just not like you? Leave me alone, girl."

"I got your girl," Panther muttered.

Sonya pushed her heavy hair behind her ears and strode into the dorm.

Friday, June 9

The office Lolly shared with a woman named Sue was on the ninth floor of the Department of Education building. Sunshine poured into the room, and through the windows Lolly could see the tops of oak trees, their branches like green capillaries covering the city, and the black roads generally filled with cars. To her left she could see the towering Capitol Building where the budget-cutting trolls lived.

Sue came in the office, carrying a stack of papers to be filed. The two of them were in charge of various webpages for the department, and they also helped devise computer programs for distance learning. It was a good job. The pay was decent enough for a single person, but best of all, over the years the department had become a haven for a number of artsy types who needed work after a decade or so of college. The halls of the DOE building were filled with overqualified, underpaid people who were generally happy to have benefits and be able to wear their Birkenstocks on casual Fridays (and many other days of the week as well). Conversations around the break room tables were often about the latest art opening at Railroad Square or poetry reading at the Warehouse or the new independent film that you just had to see. Sometimes, especially this year, the conversation drifted toward politics. They were generally a liberal bunch, and many of them didn't think it was an insult to be called a "tree-hugger." They liked trees.

These were also people who had interests outside of the job. Sue owned a coffee shop with her husband. Others were artists or poets or short story writers. One man in the office next to her edited one of the most prestigious literary magazines in the southeast. Of course, he didn't get paid for it. So most of them knew about Lolly's work with the women prisoners. "Lolly's women." They had read the poetry the women wrote, and her supervisor turned a blind eye when she needed to use the copier to copy some materials for her women.

"Hey, are you going out for lunch?" Sue asked.

"No, I need to do some personal research on the computer," Lolly said. "So I'm going to use my lunch hour."

"Oh, okay. Can I bring you something back?"

"No, I'm not that hungry," Lolly said. "I'll get some fruit from the cafeteria later."

"You seem happy today," Sue said. "I mean you're always happy, but what a bright smile you have."

She walked out of the office. Lolly hadn't even realized she was smiling. *No,* she thought, *that smile just means I'm absolutely terrified.* All week she'd had this nagging uncertainty, this amorphous fear lurking in the back of her mind; the words "what if?" softly echoing.

Lolly sat down at her computer. She typed in the word "osteosarcoma" and hit "search." There it was: "more common in young people ages 10 to 25." About two in one million people a year get it. How nice to be so special. None of this information was new to her. She had lived it. She had lived those symptoms—the way her leg had turned red and thick. The pain that kept her awake at night, and her mother's assurances, "probably nothing, but let's go see the doctor anyway." They x-rayed her and biopsied her and then left her lying on the exam table, the doctor in his white coat and serious voice saying he needed to talk to her mother alone. And the look on her mother's face as she came out of the doctor's office as if every good thing had been wiped off the earth. Seeing her mother's face, forlorn and foreign, Lolly had experienced an unspecified terror to add to the pain, and she tasted it in her mouth—dry and metallic.

Then there had been months of doctors, tests, hospitals, her body like something that didn't belong to her, just something to poke, prod, scan and shoot radiation at, something to dump chemicals in. So that when the doctor stood in the hospital room as her mother clutched her hand and said, "We have to remove Lolly's leg," she was tingly with numbness. She turned and smiled – smiled! – at her mother and said, "Don't worry, Mama. I'm brave."

Looking back on it, she understood that she had no other way to separate herself from the horror that was happening to her and that worse than anything was the anguish of her mother. It must have been a terrible thing indeed to face the possible loss of her child.

So she smiled at her mother and later she smiled at the kids at school when they whispered about her. She smiled at the adults who for some reason treated her as if she were somehow at fault, somehow to blame for not being perfect. They had. Not all of them, of course, but too many. Before high school, she thought she'd follow in her sister Jen's footsteps and go into drama. She had gone to see Jen in all the high school plays, and Jen was usually the lead role. Jen was pretty and even popular in high school though she wasn't one of that elite clique of rich kids. Still she was accepted by everyone and her dare-devil exploits gave her a certain cachet in the school. Teachers liked Jen and ignored the smell of pot smoke or the fact that she sneaked off campus to be with one of her boyfriends. But treatment for Lolly was sharply different. When Lolly auditioned for the school production of *Oklahoma*, the theater teacher had grimaced and said to her, "I'm sorry, but what were you even thinking? You can't be on stage."

Lolly remembered the feeling, like a sucker punch, her breath hard to find, but still she smiled. She smiled all the way to the girls' bathroom where she broke down and sobbed in a stall by herself until someone knocked on the door and asked if she was all right. Lolly opened the door, preparing to smile, and saw the school cleaning lady, and instead Lolly fell into her arms and wept. That day Lolly made her alliance, not with the blessed people who strode the earth obliviously crushing anything in their path, but with the invisible ones who cleaned up their toilets and swept their debris.

The Internet yielded no answers as to whether osteosarcoma could come back in some other form. It made no sense anyway. They had cut off the leg, removed the shin bone where the cancer had spread to the blood vessels. The cancer was gone. Lumps in the breast could be anything, a benign fibrous something caused by caffeine. She got up from the computer and took the elevator downstairs to the lobby to go outside and sit in the fresh air for a few minutes before her lunch break was over.

The lobby of the building was filled with light from large plate glass windows overlooking Gaines Street and the floors of the building sparkled. A security guard named Frank sat behind the desk in the lobby and waved at her.

"Hi, Frank," she said. On the walls were bright colorful paintings by school students. She loved working here. She loved her life. It had taken a long time, but she had overcome the emotional ravages of her early years. She liked the person she had become. She liked the way she laughed, the way she felt curious about everything, the way most people warmed up to her slowly but permanently.

She went outside and crossed the busy street to a park where she liked to sit on a bench underneath an oak tree. But as she came closer to the bench, she saw someone was already there. Oh, it was Rusty, a friend of hers who worked in the investigations department. Rusty was lanky with longish dark hair. On weekends he played bass guitar in an alternative rock band. He was always kind, and she enjoyed his friendship. It had been so sad last year when his wife died in a car accident. She hoped he wouldn't mind if she came over and sat with him. She approached him and smiled.

Saturday, June 10

Jen rode in the passenger seat of Lolly's Honda Civic and stared out at the passing scenery. Highway 90 wasn't much to look at except for the crepe myrtles waving in colors of white, pink and purple like girls in dresses. The sisters hadn't said much to each other, though she could tell that Lolly wanted to talk about what they'd be doing that day.

Finally Jen asked, "Why do they call it a wellness program?"

"You can never say you are there for any kinds of arts programs. The legislators would have conniption fits if any coddling of the worthless criminals took place. I am there for 'wellness.' But that's accurate enough. Words can be good medicine."

"I guess they don't see how the arts by themselves could be a benefit," Jen said.

"Are you nervous?" Lolly asked.

Jen shrugged and asked, "Shouldn't I be? I mean, these are convicted murderers and thieves, right?"

"Some of them are, but you know, that's not what they do every day. Most of them just got into some kind of bad situation and couldn't figure out how to get out. I try not to judge them."

"Well, it's not like I've been an angel my whole life," Jen admitted. She'd never told Lolly about her Miami years, and yet she imagined that Lolly must have figured out some of it by now. There were whispers, rumors around Tallahassee. That's probably why she couldn't get a fulltime teaching job and had to scrape up a living as best she could. To think of all the thousands of dollars she'd made and blown in those few short months: right up her and Lyle's noses.

"What I think you're going to find is that these women are incredibly talented and willing to take risks. You'll love them. I know I do," Lolly said.

"You would, Lolly," Jen said. "I just hope you don't let any of them take advantage of you."

Lolly glanced over at her. Lolly had thick Frida Kahlo eyebrows and freckles across the bridge of her nose.

"How much advantage can they take? They're locked up. Some of them for decades," Lolly said.

Jen didn't answer.

"You'll be amazed at how talented they are," Lolly said. "I have one who is a really good writer. I actually sent a couple of her poems out after the poetry class and they were taken by a literary magazine. And last week, when I met with them, I brought in a monolog from The Trojan Women. Wow. Some of them were really good. Of course, some of them are not so good, but we'll find things for them to do."

Jen mused. "But they're convicted felons, right? I guess I'm having a hard time imagining this. Do they have any education?"

"Some of them have been to college. In fact, Lucille has a master's degree. They all have to have a GED or high school diploma to take the program. That's their rules, not mine. Personally I would open it to everyone, but that's not the way it works."

"What about behavior problems?"

"We shouldn't have many problems. They all want to be in the program. It's like a form of escape for them, and if they screw up, they won't get to come back. You have to understand they only let twelve women in and those are probably going to be among the more peaceful."

"So, no murderers?"

"Oh, we'll have a couple of murderers, but, Jen, it wasn't like they were going around murdering people every day of their lives. One time. One moment of their life. People make mistakes. You ought to know that."

"Bite me."

"God, why do you take everything so personally?"

Jen didn't answer.

Lolly turned off the state road and drove down the long winding road that led to nowhere but the prison. Jen soon saw the turrets and the shining silvery gleam of the fences. A thick bank of purple and black clouds hung over the prison but gold fingers of sunlight snuck around and under the clouds. The parking lot was in full sun.

"One of the women once told me that it rains right on top of them," Lolly said. "She said, 'You can see the sun shining just on the other side of the fence while we're standing in the durn rain.'"

The heat rose up from the tar of the parking lot in waves.

"Let's go," Lolly said. She grabbed her satchel and headed toward the Control Room. Jen followed. "Be ready to smile. You always smile at the guards. And they never smile back. But if you don't smile, you're likely to stand in between fences forever: prison's purgatory. Or else they'll decide you need to be searched. Every time the protocol is different."

They stood at the window and Jen noticed a big barrel of sand beside the gate. A sign said it was for "spent casings." She wasn't sure the logistics of the barrel and the spent casings (from shotguns?) but it held a violent significance. Perhaps there was reassurance in that— you knew you were entering a world where you were powerless, completely at the mercy of those who wore guns and pushed buttons that swung open the steel gates. You always knew where you stood. Lolly slid her driver's license through the metal slot toward a woman dressed in a brown uniform, and Jen followed suit with her faculty I.D. since she didn't have a license for the time being.

"Lolly Johanssen with the Department of Corrections Wellness Program. This is Jen Johanssen. We're scheduled to give a workshop today," Lolly explained. "We should be on your list."

The woman looked at Lolly's driver's license, then pushed a button, and Lolly and Jen walked through the first gate. It clanged shut behind them. They now stood in a six-foot square area between two locked gates, looking out at a few pink buildings with flowers planted in front of them. Lolly pointed to the buildings

"That area is called Zone One," Lolly said. "There's a library, the drug treatment center where my classes always take place and a few classrooms for GED students. Just beyond that other fence down there is the compound."

Jen noticed that prisoners, identifiable by their shapeless gold shifts or their blue jeans and blue workshirts, all walked right along the edge of the road. She asked Lolly about it.

"See that yellow line about a foot from the edge of the road? The women have to walk in that one-foot area or they'll get written up. After three 'write ups' they could wind up in the box or lose their gain-time. On the other hand, *we* are allowed to walk all over the road."

"It seems an odd and arbitrary means of control," Jen said. "And what is 'gain-time'?"

"Like time off for good behavior."

They stood at the second gate waiting for it to open. Thunder drummed in the distance. A group of women in blue began strolling up from the compound. A tall African-American woman was in front.

"There's Lucille," Lolly said.

Lucille waved, and Lolly waved back from behind the gate at the other end of the road.

"She's wonderful. A little boisterous, but very warm. When I had her for poetry, she used to write about fishing and cooking and a life far in her past. Nicole is with her. Now, there's a diamond in the rough."

"Is she the one you mentioned before?" Jen asked.

Lolly nodded and then said impatiently, "When are the guards going to open the damn gate and let us through?"

"You're probably the only person in the world who actually wants to get inside a prison."

The gate finally opened and they stepped through. Jen jumped as the gate clanked behind her, but Lolly didn't even seem to hear it. She was intent on the crowd of women in blue work shirts and jeans standing in front of the low cinder block building to the right. She marched toward them with Jen following.

"Hey, Ms. Lolly," a short cute young woman with caramel-colored skin said.

"Hey, Nicole. Hey, everybody," Lolly smiled big and waved.

"We're so glad to see you," the tall woman said.

"I'm glad to see y'all, too, Lucille," Lolly said.

Jen felt an odd curiosity. She was used to being the center of attention. Hadn't she craved attention all her life? Some goddamn dime-store psychologist said it stemmed from the birth of Lolly which was followed shortly thereafter by the desertion of their father. Of course, Jen could barely remember when their father lived with them. But there had been a few sporadic visits that ended when she was eleven. "Some men aren't cut out for fatherhood," her mother said and left it at that. But what, Jen had wondered, would he have done if there'd only been one little girl to take care of, not two.

All of it, of course, had been aggravated by Lolly's cancer. Well, maybe the therapist was on to something. Nothing made Jen happier than to be looked at and fawned over. That was how Lyle and Irv had persuaded her to take off her clothes and have sex in front of a camera crew. But she found that it wasn't the same as an audience's applause. It wasn't the same thing at all.

Now she was not the center of attention. Once again it was Lolly. She wondered what these women saw in her goofy younger sister. They were watching her with sharp, inquisitive eyes.

"This is Dr. Jen, everybody," Lolly said. Lolly had warned Jen that she had to use some sort of title, but Jen didn't like it. The whole 'doctor' thing felt pretentious, especially since she hadn't technically gotten the degree. But one of the women—the tall one who had big freckles across her reddish-toned face, the one Lolly had addressed as "Lucille"–solved the problem.

"Hey, Doc," she said with a big grin.

Jen grinned back. "Doc. I like that."

Jen was swept up in impressions of faces. As she walked in, a woman who was distinctly Native American with thick black hair and large brown eyes said, "Welcome."

"Thank you," Jen said.

"Oh, Alice," Lolly said. "I'm so glad you signed up for the class."

"Well, I'm not much for acting, but I thought I could help with the sets and stuff like that," Alice answered with a sort of humility that made Jen suspect she had gifts beyond the ordinary.

"Oh, Lolly," the short woman said. "We missed you all week long. I've been writing some poems and I want you to see them."

"Nicole be always with her face in that journal of hers, Ms. Lolly," another woman chimed in. This woman had very dark black skin and large teeth in an enormous smile.

"Shut up, Daffy," Nicole said. Now the one with the killer smile had a name. A very quiet brown-skinned woman, who looked like a librarian, followed them. And a short blond white girl with a swagger came behind her. Then a couple of Spanish women and a slightly aloof woman who looked Middle European. There was something so ordinary looking about them all that Jen felt ashamed about any misgivings she'd had.

They filed into the room. Jen felt as if she were following Lolly's entourage as the women crowded around her, talking about what kind of week they had.

Lolly was clearly in control as she sat in the circle of women.

"We're going to open up with a quick writing exercise. Then I'll introduce our guest to you and we can start learning something about how to make plays. Does that sound good?" Lolly asked.

The women nodded.

Lolly and the women were soon writing furiously on sheets of paper that Lolly had handed out. They spent about ten minutes writing and then sharing what they had written. Lolly seemed to have something insightful to say about each piece. Then she turned to Jen with her wide smile. Jen felt she was looking at a complete stranger.

"Jen, I mean Doc, is going to be working with us to help us learn some acting techniques, and she is also going to help us put together our production. So I'll work with the writers and she'll direct the skits or whatever it is we decide to do. Doc has been working on her doctorate degree in Theater Arts from Florida State University. She's also an accomplished actress. You may have seen her in that *Pizza Delight* commercial? Anyway, she does tons of theater around Tallahassee and just recently directed the Young Actors Troupe in some Shakespeare adaptations for the Shakespeare Festival."

Jen was glad Lolly left out the dipsomania and sleeping with a married man part out of the brief intro. Lolly looked at her expectantly, and Jen figured it was show time.

"One thing actors always do is warm up," Jen said. "And this exercise will help me learn your names as well. It's called Sound and Motion. So, if you'll all stand up. Stay in your circle, though. Now what we do is each person says their name out loud and follows it with some kind of motion. Then the rest of the group has to say the name and do the exact same motion. Like I'll say, Doc," Then Jen lifted her arms and twirled once. "Now you have to say Doc and do the same thing I just did."

The thing Jen liked about this exercise was that she could nearly always identify even in this simple exercise who had the brassiness and the imagination for good theater and who was going to need work.

No surprise that Daffy with the big smile could project and come up with a fun dipping dance motion. Alice, the Native American, was a little more shy but was obviously well liked. Nicole added a snap and a strut to her motion but her voice didn't carry well. There were various levels of enthusiasm – a key ingredient for theatrical success – but one surprise was the quiet woman who looked vaguely middle European. She had been slightly aloof up till the instant she announced her name, "Sonya," with a flourish and then did a few moves from a belly dance.

"Good," Jen said with a smile when they were done. Lolly seemed to be happy with the results as well, and Jen had a tiny hope that perhaps this group of women could create something exciting, something beautiful, together.

Her initial impressions were confirmed in the next exercise—an improvisation in which one character is hiding something from another.

"Lolly and I will demonstrate," she said. "Okay, Lolly, there's something you're hiding. Something you don't want me to know."

Lolly nodded. They stood at the end of the room with the women forming a half-circle around them.

"What's wrong?" Jen asked.

"Nothing. Why do you ask?"

"You seem distracted."

"I'm not distracted."

"You just poured salt into your coffee," Jen said, indicating an invisible cup of coffee. She noticed the women register the pretense. You could tell when an idea traveled, and this was a new idea for them.

"Um, that's part of a new diet," Lolly answered. "Haven't you heard about it? I saw it on Oprah."

"Really?" Jen asked, skeptically. "You don't watch Oprah."

"You don't know what I do when you're not around. I watch Oprah, Sally Jesse Raphael, Montel. All of them."

"Why is that? Is something wrong?"

"No, I told you nothing is wrong."

"There must be if you're watching all those personal advice shows."

"I just find them entertaining."

"Really? Hey, what's this? A letter?" Jen picked up an imaginary envelope. Lolly reached out and snatched it from her hands.

"None of your business."

"But it is my business," Jen said and then lowered her voice, "I'm your husband."

Several of the women laughed in surprise. Lolly pretended to put the envelope behind her back.

"Are you going to tell me?"

"It's test results from a biopsy I had. I have a lump in my breast."

"Why didn't you tell me?"

"I didn't want you to leave me?"

"Leave you? I'll never leave you. Open the envelope. What do the results say?"

The women leaned forward, watching in anticipation as Lolly pretended to open the envelope. Then she smiled.

"Curtain," Jen said. Then she dropped out of character and faced the women. "That's how we signify the end. You don't want to drag the scene out too long. It's something you sort of develop a feel for, so until you get the hang of it, I'll call curtain for you. But do you get the idea? Good. I have a stack of cards here with secrets on them that you can use for your improv or you can make up your own. Okay, let's have two volunteers."

From the Journal of Nicole Parks

In my dream I was having dinner with my mom in a Paris restaurant. I'd never been to Paris before, but for some reason I was there in my dream at this little café on the rue something or other, eating plate after plate of delicious pastries all dripping with cinnamon and chocolate and vanilla icing. And I was saying to my mom, "Oh, you don't know how much I've missed this sweetness."

Something woke me up out of this nice dream. Someone in the dorm was moaning. The longing I felt just moments earlier turned into raw fear. Who was making that god-awful sound? It sounded like a ghost, like the dorm itself was haunted. A chill clenched the back of my neck and a shiver traveled down my body from my scalp to my toes. I finally raised my head out of the bed and that's when I thought I'd faint from sheer terror. Someone was floating over in the corner of the room. I grabbed that ugly green wool blanket and pulled it up to my chin. Quiet as I could be, I kept watching it and slowly I started to realize it wasn't a ghost. It was Viola Carpenter sitting up in her bunk. It looked like she was fighting someone.

Finally, she fell back on her bunk and the moaning ceased. It took me a long time to fall back asleep after that. Viola's moaning was just one more reminder that there were lives here I couldn't even begin to imagine.

After that I couldn't help but keep an eye on Viola. I noticed that she forever seemed to be losing things—her glasses, her coffee cup, everything but her Bible that she toted everywhere with her. She was quiet and ladylike, but not exactly approachable. I was surprised she had signed up for the drama class. She didn't seem the type but she had come to class and participated willingly so maybe she was and I just couldn't see it.

One Sunday morning I got dressed up for church. I put on my make up extra careful—we're allowed to have make up if we buy it from the canteen where the mascara is almost seven dollars, so you don't let it out of your sight ever—and my one good pair of black shoes. I wore a painted silk scarf around my neck that I'd made in a crafts class and they had let us keep. I took special care with my hair, combing it in a flip down on my neck. It's funny what a woman can do to make herself beautiful with nothing. Daffy was just as bad as me. We liked to dress for church and the two of us were in the bathroom primping when Viola came in, and I felt a burst of inspiration.

There was a row of sinks along one wall and a couple mirrors across the room on the opposite wall. I watched her bend over the sink, brushing her teeth nice and thorough like when out of my mouth came an invitation.

"Viola, why'd you come sit with me and Daffy in church today?" I asked.

Daffy's jaw dropped. Viola spit into the sink and looked up into the mirror. I could see her face in the reflection and she could see me. She still had a little spot of toothpaste on her bottom lip.

"Thank you," she said in some sort of island accent and wiped the toothpaste away with a wet washcloth. Daffy's mouth had closed but her eyes were wide and looking at me like I had lost my mind. Viola was a bit older than we were and she just wasn't part of our clique, but I wanted to find out about her. It's an urge some people have that makes you want to know, need to know about other people.

So Viola, Daffy and I signed out of the dorm and walked to chapel on that brilliantly sunny Sunday morning. Lucille didn't come, claiming she had a toothache, but she was just being lazy and sleeping in, Sunday being the only day you could do that.

Now prison churches never have a problem with attendance like some free-world churches do, and I believe I have never been so close to God as when I was locked up. For one thing you just don't have the same distractions, and you are not under any illusion that you have the slightest bit of control over anything in your life. So when we sang, "And He walks with me and He talks with me and He tells me I am his own," I could really believe it.

We had a beautiful chapel at our prison: pews made of a glossy light-colored pine and a high A-shaped ceiling, paneled in wood. The floor was carpeted in bright red and the stage area had a simple podium and a place for flowers. This was one of the reasons I loved to go to church because for a few hours every week I didn't feel like I was in prison. Just like when we had the classes with Lolly. It was a form of escape.

That day the preacher was talking about how God is looking for the fruits of the Spirit not the nuts. Of course some of those nasty-minded women took it the wrong way and were giggling. Okay, I will admit that often as not I used to sit and daydream about Antwan during that preacher's boring-ass sermons (Jesus, forgive me). And I always went back in my head to this one scene: Late at night Antwan and me walking along the beach, me wearing a sarong and him with his shirt off and pair of rolled up white trousers. I had a big old banana daiquiri in my hand, and he was carrying a bottle of Red Stripe and a blanket. Finally we found a deserted spot and neither of us could keep our hands off each other any longer. Well, I don't have to go into the details. Just picture the most ecstatic moonlight sex possible. When we came in unison, the whole earth trembled and probably caused a tidal wave out on some remote island in the Atlantic that no longer exists thanks to our moment of passion.

Viola was still there, next to me on a pew in the chapel. I could tell during the service that she was steady praying. I mean she was praying fierce, hands clenched together and head bowed, lips moving. Daffy glanced at me, and I had to hit her to keep from laughing at that wide-eyed expression of hers.

After church Viola sort of latched on to us. She came with us to the cafeteria, and so Daffy and I didn't sit with our usual cronies, which I was glad about because there was this one stud who had the worst kind of crush on me. She wasn't the only one after a piece of me, but she was damn sure the most persistent. Now I'm open-minded and all, but I just didn't have all that much time left, and I wasn't about to squander my chance at going to work release in the fall because some wanna-be-a-man type of girl thinks she's in love with me. If I were to get tangled up in something like that it would be just for kicks, and kicks aren't worth it—not when you can see freedom waving its hands at you, wanting you to come out and play in the free world.

So the three of us sat at a table down at the end of the hall. My curiosity was getting the best of me. I finally broached the subject and asked, "Viola, is something bothering you? I noticed you were having trouble sleeping the other night."

Viola took a dainty bite of the canned spaghetti we were having for lunch that day and put down her fork before turning to me and saying, "I am being haunted."

Daffy, with a mouth full of food, nearly spit it all over the table. She swallowed and said, "Oh my god."

"By who?" I asked.

"By my dead husband, Raymond Carpenter."

I was plenty creeped out by this. I have always sort of believed in ghosts since I was a child and my Granny Hazel swore up and down she ran one out of her house when she lived down near Lake Okeechobee. She said the ghost was a woman who was a victim of the 1928 hurricane that broke the dikes and took all the water out of the lake and dumped it on top of the people, killing more than 2,000 people. She knew she had a ghost because she'd find wet foot prints on the floor and wet spots on her furniture and water would overflow the sinks for no reason at all. When I asked her how she got rid of it, she said she did her own exorcism with a cross and a Bible and a stick of burning sage.

"What do he do?" Daffy asked.

"Does he do?" I corrected.

"Shut up, Miss College," Daffy said.

"He touches me and I get real cold," Viola said. "He whispers to me at night and won't let me sleep. He takes my things and hides them."

"Is he here right now?" I asked quietly.

Viola paused as if listening for something. All I could hear was the noise of six hundred woman all running their mouths at the same damn time. Viola shook her head.

"How did Raymond die?" Daffy asked.

Viola took another bite. She looked so prim and proper, even had a paper napkin in her lap. She sighed and said, "I shot him to death."

Daffy and I sat back like a couple of Siamese twins.

"Why?" I asked.

Viola's shoulders sort of slumped forward, and she looked like she was bearing a fifty pound weight on her back.

"Have you ever loved someone so much that he was your whole life, he was your reason for breathing, for eating and for waking up in the morning? Have you ever loved a man so much that if he asked you to, you would lay down on a set of railroad tracks, not getting up even when you could feel the tracks shaking and the whistle blowing?"

"Hell, no," Daffy said, dropping her little tin cup of kool-aid on the tray.

But I unfortunately knew what she meant. And now I understood what drew me to her.

"Yes," I said. "I think I have."

"He shamed me," Viola said. "He gambled all the time. And he lost all the time. One night he gave me, his wife, to another man to pay off his debt. I did it. I thought I was saving his life."

She breathed heavily and looked down at her hands.

"That other man treated me like a dog, girls. I . . . I can't even tell you the things he and his thugs did to me."

I felt a real sick feeling in my gut then because my imagination had no trouble conjuring up various scenarios.

"But I thought that Raymond would come back and get me," she said, leaning forward, suddenly urgent. "I waited, and I waited. But he never came. He just went out and got himself another girl. My brother Junebug finally found me and got me away from that man. I was locked in this little room without a stitch of clothing. My brother had tricked them into letting him in to see me. When he came in, I just fell to the ground in relief and shame. I was so ashamed for my own brother to see me like that. Junebug is a big fellow, and he carries a big gun. A .44 magnum. He pulled out that gun and told those other men, he would kill them if they came near me. Then he made one of the men take off his shirt and give it to me. Then my brother took me out of there and got me home. He wanted to go back and kill them, but I begged him not to. I didn't want him to wind up in a place like this."

I breathed a sigh of relief myself and fell nearly in love with Junebug.

Viola continued, "It took me about three or four months to get my sanity back, and even then I still couldn't hardly sleep at night. Finally, I woke up early one Saturday morning and I knew what I had to do. It was perfectly clear. I snuck into Junebug's room and I took that .44 magnum out of his dresser drawer. I took a bus over to where Raymond's new girlfriend lived in a little duplex down on the eastside of Jacksonville. I knocked on the door and her little boy answered. He was up by himself. He was just a kid, and he let me in. I leaned down and asked him where his mommy's bedroom was and he pointed to the closed door. So I slowly and quietly opened it. Raymond was all sprawled out on the bed, snoring, buck naked with the sheets thrown off him. I lifted the gun and pointed it right between his legs."

"Oh my God. I think I'm gonna lose my lunch," Daffy said.

"I shot him there, then I shot him in the heart and then I shot him in the head. He was dead when I was done with him."

Viola picked up her fork and took another bite.

Neither Daffy nor I could move a muscle. Finally, Daffy asked, "What did old girl do?"

"What do you think? She jumped out of the bed screaming and wet herself. I turned around and went outside. I walked down to the bus stop and waited for the bus, but the police got there first. I didn't mind going to jail. But I thought . . . I thought I'd at least get my sanity back. Instead I'm being haunted by a dead man."

Later that day Daffy said to me, "Child, that woman is insane."

I shrugged. I was reserving judgment, as my daddy used to say until I had some more information. I got it by surprise the following Tuesday night.

I was in the bathroom, washing up for the night. I could hear water running in the showers, so I knew someone was in there. Just as I finished drying my face I heard this terrible screaming. I froze for a second and then ran to the shower to see what was wrong.

Viola had jumped out of the shower and she was trembling and shaking and crying holding the puny towel up to her front side.

"I'm burned," she cried. "He burned me." I looked and saw blistering welts on her shoulders and back. Steam was foaming out of the shower stall. I turned and ran for the C.O. who came charging back into the bathroom with me, ordering the crowd of busybodies out. While the C.O. looked at Viola's burns, I tried to reach into the shower to turn off the water. I had to slide my arm around the scalding streams of water with a towel over my skin. I reached the faucet knobs and turned. The cold water was nearly full on but the hot water knob was just barely turned.

"What were you thinking, turning the water on that hot?" the

C.O. scolded Viola.

"Excuse me, but that hot water was barely on," I told her.

That changed her tune. I could see she was worrying about a lawsuit. She started treating Viola a little better, and ordered someone to get some ice. They sent Viola to the infirmary for the night but before she left, Viola looked me in the eyes and said, "See? He makes my life a living hell. Still."

Monday June 12

Lolly's eyes opened wide and she raised herself up from the bed long enough to look at the blue digital numbers of her alarm clock: 2:57. Her heart was thudding as she lay back down. This didn't happen very often, but there was a reason now. A reason she had ignored for about a week now. The lump. There it was, and she knew as she lay there watching the moonlight send shadows across her wall that the lump was a piece of cancer. She was 30 years old, would be 31 in October. And that meant the cancer had been waiting inside her body for sixteen years. *What was it doing all that time*, she wondered. Sleeping, gathering strength, or just waiting, waiting until it decided that now, right now, was the perfect time to spring into action.

Damn it, she whispered. Why hadn't she called the doctor right away? Why wait? She didn't even know if her old cancer doctor was still around. Probably not. She'd have to check with her insurance first thing in the morning. Probably would have to get a god damn referral from her primary care physician. She hated the medical establishment. Hated the damn HMOs, the whole crazy system. And she hated cancer. She did not want to die. She wanted to marry and have children. She wanted to quit her job at the Department of Education and work fulltime developing arts programs for inmates, for at-risk juveniles, for anyone who needed a way to cry out. Art is not therapy, Jen always said. Art is art. That was true, but if it didn't feel good, if it didn't somehow cauterize the wounds, why did anyone do it?

Not for money. Lolly herself wrote poetry, painted pictures and made things out of wire and plaster. And it wasn't so anybody else could say, "Isn't that nice?" or "Hey, let's give you a thousand dollars for that poem." She did it because, well, just fucking because. Jen was the same way with her acting and various theater projects. It was a way to make sense of life, and life had seemed pretty nonsensical to both of them. Jen thought they were so different, but were they? No, Lolly hadn't gone the bad girl route the way Jen had. That brief dance with death when she was fourteen had been enough of a walk on the wild side for her. But things seemed to hurt her deeper. Like injustice and the amazing lack of compassion that most people displayed. When she said she worked in a women's prison, most people giggled. They seemed to think that the women were having some great orgy in there. They didn't think of the tears those women shed, tears of rage at the men in their lives, at the system, at themselves. They didn't know how it hurt those women to be away from their children, to be denied the simple joy of a loving touch, and to live with the idea that you just weren't good enough, smart enough or rich enough to find a place in this society.

These thoughts churned in Lolly's head, an angry discordant throng of voices. But underneath was the one lone syllable of fear. The cancer was awake. She was awake. She and the cancer were awake together. And this time she did not have her mother to help her through it. All she really had was her selfish and self-centered sister, Jennifer Louise Johanssen.

On the way back from the prison she had told Jen that the improv was based in reality. "It's probably nothing," Jen had said casually. But Lolly knew with certainty that it wasn't nothing. She had a dryness in her throat as if she already felt the ashes her body would become.

Lolly pushed the covers off her, rolled over and turned on the light. Her bedroom was small, decorated with an antique dresser and a cabinet with glass doors where she kept excess clothes. It was an orderly room, cozy with rose-colored walls and a braided rug over the hard wood floor. Beside her big four-poster bed was a table covered with photos. She reached instinctively for her mother's photo and held it in her lap, looking into her mother's laughing eyes. She had written a poem about this photo once during a workshop with the inmates. It was an exercise that began "In this photo you are . . ." and had a set of instructions, including alliteration, similes and metaphors. You had to include a piece of clothing, a wish, a color, an animal on various lines.

Lolly began to recite what she remembered of the poem to herself: "In this poem you are young, your face framed by auburn curls that look black in this black and white photo of you. Behind you is the house where you lived with your granma and six sisters after your parents died in a factory fire. You were the blue-eyed bouncing baby. You were always dreaming. Like a peddler, you sold integers to sullen students. Your auburn curls turned silver like moonlight. I wish you could come back to life as a queen. I would polish your crown and place it on your head, gentle as a kiss."

She smiled, thinking about the poem. It was just an exercise, nothing she would send out to a literary journal, but it gave her a momentary sense of peace. She replaced the photo and turned off the light.

Lolly woke up the next morning feeling groggy from her nocturnal battles. She remembered that she had to call the doctor's office. Had to call them today. ASAP. At work she began putting together a report on distance learning initiatives for her supervisor. She made the call to the doctor during her break while Sue went out for coffee. The woman on the other end of the line said, "There's an appointment available in late June."

Lolly grimaced. "I could be dead by then. I need to see the doctor today. I need a referral to an oncologist immediately."

"Honey, it could take months to get into an oncologist. There's only four of them in town," the woman said.

Lolly shut her eyes.

"I am not going to wait months," Lolly said simply. "Now please get me into see my physician today."

"You know what? His assistant can give you a referral. Come in tomorrow morning at 8. We'll be waiting for you, honey."

Lolly breathed a sigh of relief as she hung up the phone. A brief respite from what she knew would be the battle of her life.

Sunday June 18

Alice Jaybird sat in the dayroom, playing checkers when Sonya walked in. It was a Sunday afternoon and Sonya had just finished her shift in the kitchen. She caught Panther watching her through the glass before C.O. Barbie came out and gave Panther some house-keeping chores. C.O. Barbie couldn't stand to see anyone not doing anything.

"Hey, friend," Alice called to her. "Come over and play checkers with us."

Sonya was taken aback. Growing up she had never had friends. She wasn't allowed. The only person she was allowed to play with or confide in was her cousin, Maria.

"Don't speak to anyone who isn't family," she was warned.

That left her mother, Dina, who often treated Sonya as if she were a toy, a doll to dress up and discard, or her father—a cold man whose fingers were glued to his money clip—or Ziggy, her brother, a pig-eyed boy who grew into a mean-hearted man. Or her cousin, Maria. Maria was okay as far as relatives go, but she didn't understand Sonya, her longings, her secret thoughts and feelings. She would dismiss her with a shake of her head and say, "Sonya, you don't make no sense." As a teenager she had so often wished she had friends like the other girls did, friends for sleepovers and talking about boys.

She sat down beside Alice.

"Do you want me to get you a coke?" she asked Alice.

Alice gave her a strange look and said, "No way. You're my friend, not my slave," as if Alice knew that Sonya didn't know much about friendship and Alice would have to teach her. Sonya smiled, leaned on her hand and watched the game.

After dinner there was a half hour free time when inmates were allowed to go hang around the recreation center or sit by the ball field. Sonya tagged along with Alice and Lucille. Lucille got called in to play a game of ping pong with Daffy and a couple of other women so Sonya and Alice sat down on a bench.

"This heat feels like someone stuffing rags down my throat," Sonya said.

Alice shrugged and said, "I don't mind it too much. We didn't have air conditioning when I was growing up, but somehow sitting on the cool dirt under a chickee we managed to stay cool. We Indians are like that."

"Well, we Polish have our tricks, too. We load ourselves into an SUV and drive to Montreal. That's how we deal with it," Sonya said.

"That's not a bad way," Indian said with that friendly laugh that made Sonya feel warm and relaxed. "So what do you think about the drama class?"

"It's okay," Sonya said. "I like those women—Lolly and Doc. Lolly is real nice, and that Doc sure is pretty, isn't she?"

"Yeah, she is. You know, I get the feeling I've seen her before. And not just in some pizza commercial. It's like I know her from somewhere."

"You never knew anyone like that, Indian. How long you been locked up?"

"Twelve years, four months and 13 days," Alice answered.

"Long time," Sonya said. "Anyway, I really like the acting. I mean I've always been good at it, I guess, but never thought I could do something with it besides use it to steal from people."

"You miss that life?" Alice asked.

"I miss my baby, Tomas," Sonya said. "I miss him like I'd miss air if somebody sent me to the moon."

"I never got to have a baby," Alice said, sadly. "Hope I get out in time."

Sonya looked at Alice as if seeing her for the first time. Her face had soft, rounded features. She had thick eyelashes and eyes that seemed as if they could see something far away, as if they could look past the fences and the razor wire and over the miles to a place that was wild and green.

Tuesday June 27

Jen smiled up at the black camera eye, and the man sitting at the desk clicked the button and said, "You're done."

Lolly stood over to the side with her arms crossed. They were in the uncomfortable position of needing each other more than ever. Jen pushed her hair behind her ears and went to retrieve her new driver's license.

"Let's see," Lolly said.

"I look old," Jen said.

"No, you're beautiful. You always were and you always will be," she said in a wistful tone as she gazed at the picture. Jen's thick auburn hair fell around her face in the photo and even she could see that she looked like she should be saying, "Because I'm worth it."

"Thanks, I guess," Jen said and stuck the license in her wallet. All the good looks in the world still couldn't make you happy.

"Just stating the facts."

They walked outside into the sweltering Tallahassee air. Summer in Tallahassee made you want to walk naked everywhere. *Good Lord,* Jen thought, *I feel like a fish.*

Of course, there was a price to be paid for Lolly bringing her out to get her license. Neither of the sisters ever did anything for each other out of the goodness of their hearts. Jen would be expected to cart Lolly around to hospitals and doctor's offices until this breast lump thing was figured out. Ever since Mom's funeral they had managed to live in the same town and not see each other more than once a month, maybe less. Lolly came to Jen's shows, of course, and sometimes they ran into each other at an art gallery or a restaurant. But now, suddenly, it was like they were old pals. Driving to the prison every Saturday to work with the drama group. And now this—Lolly's lump.

"What ever happened to that guy you were seeing?" Lolly asked as they got into the car and drove away from the DMV office.

"What guy?"

"The tall one, what was his name?"

"Daniel. Daniel whose wife found my bra in the glove compartment of his Mercedes and called me up and said she would eviscerate me if I ever saw him again."

"I didn't know he was married," Lolly said, her eyebrows furrowing. *Sleeping with a married man was not the sort of thing Lolly would do*, Jen thought. It wasn't that she was too good to do it, she was too smart. "Did she really use the word eviscerate?"

"Yes, it made me admire her dreadfully. I hate those sweet, simpering types of women. The kind Lyle always liked. He liked women who drew hearts instead of dots on their 'i's. Like that bitch with the Farrah Fawcett hair that I caught him in bed with."

"You've never gotten over him, have you?" Lolly asked.

Jen took a deep breath.

"Oh, I got over him all right. But this one was a little harder. I don't even remember leaving my bra in the car. I must have been plastered." She paused and then asked, "So, where do you have to go today?"

"To the hospital," Lolly said in a quiet voice. "They're going to take off one of my breasts. They did a biopsy last week. It's malignant as hell."

Jen sat in the passenger side of the little Civic. She felt as if the sun had suddenly eclipsed. Her hands shook. The air from the air conditioner was nowhere near cold as it blew pathetically against her skin.

"Why didn't you tell me?"

"I know how you don't like things like this," Lolly said.

"Jesus Christ, Lolly, I'm your sister. Why the hell didn't you say anything?" Jen asked. "How could you . . .? My god. Not again."

Lolly's face was set like a plaster cast. Nothing, not even a tremor of sorrow, passed over those pinks cheeks.

From the Journal of Nicole Parks

Every year on the compound there is a yearly review by the Department of Corrections. Everyone got off their regular job assignments and had to paint and clean from sun up to sundown. Then some of us got pulled off duty to load up TVs from the offices and pile them into a bus. I couldn't believe it when I found out the staff was going to hide the TVs off in the woods. I guess they didn't want it known that they were busy watching soap operas instead of doing their jobs.

It was about this time that Viola showed me a picture of her brother, Junebug. There wasn't nothing subtle about it, though she tried to play it off.

"Don't you think he's a fine looking man?" Viola asked me. I was doing some ironing in the dayroom.

I had to concede that he wasn't hard to look at. He had a red tone to his skin and deep eyes. He was wearing a thick gold chain around his neck but not all that flash that them ghetto thugs think they have to wear.

"He's a hard worker, too, girl," Viola said.

Daffy strolled up and stuck out her long neck so she could see the picture.

"What kind of car do he drive? Hmm?" she asked.

"Um, a Ford Taurus, I think," Viola said. "It's blue."

"A Taurus?" Daffy opened her eyes wide like she was impressed when I knew she was making fun of Viola's brother, so I had to stick up for him a little bit even though I didn't know the man.

"It doesn't matter what kind of car a man drives. What matters is how he treats you." I pressed down hard on the iron, thinking that Antwan had treated me so good all the way up to the moment he let me do his time for him. And it occurred to me I didn't know jack about the way a man ought to treat a woman. I used to think my daddy wasn't good to Momma. He didn't spoil her and all like that. I'm not even sure what broke them up. On the other hand, I could remember coming into the kitchen and seeing them cooking together – Daddy making stew and Momma cooking greens and biscuits. And there was something about the way they moved about the kitchen together, stepping around each other in constant motion, never getting in each other's way. It looked like they were doing a dance together. Maybe they had more going on than I realized as a fourteen-year-old girl.

Daffy walked out of the room, and later in the cafeteria, she said to me, "Child, please. What is Viola thinking? Like you would dump Antwan for her chump of her brother."

I just crossed my arms and nodded. I had gotten a letter from Antwan just that day full of his sweet sexy words (though he couldn't spell worth a damn). And he had put fifty dollars in my bank, which was nothing out of his bankroll, but meant a lot to me being locked up.

But that night, don't you know, as I was standing with my head stuck in my locker, I overheard Daffy telling Viola that her brother Junebug could write to her—Daffy, that is—if he wanted to. And poor Viola started stammering something. I just held in my laughter and pretended like I didn't hear a thing.

Wednesday, June 28

Jen watched them wheel Lolly on the gurney into surgery. She had no idea how long it would take or when Lolly would be able to talk. Lolly was scheduled to stay in the hospital for at least one day after the surgery; the insurance companies didn't let you lounge around for long. Jen stood in the hallway at a loss, the raw hospital smell like detergent in her sinuses. Any number of Lolly's friends would have been happy to be here. They all doted on Lolly, but Lolly hadn't wanted to tell people. One thing Lolly hated was pity. Maybe that's why she asked Jen to bring her; Jen had never been capable of pitying her.

A couple of nurses bustled past Jen, and Jen looked around at the various doors leading to mysterious rooms of equipment and wondered where they kept the good drugs. Oh well, she did know where a good bar was located quite nearby. She could while away the afternoon there and come see how Lolly was doing later that evening.

Jen left the hospital and headed straight to the bar. She started drinking about three in the afternoon; rum and coke seemed like it would do the trick. The sugar alone would kill her. The bar was decorated in an island theme with a large patio area out back where bands sometimes played.

She had moved to Tallahassee when she was 26, already a senior citizen in the eyes of the college-going populace. In the past six years, she'd met her share of fellow imbibers.

A loud thunder crack overhead shook the place, but they all knew in fifteen minutes or so it would all be over.

Oh Lord, here came big tall Howard toward her table. He would surely offer to buy her drinks all night. She was a magnet for easy men. Lolly's surgery would be done soon. She couldn't allow herself to get sidetracked.

"Whatcha drinkin', Lady?" Howard asked with a big smile.

It had been dark for a while when Jen sped along Tennessee Street in Lolly's Civic. Howard had eventually gone home to his wife, and Jen had stopped at her place to change. Now she was out with the sultry night air licking her face. Amazing what power this little car had. She flew past the bars crowding against the strip, the stereo was screaming out "Radar Love" and she was screaming with it. She felt electric. She felt good for the first time in weeks. Sure, her sister was in a hospital somewhere with her breast lopped off, but Jen's boobies were still there firmly planted and oh, the rum sang inside her. And she was ready to party. Where were her friends? Where was anyone? The sky above was a swirling gray and black. The young night was full of possibility and green lights. Go, she heard her blood whisper, fly.

The whoop of a police siren broke the spell. Jen slowed the car down. How fast had she been going anyway? The police car with its siren and steady beating blue light followed close behind her, admonishing her. Damn, she said, and I just got my license back. This struck her as terribly amusing. She pulled into the parking lot of a wooden building designed to look like a saloon where college students regularly obliterated their busy brain cells. Now, she was busted. At least she looked great if she was going to the hooskow. She was wearing her red dress that hugged her body and a pair of black, strappy sandals. Boy, it would really look bad if any of her former students were around. She laughed again at the thought of it and turned her car off.

The police officer shined a light into her car.

"Ma'am, have you been drinking?" he asked. There were two

police cars.

"Yep," she answered with a smile and handed over her license.

"Get out of the car please," he said. She opened the door and stood up. My, my. A low whistle came from the other car, but they merely watched.

"Jennifer Johanssen, is it? Do you know how fast you were going?"

"No, I'm sorry. I wasn't paying attention."

"You were going about 90 miles an hour."

"Wow. Ninety on Highway 90," Jen said. "Sorry. That's way too fast." *Way to go, friggin', Einstein*, she thought. Mmmm, stupid, stupid, stupid.

"I'm going to need you to take a sobriety test," he said. "Please walk along this line here, placing one foot in front of the other." He indicated a yellow line in the parking lot.

The thing about Jen's drinking was that there was a little window in the intoxication process when she could perform all things flawlessly. She'd once won a pool tournament in the very bar next to the parking lot after having imbibed a considerable amount of tequila. Generally, after drinking a bit, her vocabulary suddenly improved. Big words—obsequious, quotidian, voluptuous, chastisement, loquacious, puerile—peppered her sentences and entranced more than one hungry man to follow her home. At these times things were sharper, clearer and easier. And then she usually went home, passed out, unable to remember the adventures of the night before. But she was nowhere near the passing out stage. She was in perfect form and easily moved over the line like a circus tight-rope walker.

"Okay," the officer said. "Now stand on one leg."

Jen did as she was told. *Didn't they have a Breathalyzer with them*, she wondered, but somehow she knew she'd pass that, too. Speeding, reckless driving, they could charge her with those, but she was going to beat the drunk driving. She felt exultant. She felt charming. She tilted her head at the police officer. Did he want her to recite the alphabet. Backwards? Z-Y-X-W-V-U-T . . .

He shook his head and told her to get in his car. She slid into the front seat and he got in the other seat. He glanced over at her and she smiled. His glance lingered. *Gotcha*, she thought.

"So do you like being in law enforcement?" she asked.

"Well, I do meet some interesting people," he said.

His radio crackled. "We've got a break-in in progress on ...." The other police car pulled up alongside his and the officers spoke to each other through their open windows.

"We've got to get over there, Zack," the woman officer in the passenger side of the other car said.

He turned and looked at Jen again.

"What are we waiting for, Zack?" Jen asked. "Let's go bust someone."

Zack rolled his eyes heavenward, chuckled, put down the ticket he was in the process of writing and sped out of the parking lot. Jen was thrilled. She hoped it would be full of drama, a hostage situation, and she would be called upon to negotiate with the desperate gunman. But the excitement turned out not to be much. A homeless man looking for a place to bed down for the night had set off the alarm of a barber shop. The cops ran him off. The other two gave Zack a knowing grimace and drove away.

"You hungry?" he asked.

"Starving," Jen said.

"Let's get something to eat."

After a few cups of coffee and a couple of waffles at the Waffle House, Zack drove to the two-story brick apartment building on Franklin where Jen lived. She liked being in the front seat of the cop car. It was like auditioning for a role on "Law & Order." Now that would be a good gig. He pulled onto the hard-packed driveway and into the lot behind the building.

"I'm going to walk you upstairs," he said.

"Good idea," Jen said. "Who knows how much trouble I might

get into."

He followed her up the stairs to her apartment. The hallway illuminated him. He was attractive, but she'd already seen that at the restaurant. She wasn't sober yet, but she wasn't sloppy drunk.

"Want to come in?" she asked, slipping the key inside the lock and turning.

She shoved the door open and turned toward him expectantly. He grinned but shook his head.

"I'll take a rain check," he said. She shrugged and walked inside.

"See ya later, copper," she said flirtatiously and shut the door. Oh, what a night. She'd almost gotten busted bigtime and instead had spent the late hours of the night hearing about Zack's exploits. It was funny. She was spending her Saturdays with convicts and her Wednesday nights with cops. And she found both of them fascinating.

Teetering in her heels, she fed her cat, Manny, who was meowing cantankerously. Manny was an assertive beast, and she did her best to appease him.

Then she pulled the red dress off and crawled into bed. Shutting her eyes she suddenly remembered Lolly. She sat bolt upright. She didn't even know how the operation went. She was supposed to have gone back to check on her. But not only had she not gone back to check on her sister, she had gone and left Lolly's car in the parking lot of a student bar on Tennessee Street. Then another thought occurred to her: What if Lolly had died? Jen felt a ball of lead in her gut as she slowly sank back into the bed.

Thursday, June 29

"We got out as much as we could. The tumor was five centimeters and we took out thirteen nodules," the doctor said, looking down at Lolly. He was a young, corpulent man with a helpless expression on his face.

"But you didn't get it all," Lolly said. The incision hurt. There on her left side was a line of folded skin; no nipple, nothing, just a scar. A red slash. They offered to put in an implant, but she refused.

"No, I'm sorry. We didn't. It was just too advanced. We'll have to start you on weekly chemotherapy right away. The nurse will go over the procedures with you and you'll need to sign a consent form."

Lolly didn't say anything, just turned to look out the window at the parking garage and the hazy sky beyond.

"When can I leave here?" she asked.

"Well, we've got to keep these tubes in you for another couple of days to drain the fluid. And you'll probably be feeling pretty nauseous for a few days after that, but I guess we could let you go home on Monday."

"Monday?" she said, trying to keep the bitterness out of her voice. "I have work to do Saturday."

"You can't work. Bed rest for the next week."

Yeah, right, Lolly thought. The doctor checked his watch and left without even saying goodbye.

For the next thirty minutes Lolly lay in the bed snatching at pieces of silence. They had cut her up in pieces and now they would poison her body. She thought of all the people who believed they'd been abducted by aliens. She was the one abducted, and the doctors were aliens, pod people. She didn't have to go into a space ship to experience it.

"Hey."

She looked up. Jen had finally come. Lolly didn't know whether to scream at her or cry.

"Are you okay?" Jen asked.

"I'm fine. Wonderful. They cut off my breast but that's okay. They didn't get all the cancer out. But that's okay, too. I'll just get chemotherapy again. It's fine. It's all fine."

Jen sat down in the chair by the end of the bed and was mercifully quiet.

"So what have you been doing?" Lolly asked.

"Making a fool of myself," Jen said. "Drank too much last night. A cop pulled me over for speeding."

"Did you lose your license again?" Lolly asked, dully.

"No, the cop liked me."

Lolly laughed. "Of course. You live a charmed life, Jennifer."

"No, not really."

Lolly looked hard at Jen—that thin, pretty face, the brown eyes and pouty lips. So many angry thoughts burst into her head that all collided with one another; she was left with a big blank. She sighed and looked up at the ceiling.

"Do you want me to go to the prison without you on Saturday?" Jen asked.

"I guess you'll have to," Lolly said. "I don't want to tell them about this, okay? Not yet anyway."

"Okay," Jen said.

"I don't want to tell anyone yet." She knew that everyone talked about everything now, but when she had been young, the first time she got cancer, it wasn't something you told people. It was something to be ashamed of, as if you had done something wrong. At least that's how the people she knew treated it. Was it still something shameful? Would people tell her she caused the cancer because of her "unresolved emotional issues"? Why couldn't it just be one of those things that happened to you?

Jen stood up and went over to the window. The sun laid a harsh hand on her face and Lolly saw that she was tired. Maybe she actually cared about what happened to Lolly. Or maybe she was just hungover.

"Are you going out tonight?"

"Probably," Jen shrugged. Which meant yes.

"Try not to get in trouble, okay?"

"I thought Momma was dead," Jen said. She stood up. "When do you get out of here?"

"A few days. Aunt Jewel will take me home," Lolly said.

"All right. Well, uh, I'll try to come by tomorrow," Jen said. And she was gone, leaving only the imprint of her perfect face and golden hair. *Time to self-destruct,* Lolly thought. She cranked the bed down and gazed out the window as the sky turned periwinkle blue. Now more than ever, she identified with those women who lived trapped behind the razor wire. She was in prison just like they were. But she would not feel sorry for herself, damn it. She would not do that.

Saturday, July 1

Jen stood between the two fences, waiting for the gate to open. Her throat felt dry, and as usual thick purple clouds hunched their shoulders and glowered over the compound. The coils of razor wire glittered. Jen stared at it, imagining how it could slice your flesh into strips of bacon. Then Jen thought of the poisonous gown Medea gave to Jason's new wife. She had played the role of Medea in college, and it had been one of her favorites—a murderous villainess. Now she was walking into a den full of them. Why had she let Lolly talk her into coming here by herself? These women didn't like Jen. They didn't trust her, not the way they trusted Lolly.

Suddenly the gate lurched open. Jen glanced over at the control room, but no one was paying any attention to her whatsoever.

The women were all seated in orange plastic chairs, talking among themselves as if she weren't there. It was the fourth week of the program and it was time now to get some material written if they were going to have a production in another ten weeks. She swallowed hard. It didn't matter if they liked her or not. They had to get some work done.

"Drama," she said, "is something you all should know fairly well."

"I heard that," Lucille said, smacking her lips. Alice was drawing a picture, and Daffy was joking with Nicole.

"The trick, I guess, is how do you turn drama into art?" Jen continued.

No one answered for a moment and then Nicole looked up and said, "It's how you present it like a structure or something."

Jen nodded.

"Yes, that's important. You want a beginning, middle and end. I've got an exercise that I'd like everyone to do. I want you all to relax for a moment, close your eyes. Go ahead, it's all right. I promise."

She watched as they closed their eyes. Sonya was the last one with her eyes open but when she saw that everyone else had shut their eyes, she lowered her lids.

"Okay," Jen said. "Think back to some point in your life when something changed, when you realized or learned something. What was the beginning? Then what happened? How did it end? As always, everything said in this room is confidential. It never leaves the room unless the person who shared the story wishes to take it out."

She paused and let a healthy silence hover in the air, before she said, "Okay, open your eyes. If you need to jot down a couple of notes, go ahead."

They opened their eyes and a few of them desultorily made some notes on the legal pads that Lolly had given them in the beginning. Jen waited a moment and then asked, "Okay, who wants to go first?"

She looked around the room. No one met her eyes. No one volunteered. Sometimes her college students were shy, but this felt like more than shyness. They were making a statement: Jen was no Lolly. She rolled her shoulders and said in a softer voice, "All right, I'm going to tell you my story first as an example. It's just one of many, but I guess it's the one that still affects me even though I try to pretend like it doesn't."

A few of the women turned to her with curious faces. Alice lowered her eyes to the floor to listen. Nicole leaned forward. Viola tilted her head and sat up straighter. Curly lounged back with her feet sticking straight out in front. Lucille sat with her hands folded in her lap, and Sonya looked furtively around the room.

Jen began: "This is the story of the moment I realized I had to leave my husband. We lived in Miami, in a little stucco house on Biscayne Bay. I used to love to watch the sun rise over the pale blue water. Of course, usually the reason I was up at sunrise is because I hadn't slept the night before. Both Lyle and I had gotten into cocaine. But about August that year I quit. For one thing it was damaging my nasal passages, and I refused to smoke or inject it. I never did get into the whole crack thing, thank God. The other reason I quit was that we were just about broke.

"I'd made about 50 grand that year acting in some small films, and Lyle and I had burned that money up so fast you would have thought we hated it. We couldn't get rid of it fast enough."

Several women nodded. They understood the drug mania.

"But, you know, I thought I loved him. He was so good looking and Lord, he could be a charmer. Wherever he went, he had women fawning over him like was a friggin' celebrity when all he was was the lighting technician for a bunch of crummy low-budget flicks."

Suddenly Alice Jaybird looked up at her and stared hard.

Jen stopped talking. And the other women glanced around.

"I thought I'd seen you before," Alice said. "My cousin sold you and your husband some coke one time. Your husband gave us a copy of a movie you were in. It was my cousin's favorite movie. He watched it over and over."

Jen grimaced. She looked around at the women, wondering what to say. The truth was sitting on her tongue ready to dive into the ocean. She glanced into Alice's deep brown eyes. Alice's mouth was shut tight. She wasn't saying anything else, and Jen had the feeling her secret was safe.

Then she blurted out, "They were porn movies."

"No shit!" Daffy cried out. "You was a porn star?"

"Not a star, really. I only made a few movies before I got out," Jen said, embarrassed. Here these women thought she was a real actor and now they had to find out she had done porn. She felt her credibility doing a Kamikaze. No one said anything for a moment.

Then Lucille laughed, "Girl, you are one of us."

Alice was smiling at her, and Curly reached out to give her a high five. Jen felt as if she'd stepped into a Fellini flick, but it was a happy scene. And she was grateful that Lolly wasn't sitting across the circle.

"Y'all, she needs to finish her story," Nicole said impatiently, her almond eyes flashing. "I want to find out what happened with her and her man."

The afternoon sun was shining through a row of windows, and the air conditioner hummed in the background. Jen felt as if she were suddenly with twelve of her closest pals.

"Anyway, it turns out I was pregnant." She paused again. This was the hard part, the part where her chest tightened up like a key was poking out of her back, turning. "When Lyle and I first got married, I used to imagine what his babies would look like. Our babies, I mean. But a week after I found out I was pregnant I had this weird thing happen. I was lying on the couch, watching TV and thinking about baby names. Of course, I wasn't going to work anymore. Frankly, without the drugs I didn't think I could work. I was just lying there, my feet up, and I had this sudden urge to go look in Lyle's desk. It was like some force took hold of me. I stood up and went over to the desk where he kept all his receipts and bills and stuff for his lighting truck. I opened the middle drawer and there was a card. A birthday card from a so-called friend of mine. Tiffany. It was the most explicit thing I'd ever read," she said.

"What did it say?" Nicole asked.

"It said that she loved riding his big hard cock, which wasn't all that big, and that she had been a bad girl and maybe he should come over and give her a good spanking again."

"No, she didn't," Lucille said. Lucille's pop eyes got even bigger.

"Girl, please," Daffy clucked.

"Yes. I found them together that afternoon in a back room at the production office. They didn't see me, but I watched them having sex and suddenly I realized that it was just like watching myself. And what I had been doing seemed so sordid and so wrong. Love shouldn't be like that. And what good was sex without love? It was like watching dogs have sex. And right then I blamed Lyle for having conned me into being in those movies. Later I realized that he hadn't held a gun to my head. I mean, I could have said no. But that day I was so angry I went down to a clinic in South Miami and I aborted the baby."

The women were quiet. Then she continued.

"I came out of that place feeling sick and had a friend drive me home. Lyle didn't show up that night. I got sicker and sicker. The next day I was hemorrhaging, big clots of brown blood on the bathroom floor. I knew I had to go to the hospital, but before I went, I left a note for Lyle, telling him it was over, and I pinned the note to the kitchen table with a butcher knife. Never saw him again."

A large, heavy silence lowered itself over the group. The women seemed to be thinking. Sonya reached over and squeezed Jen's fingers. For a moment, Jen's chest got tighter. Such an odd feeling. She never cried, not unless the role called for it, but she felt as if she could have wept like a child at that moment.

Then Nicole opened her journal and spoke up.

"I got one already written down," she said.

Nicole Parks'
Monologue

When I met Antwan, I was attending the University of Miami. I was a small town girl from Maitland, Florida, but I had enough brains to get a scholarship to college and move to a big city where I could get educated not just through books but in the ways of the world. I loved everything about my new life—the clubs, the crazy people parades we saw down on South Beach, and the football games where the University of Miami Hurricanes steamrolled every other team in the nation.

One night after a particularly wild game against the Florida State Seminoles, my girl Teshaun and I were walking away from the stadium, hollering just like everybody else: "Wide Right! Wide Right!" 'til our throats were dry, papery chutes of air. Teshaun looked at me and said, "I'm 'bout to starve to death, girl. Let's go get some Chinese."

I remember everything about that night, the feel of the passenger seat in Teshaun's Toyota, how we cranked up her CD player and let Tupac rap his way inside our bones. We were so full of the absolute joy of being young and fabulous, we were a couple of conquistadoras, ready to take on anything.

This Chinese restaurant also had a bar which was frequented by your higher class sort of players, and Teshaun and I had noticed them before sitting in there, sipping on Courvoisier in their brandy snifters like they were all that. Mostly we just ignored them. This night we plopped ourselves down in a red leather-seated booth not far from the bar so we could watch the TV in the corner and see replays of the sad, sad field goal attempt that would live in infamy for years to come.

We had just ordered some egg rolls, Chinese barbeque shrimp and Lo Mein, when I shivered. My granny used to say that someone was walking over your grave when you shivered like that, and I believe that's exactly what happened. I looked up at the bar and noticed this dark-skinned guy sitting there, his shoulders cocked as he looked over at me. It wasn't that he was so fine. I mean, he looked good, but not like you'd fall out from the sight of his sheer beauty. No, it was way more than that. He had a presence. It was like he was wearing a magnet so strong that the snaps on my jeans were about to drag me over to him.

"Lord have mercy," I whispered. Teshaun glanced over her shoulder and she saw him, too. Just then he swiveled his chair back to the bar, showing me his back. That bit my ass like a platoon of fire ants. I jumped up, grabbed my knock-off Dolce & Gabbana bag and swished by him on my way to the restroom. I made sure my hips were rocking like a pendulum back and forth, and I smiled and waved at the bartender as if we were old buddies. He played along, winking at me and saying, "Hey, girl." But I pointedly ignored the 24-karat man sipping his brandy as if it was elixir from Valhalla, which I knew all about from my mythology class.

In the restroom I checked myself out, freshened my lipstick and pulled my green Hurricanes t-shirt tighter around my chest, puffing out my 34C's. I did look good, but I had just come from a football game and I was wishing I looked more glamorous or something instead of like the little college freshmeat that I was. I didn't know that was exactly what would appeal to a man like Antwan. He told me later that he liked innocence and wholesomeness. He didn't want to be seen with a down and dirty street girl. He couldn't afford it. I learned the hard way what that meant.

Antwan wined me with Pouilly Fouisse, a rich dry white wine from some place in France that you drink with seafood. He was always trying to teach me about stuff like that. He dined me on blackened snapper and stone crab claws. We did Miami, tooling around in his Black Lincoln Navigator, going to the best parties and rubbing elbows with rap stars and promoters as well as Mafia types and people you thought probably took out contracts for a living and I'm not talking about lawyers. Then when we got tired of that, we took this little seaplane called Chalk's over to Bimini and we'd eat lobster and drink Pina Coladas. This was the life I was born to live. This was so far away from the neck bones and rice that my momma thought was good eating that I might have flown to the moon. Those rich University of Miami girls had nothing on me. Antwan made me feel like a queen.

And sex . . . all I'd ever known was the back seat fumblings of a boy back at my high school, when he'd get his stuff all over my jeans rubbing on me and shit. Oh, I hated it. He'd yank on my titties like he was gonna milk me and put his big calloused collard-picking fingers down between my legs. Nothing about sex felt good, and I had no idea what all the fuss was about until Antwan started running his tongue over my ribs and down the front of my body 'til he was gently kissing me just above my bikini line. Then when his tongue plunged down there I almost screamed. Okay, I did scream. I screamed and writhed and begged him for more. Then he'd slide back on top of me and roll me over so I was on top, and well, you know how it went from there.

Antwan taught me how to fall in love with my body. He showed me that every postage-stamp size piece of my skin could be erogenous from my scalp to the soles of my feet. He rubbed me in oil, he draped me in silk, and he waved his magic wand and turned me into a woman. Was there anything I wouldn't do for him after that? Even claim that the drugs in my apartment and the gun in my purse belonged to me when the police came swooping down on my place when I was in a dead sleep about three a.m. and Antwan was out the window and ghost before I even knew what was happening?

"Baby," he said when I called him. "You won't get nothing but probation. But I been busted twice before and you know they mean it when they say, 'three strikes and you're out.'" But I didn't get probation. I got three years in the state penitentiary.

"So what do you think, Doc?" Nicole asked. "Can that be my monologue?"

"I love it. It's dramatic and exciting—lots of details."

"I'll say," Daffy interrupted. "She could go on Sally Jesse Raphael or some shit."

Jen smiled and looked around the room. "Not all of these stories will wind up in the production. It's up to you. I just want us to start thinking about aspects of your lives that are dramatic, those that have some sort of emotional impact. Okay, anybody else?"

Shy, little Bonita raised her hand as if she were in school. Bonita was the youngest of the group, probably around 20 years old. She had a sweet childlike smile and never caused trouble.

"I have a story. This happened when I was eleven. I was a very happy little girl. My mother raised me and my big sister. We lived in Hialeah in the back half of a little bright blue house. That house was so pretty. We had a little fenced-in yard and we kept a couple of chickens even though you weren't supposed to have chickens in the city. Mama said her family always had chickens and she wasn't going to stop just 'cause in America everybody got their eggs from the store.

"The school was right down the street. My mama had a job at Burdines during the day and worked at a restaurant at night. My mama had this boyfriend named Joe. And he lived with us for a while. When he lived with us, Mama didn't have to work so hard and we liked that. But then they broke up and Joe moved out. One day after school, my big sister had to stay after to make up some work. So I went home by myself. But on the way home I saw Joe's car. I was happy to see him because I didn't want to go home alone. He said I could come to his motel room until my mom got back from work. And he would help me with my homework. He was staying in a motel because of breaking up with my mom. I got in his big yellow sports car with black leather inside. I loved that car. It had a big engine and roared when he pushed the gas. He liked to push the gas while it was idling just to make me laugh. I can remember everything about that day. There was a six pack of bottled beer on the floor by my feet and a laundry basket of clothes in the back seat. He had a crucifix hanging from the rearview mirror. We pulled into the motel and when we went inside his room, there was another guy there."

Bonita paused. All the women seemed to hold their breath, hoping that she was not going to tell the story that she was about to tell.

"They beat me and they raped me. One at a time."

"Shit," Curly whispered.

"I was eleven years old. It hurt so bad. Joe was laughing, but I could tell he knew what he was doing was bad. Afterward, he made me take a bath and wash all the blood off. He said, 'That will teach you not to go into motel rooms with guys. Only bad girls, *puta*, do that."

"Then he took me home. And when I told my mother what happened, she slapped me and said I was a liar. A week later she and Joe got back together. And he moved back in. That was when I started staying away from home."

After Bonita finished her story, the women sat silently as if they were grieving for some lost part of themselves. Jen looked down at the brown sandals she was wearing and felt a helpless rage. An eleven-year-old girl. And a mother who had betrayed her. Bonita had her hands clasped. Her soft brown-skinned face was damp with tears. Jen thought about her own mother. Her mother would have single handedly beaten to death the man who harmed either of her daughters. She had never really appreciated her, and now it was too late.

"I would like to strangle that motherfucker with my bare hands," Lucille said.

Jen spoke up, "I'm sure we all would."

Somehow that broke the tension. Nicole reached over and hugged Bonita. Then Lucille began the story of the Christmas Eve when her family was evicted from their home.

"Mama had no idea that Daddy had spent all our rent money on drugs. She was so naïve." Lucille was a pull-yourself-up-by-the-bootstraps type gal, and Jen could see how her experiences must have toughened her up.

"So there we were, standing out on the lawn with our Christmas tree, all our wrapped presents and our groceries, including the frozen turkey, and our suitcases. They only give you ten minutes to get up all your stuff. Of course, Daddy wasn't there when it happened. So all us kids were dragging our stuff out into the cold. I grew up in Virginia and it can get mighty cold there in December."

She paused. Jen asked, "What did you do?"

"We stood out there for the longest with Mama crying and cursing. Finally my brother and I were picked up by my dad's sister. A neighbor took in the two younger ones. I don't know where Mama went.

"People from the neighborhood got all our furniture and stuff. Like vultures. My brother and I came back the next day and all that was left was a broken bicycle and a headless doll. Mama came to get us from our aunt's house a few months later. It was a hard year."

"Well, that story has a lot of dramatic potential," Jen said. She couldn't help herself. She was already imagining the staging of it.

Sonya spoke up. "I can't imagine," she said. "We never had anything happen like that to us in our family."

"'Course not. You TC be some rich suckers, conning them old people out their life savings and all," Daffy opined.

"What's TC?" Jen asked.

"Traveling criminals," Daffy said.

"Gypsies," Mariposa added.

"See, they got all kinds of scams," Daffy explained. "Come and tell you you need to get your driveway repaved or your roof reshingled. They charge a couple grand for something that costs maybe two hundred dollars. They be raking in two, three hundred grand a year. Sometimes you see them all in a caravan in their big fancy SUVs and pickup trucks."

"How you know so much?" Curly asked.

"My daddy's a roofing contractor," Daffy said. "And there was a camp of them not far from Tampa where he lived. I used to stay with him in the summer and one year he did real well, going around, fixing up all the roofs they had ruined or left half-done. He told me all about 'em."

"Your daddy's a roofing contractor?" Nicole blurted out.

"Yeah, I know you think I'm all ghetto, but my daddy's a working man. If I hadn't gotten messed up on these drugs, girl, I would not be here in this mess. He didn't raise me to be no cheap street ho, but that's just what I was. And now I don't see how I can ever go back to being nothing else."

"Lolly would tell you that you can do anything you put your heart to," Nicole said. Now Jen could never have said that without sounding corny and condescending. She was glad Nicole chose to "channel" Lolly.

Daffy then launched into a story unlike the previous ones. She recalled a trip to Weeki Wachi with her family when she was a little girl.

"I thought they were real mermaids," she said. "That's what I wanted to be. A mermaid just like that, with a big tail instead of legs."

"Well, you got the big tail," commented Lucille. Daffy laughed.

The odd—or interesting—thing about this work was that the women evinced a return to some essential personality. All of them seemed to be a portrait of the person they might have become if circumstances and lousy judgment hadn't interfered.

All except Sonya. Sonya was the one she couldn't quite figure out.

Then Sonya spoke.

"I did not have a life of hardship. You call us gypsies, but we are Polish, and we are very, very close. We do not have anything to do with anyone outside of the community. We take care of each other, and yes, we live well. But I was raped once," she said. "I was not eleven. I was twenty-one. Five years ago."

Jen glanced around the room. There was an odd tension. She noticed how still and alert Mariposa sat as Sonya began her story. *What is going on*, she wondered.

"Some of my family members went to Orlando for a vacation. We like to go to Disney World. I was there with my mother, my cousin Maria, my Uncle Jan, and my brother Ziggy. One night after we had been doing things all day I felt sick so I didn't go to dinner with the others. Then they went out after dinner, back out to watch the fireworks. I heard a knock on the door, and I thought they had come back, but when I opened the door, this man pushed his way into the room." Sonya began to tear up. "He beat me, and . . . and he raped me."

Something was odd about this story. But before Jen could say anything, Mariposa said in a cold voice.

"And how much money did the hotel pay you to keep your mouth shut about this so-called rape?"

"What do you mean?" Sonya stammered.

"This rapist. He was a Hispanic man, wasn't he?"

Sonya nodded her head.

"And then you threatened to sue the hotel, didn't you?" Mariposa questioned.

"They shouldn't hire people like that!" Sonya said.

"No, they shouldn't hire decent law-abiding men who might get tricked into fucking some gypsy whore who will later scream rape," Mariposa had risen at this point and before Jen could move, she had pounced on Sonya and clutched her by the throat.

"Holy shit," Nicole said.

Jen leaped up and approached the two women but Lucille got

there first and pulled Mariposa back.

"Easy, girl," she said. "You don't want to get a D.R. now. They'll put you in the box you mess around and hurt someone."

Now Mariposa was crying with rage as she pulled free from Lucille's grip. She slapped Sonya hard across the face.

"That was my brother, you lying *puta*. He never raped you. He never did. He was the bread winner of our house, and he sits and rots in prison because you lied. You lied for money. He didn't beat you. Your own brother and uncle beat you up."

Jen turned with a shocked expression to Sonya, who had backed away from the group, holding her face where Mariposa had slapped her. And in that instant Jen knew that Mariposa was telling the truth.

"How dare you let her attack me!" Sonya cried out.

Lucille just laughed.

"Honey, I don't think you gonna get much if you try suing Doc."

Jen took a deep breath.

"Sonya, would you like me to call a guard?"

Sonya shook her head.

"All right then," Jen said. "We all need to calm down. Mariposa, there will be no violence in this program. None. I won't accept it."

Her breath came hard out of tight lungs. Of all the days for Lolly not to be here. Now she was sorry to be all alone with these women. Lolly, Jen was sure, would not have let this happened.

Mariposa looked chagrined.

"Yes, I'm sorry. It won't happen again."

Jen looked around the circle.

"What happens here stays here. Is that clear?"

The women nodded. Sonya sat back down in the chair, holding her head as high as she could. She was frightened, Jen could tell, but trying to maintain her dignity. Not an easy task. *How could these two women have wound up together in this room*, Jen wondered.

"Now, this is not a court of law. We can't judge anyone's guilt or innocence here. We're here to make art together, to do theater. I need to know if you can still do that." Jen looked directly at Mariposa. Mariposa's eyes were hard and angry, but she nodded her head.

"Sonya, can you?"

Sonya's chin quivered, but she nodded as well.

As Jen sat down, her heart continued to beat hard in her chest. She wondered if she should say something to the authorities about this episode. It wouldn't take much for them to cancel the program altogether. And that would crush Lolly.

"All right. I guess we'll continue," she said, swallowing her anxieties.

She looked around the room at the silent faces. Then quiet Viola took off her thick black-framed glasses and said, "I killed my husband."

Saturday Night, July 1

Dinner that night was Salisbury steak, green beans from a can and squares of yellow cake with chocolate frosting. Sonya walked through the line slowly, glancing carefully around. She was accumulating enemies in this place and not winning any friends. Panther sidled up behind her.

"Hey, whassup, Gypsy Queen?" Panther asked. Sonya could feel her long lanky presence. Sonya shrugged. Maybe Panther hadn't heard about the blowout in drama. That would be odd since news generally traveled fast in the prison like water running downhill.

"You gonna sit wit' me?" Panther asked.

"No," Sonya said. "You sit with your friends. I need to think about some stuff."

"Okay, no hurt in trying tho," she said.

Sonya found a corner spot at the back of the large noisy room. She didn't like to admit that she didn't hate Panther's attention. Sometimes she wished she could turn to Panther, let Panther wrap her arms around her, but she was afraid. She didn't want to be owned. Duke had owned her. It was pure and simple.

She tried a bite of the steak and couldn't decide which was worse— the taste or the texture. She pushed the beans around with her spoon and thought about her marriage. At twenty-two she was an old maid and not the prettiest girl in the clan though her figure had earned her the interest of more than a few men. She hadn't responded. The only men she allowed to get close to her were strangers she met in bars when she could get away from the constant watchful eyes of her parents and brother. When Dina figured out what Sonya was doing, she found Duke and invited him into their lives. Duke was a distant relation of her mother's best friend from Poland. He'd been in Canada, but when Dina called, he answered. He got in his big midnight blue Dodge Ram truck and drove down to Florida and presented himself as a suitable match. It was decided in a day.

It had all seemed inevitable and Sonya was glad not to have to make any decisions. There were worse men than Duke to be married to. He did not scream and berate her the way her own brother did his wife. And he had only hit her once. Not a punch, just a quick cuff on the side of her head, and she couldn't help but believe that she had deserved it. She had been so bitchy that day, probably on her period, and had not wanted to go to work. But she had not been brought up to be lazy and to make excuses. As Dina had said so often, "Fishermen never say no to the sea."

Indian sat down across from her. Sonya smiled.

"Damn," Indian said. "I don't see that very often. You have a really pretty smile, Sonya. It lights up your whole face."

Sonya looked down at her metal tray.

"Alice," Sonya said, tasting the word. "Your name is Alice. I don't know why everyone calls you Indian."

"Same reason they call you Gypsy, I guess. We're not really white and not black either and we don't speak Spanish. They have to put us in some category."

"From now on, I'll call you Alice," Sonya said.

"Thanks," Alice said. "I mean, it doesn't bother me what people call me. But it's nice to be known by my name. More friendly."

"I wonder why they aren't buzzing around, gossiping about what happened," Sonya said, gazing around the room. Mariposa was at a table with her friends but didn't seem to be paying any attention to Sonya.

"It's like Doc said, what happens in workshop stays there. Mariposa won't mention it again. I mean, she might shoot you some stink-eye, but that's probably all."

"The hell with her," Sonya said, but her tone was weak.

Alice didn't say anything. Sonya didn't either. She couldn't admit the truth. When they had pulled the scam, it had seemed a brilliant, beautiful stunt. She remembered the celebration when the check came from the hotel, the settlement to keep from going to court without having to admit their security was lax. Hotels hated bad publicity. That night the family rented a restaurant in Tarpon Springs, where they could blend in with the Greek community. Florida's cracker cops wouldn't know the difference. She wore a brand new Dior dress, white with little beads around the neckline. Maybe twenty people from the family were there, drinking champagne, and that strong Greek liquor—Ouzo. She got a little tipsy, too. But she was the belle of the ball that night.

Her uncle came up, rubbed his finger along her cheek and said, "This kid can really take a punch."

Then Ziggy was behind her, breathing down her neck with his hot sour breath the way she had always hated when they were kids. She stepped away and turned to face him. He'd smirked at her and said, "Yeah, that was fun. Let's do it again, Sonya."

She had turned her back on him. That was the same night her mother brought over a man and said, "Sonya, this is Duke. He'll be working with us. Why don't you get to know him?"

Duke was tall with heavily hooded eyes, a barrel chest and a shy grin. He stuttered a little bit when he talked, but she soon learned that he didn't speak often. He could be quiet for hours, and after growing up with her family of non-stop monologists, she found she rather liked him. They were married two months later. The night of their wedding, Duke lay next to her in the king-sized bed at the Sheraton in Miami Beach, and gently running his finger over the slight lump in her nose, he said he'd never let her pull that scam again.

Monday, July 3

This time last year, Daniel had told his wife he had a shoot in California. He did, but he didn't mention that he had flown Jen out to be with him. The worst part of the whole affair was that she had actually been in love with Daniel. It was on a shoot for the chamber of commerce in Destin, Florida—promoting the "Redneck Riviera." She had been cast as the spokesperson and Daniel was the director. In one week she'd fallen like a rock for the man and he apparently had fallen for her, too. Then she found out he was married. Not long after that her drinking started to become a problem.

She was still a professional. She never got drunk on the job. In fact, she could go weeks without drinking or just be content with a beer or a glass of wine, but then something would happen and she'd stalk the night like a vampire. At those times she never had just a friendly beer or two but always drank until all the locks had been broken and the wild exuberant spirit she kept trapped inside could be let loose.

Now, Daniel was gone from her life forever. There was no doubt about that. But still when she came home sometimes just before she played her messages, she had a hope that he would have called if only to say hello and ask her how she was doing. Instead there was a message from someone named Zack Holtz.

"Hi, Jennifer Johanssen. This is Zack Holtz. We met the other night—uh—when you were driving at an excessive speed down

Tennessee Street. I wondered if you'd like to go to the lake with me tomorrow. Some of us are going out on my friend's boat and I thought you might be able to join us. Call me," he said and left a phone number.

Jen hardly remembered him except that he was sort of attractive. He had a nice voice, too. But for God's sake he was a cop. What could they possibly have in common?

She dialed the number. She would politely decline the invitation and be done with him.

"Hi, Zack," she said when he answered. "It's Jen. I got your message about going to the lake."

"Hey, you called back," he said, sounding surprised.

"Um, yeah. Listen, I can't do anything tomorrow. I have to go out to the prison."

"What? What did you do now?"

"I didn't do anything," she said. "I'm working on a drama program at the women's prison."

"You've got to be kidding," he said.

"No, I'm not. It's a grant-funded program my sister got me into. I'm helping them put together a drama production."

"This, I've got to hear about. Okay, how about we meet afterwards for dinner and a movie?"

"You mean like a date?" Jen asked, realizing the absurdity of her skittishness. She had probably been willing to fuck him the other night when he brought her home. Manny, her cat, crawled into her lap and was purring full throttle.

"We can go Dutch if it'll make you feel better," he said.

"No, not this time. It's just not a good time for me, okay?"

"Okay," he said. "Maybe later."

She hung up the phone and rested her head against the back of the chair. She absently stroked Manny's orange neck and wished she didn't have this suffocating cloud of depression. Manny, short for Maniacal, twisted onto his back and grabbed her hand between his claws as if it were a fat, hairless mouse. He sunk his sharp little teeth into her flesh as she watched dully.

Then that interlude between day and evening sent a splash of cool light into the room. Jen remembered sitting in the room at the prison with those women, their faces friendly for the first time, accepting. She remembered how she had felt carefree for a while, like she was naked and it didn't matter to anyone. A realization came over her and she gazed out the window at a heavy-limbed magnolia tree with thick white blossoms.

"Lolly, you devil," she whispered, cupping her cat's head in her hand. "You aren't a do-gooder 'cause you like to help them. It makes you feel better, doesn't it?"

Tuesday, July 4

Alice leaned back against the concrete wall, her blue-jeaned legs stretched out across the grass. The small gold posts in her ears. No hoop earrings were allowed, but most everyone wore posts of some kind as long as they weren't worth more than fifty bucks. Sonya looked down at her sneakers, ran her fingers along her shin bones and tucked her dress underneath her. Alice was slowly, luxuriously enjoying a large piece of watermelon.

"Don't get fresh fruit too often," she said, with juice dripping from chin.

"And right off the truck, too," Sonya said. It wasn't such a bad day for once.

"So tell me about your family," Alice said, curiously.

Sonya shrugged. A couple of the women were doing jumping jacks in the yard, trying to shake off the prison pounds.

"We run scams," she said finally.

"How do you go so long without getting caught?"

"You have to be smart. When you steal, you don't take the whole wallet. You get the license and one credit card. Sometimes you even leave the cash. You find a checkbook, you only take the last two checks. You never write the check for more than 950 dollars. Sometimes it may take weeks before those old people know what happened. Most of them are little senile anyway so they're not following their accounts. By the time they realize they've been bouncing checks like Michael

Jordan, they don't remember exactly what you looked like, or if there was one or two of you, or when you were even there. Did you go in their house? They don't remember. That's why you go after old people."

Alice crossed her ankles and stared up at the sky.

"What's wrong?" Sonya asked.

"I was just thinking about my grandma. She's so sweet. She married a white man in her old age and now she lives in one of those retirement villages. Sometimes my moms brings her up to see me. I'm trying to imagine what she would do if she got ripped off like that. Or how I'd feel about it."

"Oh, man, it's no big deal. The bank is insured so they don't lose any money. We don't hurt anyone."

Alice shrugged and didn't say anything for a few minutes. Sonya turned the other way and thought a murderer had some nerve criticizing her.

"It's just that I've been locked up a long time," Alice said, "and I figured out one or two things. The main thing I've figured out is that what we think we're doing to someone else, we're really doing to ourselves. Like when I shot that guy. I killed something in myself, something I'll never get back. Everything you do—it affects everyone else whether you realize it or not. Every time you say something, whether it's kind or cruel, it ripples out. Every time you do something, other people feel it, people you never even saw. When I was little my father got drunk and beat the hell out of me with the wrong end of the belt for no reason at all, beat me so bad I wanted to die. A few years later, a man dies of a gunshot wound in a botched robbery by a couple of teenagers with a stolen gun.

"I'm not making excuses for myself. Like I said, I've had a lot of time to think about things and it's never as simple as it seems."

Sonya plucked a blade of grass as she thought about Alice's words. She looked up and saw Panther watching them from the doorway. The afternoon light glowed on Panther's skin, and Sonya felt a strange stirring inside. Alice was right. Nothing was as simple as it seemed. The buzzer sounded, and they had to get back to the dorm for count.

Tuesday Night, July 4

A huge crowd of people had spread over the large park field while patriotic songs played on the loud speakers. Lolly sat in a canvas folding chair next to the blanket where Sue and her husband and two kids—Laura and Kevin—were sprawled. Aunt Jewel had her own little lawn chair on the other side of the blanket. Aunt Jewel and Sue's husband were engaged in an impassioned discussion of the upcoming election. Sue's husband was on-the-fence and Aunt Jewel was proselitizing with the fervor of the truly committed. Politics, it seemed, was on everyone's mind.

Lolly was not interested in national politics this year. She had enough politics to deal with at the prison. Jen had told her about the incident between Mariposa and Sonya, and it gnawed at her. She hadn't had either of them in a previous class, and so she didn't know them as well as she did several of the others. She couldn't stop thinking about Mariposa's brother, locked up for a crime he didn't commit—if Jen was right. She gazed down at 10-year-old Kevin with his shaggy blond hair and round impish face. He was one of her favorite children in the world—all mischief and bravado and curiosity. What if he were to wind up someday in prison because he trusted the honeyed words of a con artist?

Kevin caught her looking at him. He twirled a glow stick in his hand.

"Why were you in the hospital?" he suddenly asked.

"I had to get a brain transplant," Lolly answered. "I'm a lot smarter now."

"Really?" he asked, sitting up and continuing to twirl the glow stick.

"Kevin," Sue interjected. "It's none of your business why Lolly was in the hospital. The fireworks are going to start any minute. Why don't you go get something to drink with your dad?"

Kevin dropped the glow stick on his sister's head and got up to follow his father to the concession stand. Sue grimaced apologetically to Lolly. Lolly shrugged in response. So far no one besides Jen and Aunt Jewel knew about Lolly's cancer. She had only told her co-workers that she had to go in for a "minor procedure", but she knew she would have to tell Sue soon. Lolly's work schedule would need to be rearranged to accommodate the chemotherapy.

"Lolly," Sue said. "I heard that your sister is going to be directing the summer play at Kevin and Laura's camp. I didn't know she worked with kids."

"Well, she teaches college and has worked with teenagers. Maybe it's not all that different," Lolly said. Just then the sky erupted with red, white and blue bursts of fireworks. The audience gasped. Laura jumped on Lolly's lap and Lolly winced as the child bumped against the incision on her chest. Sue coaxed Laura back down on to the blanket and looked at Lolly curiously. Lolly covered her pain with a smile.

Then she bent down and said to Sue, "Could you come over to the house after the fireworks? Let Marty take the kids home. There's something I need to talk about."

Sue reached up and took her hand.

"Of course," she said.

Lolly leaned back and watched as the explosions burst one after the other on the night screen.

Wednesday, July 5

Jen stepped out of the cool building with the script pages in her hand. Joe held the door open and said, "See you tomorrow, Jen. Seven a.m. call time, okay?"

"No problem," she said.

"Stay sober tonight, okay?"

She turned to him and glared. "What do I look like, Judy Garland?"

Joe grinned and began singing "Somewhere over the rainbow . . ."

Jen turned and walked toward the Blazer. She had gotten wasted with Joe and his crew a few times over the years, but she never missed a call time, and he knew it.

In spite of the oppressive heat and humidity weighing down the moss-draped oak trees, Jen felt light. Summer was usually a barren time for work in the Capital City so she was glad to have even a public service announcement job that didn't pay squat. It was always good to have work.

As she got in the sauna which her Blazer had become and wiped the steam from her sunglasses, she remembered that she was supposed to take Lolly to her first chemo session the next day. Well, she'd have to stop by and tell her she couldn't do it. She was grateful for the excuse. She hated hospitals. They made her think of that movie where Jessica Lange plays an actor who has lost her marbles. A riveting performance Jen had watched countless times. Maybe Aunt Jewel would take Lolly instead.

As Jen pulled up in front of the house, Lolly came out of the front door of her house, and Jen stared in horror.

"What have you done to your hair, woman?" she asked as Lolly approached the Blazer. It looked as if she had whacked it all off with a pair of blunt scissors.

Lolly stood before her and answered, "Well, I remembered how I lost it all the last time. It was probably the worst part of the whole thing. Maybe not the worst, but it was bad. And I just couldn't go through that again."

Jen remembered once getting in the shower while Lolly was going through her chemotherapy treatments. She had found a mass of long, dark hairs covering the drain, and in a rage stormed into Lolly's room to scream at her for being so gross. But when she threw open the door, she found Lolly curled up in a ball on the floor in front of the full-length mirror hanging on the closet door, shaking with sobs. Her hair was so thinned out that patches of her scalp were visible.

Lolly's hair had been a source of pride, and even Jen had to admit it was gorgeous until it disappeared strand by strand. Lolly became a bald teenager, which was almost as bad as later becoming a one-legged teenager. Jen had been young and angry and even ashamed, unable to feel much sympathy for this person who required so much. Now it seemed that Lolly didn't require anybody or anything, least of all a head full of gorgeous hair.

"I'm going to beat the bastards to the punch before even one chemo treatment. I'm going to the barbershop in Frenchtown and have the barber shave it off."

"Well, I'll take you then," Jen said. "Hop in."

Lolly walked around and got in the passenger seat of the car. Jen studied her for a moment before shifting into drive. Lolly's expression was not one of bitterness. It was more like determination.

"Listen, I can't take you to the hospital for your chemo tomorrow," Jen said. "I've got to do a PSA for some new insurance program that the government wants people to vote for."

Lolly shrugged. "I'll get Aunt Jewel to take me."

Jen turned on the radio and a song about the Age of Aquarius came on the oldies station. Love would steer the stars they said. Mystic crystal revelations would happen. Jen didn't believe a word of it.

Lolly leaned her head out of the window for a moment and then pulled back in.

"God, it's hot out there." She rolled up the window and Jen turned up the AC.

"So why Frenchtown?" Jen asked.

"I don't know. I just figure those old black men will know how to shave a head and I think they won't judge or refuse me," she said. "Plus it's the only place they still use the razor. I want to feel it happening."

Jen drove on. The houses in Frenchtown were small and wooden, painted bright colors or in need of a paint job. They were crowded close together, separated by chain link fences surrounding small yards, sometimes boasting a plethora of flowers.

"I love these yards," Lolly said. Jen had never paid much attention to them. They were just the homes of the disadvantaged, the result of centuries of slavery followed by a century of systematic discrimination. But, of course, that's not what Lolly saw. Lolly saw the charm and beauty and tender care of gardeners.

"That's Mary Thompson's house," Lolly pointed out as they came to a corner with a stop sign. The yard was practically overflowing with flowers of every description.

"How do you know her?" Jen asked.

"Oh, I come over and get gardening advice from her all the time. Don't you love her little pansies?"

"Nice," Jen said.

"Look, there she is," Lolly said and waved madly out the window at a surprised elderly lady. When the woman finally recognized Lolly, she broke into a wide smile and waved back. Jen turned the corner and headed down into the historic Frenchtown district. This is where

Tallahassee's black history had often been made. The buildings were old and some of them were derelict. The windows were covered with thick black burglar bars. In winter the men stood in the parking lot next to the convenience store and warmed themselves beside a fire in a wire trash can. In summer they sat in plastic lawn chairs around a square crate and drank tall cans of malt liquor under a sprawling oak tree. Supposedly this is where you came to buy crack. And this is where police cars often cruised by if there was room in the jailhouse.

Though only a few blocks from the university and a few more from the halls of the capitol building where the state's power brokers decided what to do with their abundant resources, Jen and Lolly would likely be the only white people to park and exit their vehicles along this strip. Jen found a parking spot near the barber shop. Outside there was actually a red and white striped cylinder encased in some kind of plastic case with brass knobs on either end. The classic barber shop pole. The heat rising from the cracked sidewalk licked at their faces. Lolly watched the ground as she walked, always careful where the leg landed. She wore an old-fashioned summer dress from a thrift shop. Jen thought that Lolly's chop job made her head look like a Q-tip.

Lolly entered the barbershop and Jen followed. A long wooden bench was placed by the front window, and on it sat a man in a fedora. He lowered his girlie magazine to eyeball the two women. A man who seemed to be in charge, dressed in brown pants and a barber's tunic, looked curiously at Lolly and asked, "Can I help you?"

"I want to know if I can get a razor shave?"

"For your head?"

Lolly nodded.

A television bolted to the ceiling in the back played an afternoon soap opera and a wheezy air conditioner blew over head. A couple of small rotating fans pushed the air around. The smell of hair pomade and coconut and one man's spicy chicken wings filled the air. Jen watched as if she were invisible.

"I'm getting chemotherapy tomorrow," Lolly said. "I want to shave my head."

Suddenly everything in the room changed. A big man with a nametag that said Ronald beckoned Lolly to his chair. And the man in the fedora said, "Go on, baby. They'll take care of you." Then he scooted over to make room for Jen. The other men who had been waiting looked at the television screen as if they had been waiting all day for this particular show. Jen sat down and studied her hands.

The man in the fedora asked, "You with her?"

"She's my sister," Jen answered.

"My aunt had cancer. Lived a good while with it. A good while."

Jen took a deep breath. She'd been denying cancer's power to kill. After all, the last time it hadn't killed Lolly. Why shouldn't she beat it again? But it could kill. She had to admit that much.

Lolly looked in the mirror at the alien looking back at her. She hadn't realized what a long neck she had. She looked like an ostrich, she decided, and smiled a goofy bird smile at herself. Now her thick dark eyebrows were so noticeable. Of course, the chemo would get to them and they'd be gone. On second thought, maybe she didn't look like an ostrich. She was more like a Nubian princess, only with pale white skin.

"Thank you," she said. Ronald dusted off her neck and winked at her in the mirror.

"You take care of yourself, Miss," he said. "And come back and see me."

"I will," she smiled brightly, picked up her purse and tried to pay him twenty dollars.

"No, ma'am," Ronald said, tucking his hands in his pockets. "You can't pay me for that. That one was on the house."

Lolly felt hot tears of gratitude well up in her eyes. She nodded and put the twenty back in her purse.

Jen had gone out turned on the Blazer to get the AC going.

"Why do you have to have this big, obnoxious vehicle?" Lolly asked as she got in the passenger side.

"Because it's paid for," Jen answered. "And I didn't pick it out." Then Jen paused and gazed at her. "You look like a Vulcan."

"A Vulcan?"

"Yeah, like from one of those Star Trek movies. I forget which one, but there was this beautiful bald Vulcan woman in it."

"Well, that was probably a career-ending role," Lolly said, gazing out the window. She ran her hand over her newly bald head. It felt so odd, so bony. "I think I'd like to decorate my scalp with a tattoo."

"A tattoo? You've been working with prisoners way too long," Jen said.

"A henna tattoo. They're not permanent. And they're so pretty. Will you do it for me?"

Jen didn't answer. She pulled into the heavy traffic of the main road and stopped at the Taco Bell. She pulled in and ordered soft drinks for both of them, then looked over at Lolly. "I don't know how to do a henna tattoo. Why don't you get one of your artist friends to do it?"

Jen reached out to hand some bills to the girl on the other side of the drive-thru window.

"You're my sister, Jen. My only relative besides Dad and who knows where he is. And since I might not have that much longer to live, I want to get to know you, if it's the last thing I do."

Jen drove silently for a few blocks and then turned onto Lolly's street.

"I wish you wouldn't say that about dying, Lolly. Many, many people survive cancer and live for years to come," she said.

"I know. I was one of them. But this is the second time, and the doctors said it is fast and aggressive. It's stage four, Jen. Do you know what that means?"

"Yes, I think I do," Jen answered.

Lolly leaned back and crossed her arms. It meant that they didn't bother to pretend there was a cure. They didn't come right out and say it, but she knew the chemo only bought a little extra time, a few weeks or maybe a few months.

"So are you gonna tattoo my head or not?"

They pulled in front of the house, and Jen turned off the ignition. *Just this once*, Lolly thought, *do something for me.*

"Okay," Jen said.

Lolly helped Jen mix the reddish-brown powder with the special oil. They were in Lolly's kitchen. Lolly sat in a wooden chair that she had painted turquoise with snakes winding around the legs and little black stick figures dancing on the back. She had touched every piece of this house and made it her own.

"You know I have no artistic talent whatsoever," Jen said, stirring the brown paste.

"Don't worry, I've made some stencils you can use," Lolly said, smoothing oil over her scalp. "Can you get the back for me? Make sure it's even."

Jen rubbed her hands gently over Lolly's bald head. They were quiet for a moment. They hadn't been this intimate since they were children. Then Jen placed the stencils on Lolly's blank scalp and began to apply the henna.

From the Journal of Nicole Parks

The next Saturday after Mariposa jumped on Sonya, Lolly was back. She looked kind of tired, but she smiled and ran us through our writing exercises all the same. She wore a little knit cap over her head and said she'd cut her hair. At the time I didn't think anything of it. I mean, you look at someone that young and you don't think that there might be something wrong. And once Lolly got involved in talking about how to structure our skits, she was her usual enthusiastic self. I was feeling worried the week before about how we were going to pull this production off, but Lolly grinned and said, "Honey, you can do anything. Wait and see. It's gonna be great."

Viola was kinda quiet in the class. No one was really sure how she'd gotten in, but she had taken two years of junior college learning secretarial skills and so her classification officer must have thought that meant she'd be good in a drama class. Yeah, the people who run this joint are kinda stupid sometimes. Anyway, I'd had an idea that somehow in the drama class, Daffy and I would be able to help Viola. I just couldn't figure out how. But a plan was starting to form in my head.

That night was kind of spooky. An inmate in another dorm tried to kill herself. She was real young and pretty, and the rumor was that one of the male sergeants had raped her but no one could ever prove anything. Rumors buzz around a compound like flies around shit, you know. All I can say for sure is that there was an angry, sickly feeling over the whole cafeteria at breakfast that morning. I was glad to be going to church and hear some hymn singing.

Viola had taken to tagging along to church with me. Daffy had joined the choir, of all things. She was really trying to look good and scrape all the gain time she possibly could. Daffy had changed in prison. I somehow got the feeling she wasn't going back to the streets when she got out. I hoped she wouldn't.

That Sunday as Viola and I sat in the congregation, we noticed a little buzz among some of the ladies in the choir. I noticed Daffy looking at the very back of the chapel where the "fresh meat" had to sit. They were kept out of the general population for three or four weeks while all their paperwork got done. So people liked to come to church to see if anyone they knew was out there.

I finally couldn't stand it and I turned around. Didn't recognize anybody, but I did notice a white chick who looked like some kind of model. She had dark hair and even from where I was, I could tell she was pretty and would have all the studs in an uproar. I didn't like her. Didn't know her, but white girls can be hard enough to put up with when they are ugly. One like her would probably be intolerable.

On the way back to the dorm the buzz was going. Seems she was famous. Not as a model or movie star, but for gunning down a couple of tourists in a bad robbery. Most women who kill don't do it like that. They're usually too smart and leave that kind of stupid go-to-prison-for-life kind of thing to the men. Once everyone started talking I realized I had heard about her on TV. Her name was Riley something.

I didn't think much of it. Didn't know she'd wind up in our dorm or that she was a bad seed.

I remember the next day pretty well. It was a Monday, of course. And I had gone to the mailroom after lunch before the one o'clock count. I really didn't want to go. For two weeks, I'd been checking my mailbox and each time it was empty. Antwan must have dropped off the face of the earth. At first I was worried, but after a while I was just mad. If he'd been killed or busted I would have known it, so the only explanation could be that he was out there messing around.

Viola came sliding up next to me. She wore a pair of ugly black state glasses and grinned her little buck-toothed grin. Viola was not ugly, but she was no Janet Jackson either. I wasn't feeling very happy that day. Truthfully, my smiles and cheerful voice were an act I put on. Lots of times I was deep down in the dumps. Even among all those women, I felt lonely, and sometimes a darkness would fill me up. Other times it would drain back out and leave me feeling so empty I wasn't sure what held my skin in place.

"You going to the mailroom?" Viola asked.

I was 'bout to say, "no, I ain't" and go to the canteen and get candy. But then I realized Antwan didn't send me any money so my bank was empty. Also there was another reason I should check my mail. So I walked in with Viola and turned the lock to my box. Inside there was a square envelope. The hand-writing sure wasn't Antwan's, but I had a feeling from the postmark who had written me. I looked over and Viola had already torn into her letter.

"It's from Junebug," she said, smiling up at me.

"Oh, that's nice. What does he say?" I asked, not really giving a damn but trying to be polite.

Viola read down a little ways and looked back up at me.

"He wants to write you if that's okay. I told him all about you, about how you went to college and how nice you are and how you are gonna be a writer."

I was shocked. I wasn't sure I wanted to be writing to some dude name of Junebug. But on the other hand, my bank was bare and what if Antwan had dropped me for good?

I waited till I got back to my bunk to read my card. The front cover showed a pair of praying hands. Yep, I thought. That's about right. I opened it and inside was a little note: *Dear Nic-nak, I got down on my knees and thanked Jesus when I got your letter. I will come visit you soon as I can. Just make sure I am on your list. In the meantime, keep your chin up and your eyes on the prize! Love, Granny Hazel.*

My Granny Hazel was my daddy's mother. She was a hellfire and brimstone street-corner preacher since she was about fourteen. As Christian as she was, she never married my daddy's father. Said he was a no-good drunk. As far as I know, he was the only man who got close to her sacred parts.

Those nasty women started coming in and getting on their bunks. Daffy came swishing her hips down the aisle in that languid walk of hers.

"Girl, who wrote you?"

"My Granny Hazel."

"Your man ain't write?"

"Naw."

"Better get your granny to come visit you. I'm tired of seeing you mopping up the floor with your big old sad lips every time Sunday afternoon comes."

"Girl, please," I said to her. The buzzer went off and I put the card in the top drawer of my dresser. I didn't realize how obvious my sadness was, but now I had something to focus on: Saving Viola from the ghost.

Monday July 10

Jen would never have imagined herself as a camp counselor, but a job in the summer was a job. And she wasn't a counselor, but actually the director of the summer drama camp for a group of precocious kids aged 5 to 13. Two other women were working fulltime to handle things like potty breaks and helping with the set designing and prop gathering. So Jen just decided to think of the job as "summer stock."

The school where the camp was held was actually a rambling wooden house. Doors had been taken off the closets, and the closets turned into reading nooks. The little work tables had been cleared away to make room for rehearsals and set building. The walls were bright and a full working kitchen meant that lunches were pretty good since one of the mothers was an organic chef and would often come in and fix meals for Jen and the two teachers.

The first week she spent doing improv classes with the kids and choosing a couple of plays. She usually got home around six. Then after a romantic dinner with the cat, she might stop by Lolly's before going out for a drink. Sometimes she skipped the visit to Lolly, but then Jen's guilt over abandoning Lolly after her surgery made it hard to enjoy her buzz. A few times Lolly had been cranky and unbearable, but usually she was in good spirits. It was hard to know what she was thinking. Was she afraid of dying? Jen was glad not to have to go to the chemo room with her anymore. Several of Lolly's friends were taking shifts, and some of them were positively martyrs, trying to outdo each other in taking care of Lolly. But in the evenings it was Jen's job to come over and make sure that Lolly wasn't in need of a trip to the emergency room.

She had just gotten home Wednesday night when the phone rang. It was probably Lolly with some more things for Jen to pick up from the drugstore. Lolly was so forgetful these days she wouldn't realize she'd already given Jen a list. 'Chemo brain', she called it. Jen had realized when she was young how cancer always had more victims than just the sick person. Now, she was learning that lesson all over again.

But it wasn't Lolly calling. It was that cop—Zack Holtz.

"Hey," he said. "How was your day?"

"You really want to know?" she asked.

"Sure, I do. I asked, didn't I?" he said.

"Well, I spent the first eight hours with 27 of the most high energy kids on the planet and then got an oil change for my car and then had to do some errands for my sister and now I'm home," she said. "And tomorrow it starts all over again."

"You need a break," he said.

"I do. I could use a two-week Caribbean cruise," she said, sinking down onto her bed and pushing her shoes off.

"Well, I can't help you with that. But I do have a Harley Davidson if you like bikes," he said.

"No way! You're a cop. Do you mean to tell me you transform yourself into a biker on your days off?"

"Yeah, I put on my colors and go bash in a few heads. I'm really a member of the Hell's Angels."

"You're a piece of work."

"I'm serious. Let's go out on the bike Sunday. We'll cruise down to the coast."

Jen closed her eyes. A whole day away from kids and away from Lolly. Where no one could find her. It sounded like heaven. And there was something about his sweet cajoling voice that lured her in this time. She felt that hook catch in her cheek. There was still time to get away later.

"Okay," she said. Manny curled up on her chest and began to purr.

Thursday, July 13

The rain fell in large hard pellets and brought an odd chill to what had earlier been a sweltering summer day. Sonya stood at the kitchen door watching it fall and puddle. Sonya liked rain, but she wasn't looking forward to walking back in that downpour to the dorm.

"Break's over," C.O. Dawkins said, waddling past Sonya. Panther had just finished a cigarette and turned to face her, smoke still trailing from her nostrils.

"You look like a dragon," Sonya laughed.

"Well, you look like a piece of cherry pie," Panther said.

"When are you going to stop?" Sonya asked, but her voice was not harsh.

"Yakowski and Goldberg, get in there and clean the steam tables," Dawkins lazily ordered. Curly handed Sonya some rags and a bucket, and together they went into the dining room to wipe down the steam tables.

Magna was already in there, mopping the floor with large angry sweeping motions. The water and vinegar solution for the steam tables wafted past Sonya's face. At least with the rain, she wasn't sweating today. She glanced warily over at Magna. Magna jammed the string mop down in the water of the bucket and then lifted the dripping mop head and shoved it into the wringer and pushed down the handle. The muscles in her upper arms bulged as she squeezed the handle down.

Magna had never liked Sonya after the cigarette swiping incident, but she hadn't threatened her again. Sonya thought it might have blown over until she noticed Magna sitting at Mariposa's table at dinner last night, the two of them all buddy-buddy, laughing and leaning together. When Sonya had to walk by them on her way to dump her tray, Mariposa said something under her breath and Magna said loudly, "I know that's right." And then she had laughed directly towards Sonya's back. Sonya had never known that laughter could feel like a blade between your ribs.

After Sonya wiped the steam tables, she cleaned out the Kool-Aid canisters and wiped down the disposal area. The sight of the food all mixed together, pieces of half-eaten white bread, peas, and chunks of chicken disgusted her. She was tired by the end of the workday, getting up at five every morning and engaging in physical labor six days a week. She'd never had to work hard at home. Duke was pretty good at cleaning up after himself and was a good father, helping with the baby whenever he wasn't out on a job. She had been bored with Duke but now she realized she'd had it pretty good. Maybe love wasn't all that important after all.

"Okay, ladies, you're done," Dawkins announced at ten minutes after two, purposely keeping them an extra ten minutes even though the second shift had already shown up. Nearly all the kitchen crew went back to their dorm and showered and napped in the afternoon. Sometimes they had dorm duties. Sometimes they got permission to go to the library. Sonya liked to go to the library and meet up with Alice. Sometimes they just sat there and read magazines. Sometimes Alice would be drawing something and she'd let Sonya watch. Alice worked as the teacher's aid and after the classroom time was over she was free to hang out in the library until the five o'clock count.

Today, as they hurried through the rain to the dorm, Sonya decided she would nap instead. She didn't feel good. Like maybe she had the flu or something. Or maybe she was just exhausted from working so hard in that kitchen. A shower would feel good.

She stood under the beating water and let it fall around her. She wanted her freedom so badly, and she wanted her son. She liked to daydream about Tomas. In her daydreams, Tomas was never a thief, never a "traveling criminal". She hated that phrase, but it was accurate. Instead he was a lawyer, living in a fancy house with a wing just for his mother. She didn't miss scamming people. And yet if you'd asked her a year ago, she would have told you there was nothing else she would do with her life. Now she considered, there was plenty to do. You could just have a regular job maybe and a house. What if Duke really just fixed people's roofs, and what if she worked with elderly people? Lord knows she got along with them well enough. It might not bring in a lot of money, but it would be better than this. And what happiness had all that money brought them? She knew that Ziggy, her mother and father and uncles and cousins, they'd all laugh at her. And she would miss them. But maybe she could be the legit one of the family.

She turned off the water and stepped out of the shower. The towels were so measly in this place. She missed big fluffy towels, but she could do without them. She could do without a lot of luxury if she could have her son back.

"Hey there, Sticky Fingers," Magna said, walking past her.

Sonya ignored her. She didn't like being in the bathroom alone with Magna even if there were windows that people could see through. There was no privacy in this place. Magna reminded Sonya of her brother Ziggy, who was neither clever nor handsome and had resorted to bullying his way through life. The family admired finesse, and Ziggy had none. Ziggy would have been more suited to an Italian family, her father used to say, where he could make a living cracking heads. Sonya wondered what Magna's crime had been. Probably a baby killer.

As Sonya slipped on the gold shift that was comfortable enough to nap in and yet still qualified as being dressed, Panther walked in, carrying her toiletries. Sonya instantly felt safer. Panther had a habit of showing up whenever Magna and Sonya wound up alone anywhere.

"Hey, Magna," Panther said when Magna came out of the toilet stall. "Girl, what are you in here for?"

"I just took a piss, what's it to you?"

"I mean here in the joint. I'm just curious."

Magna scowled and said, "Armed robbery. What about you?"

"Dealing," Panther said with a touch of pride. "I used to deal plenty weight. Ask anybody from Tampa who had the best stuff on the block and they will tell you it was me."

"I guess that's why your shit got busted," Magna said. "Everybody knew about you."

C.O. Barbie stepped in at that moment and announced, "Ladies, I need all of you dressed and in my office right now."

Magna glared at C.O. Barbie. That was one thing that united them—their hatred of C.O. Barbie. The three of them followed her wiggling little butt down the hall to her office. Curly was already in there. Sonya looked at Curly with a question in her eyes. Curly shrugged.

"What is this about, ma'am?" Panther asked.

"Hmph, you'll find out," she said in a low voice as if it took too much effort to speak to them.

Magna kept a cool impassive look on her face, and Curly looked annoyed. Sonya felt nervous. She did not like not knowing what was going on.

Magna leaned over and whispered, "What did you steal this time, sticky fingers?" Sonya jerked away and frowned at Magna. Magna smirked at her and then turned her attention to C.O. Barbie on the phone.

"Yes, I've got all four of them right here in my office," C.O. Barbie said. "Yes, I understand."

C.O. Barbie hung up the phone and said, "Ladies, I need to you to strip down to your bras and panties."

"Right here?" Sonya asked. There were windows on all sides of the office. Not that it mattered. The male guards could walk by and see them in the shower any time they wanted, but this was so humiliating.

"Right here, Inmate Yakowski. Take off your dress now."

Sonya and the others did as they were told. C.O. Barbie made each one rotate in a circle as she inspected them. Then she carefully felt through their clothes.

"Okay you can get dressed again," she said.

Sonya hurriedly put on her dress. The others got dressed, too. Three male guards came trooping into the building, their walkie talkies bouncing on their hips. One of them carried a shotgun.

"Damn," Panther whispered. "These po-leece love them some drama. Maybe they oughta take that class wit' y'all."

"You better shut up, Inmate," C.O. Barbie said coldly and walked out of her office to talk to the men.

"She thinks she's the shit," Curly said.

"I'd like to slit her throat," Magna said.

Sonya glanced at Magna and was sure that she could do it. C.O. Barbie was obviously telling them which bunks to search. She returned to the office and sat down while the four women stood silently waiting.

"Did any of you all go anywhere between the time you left the kitchen and the time you got here?" C.O. Barbie asked.

"No, ma'am," Curly said.

"None of y'all? Did you all walk back together? I don't remember seeing y'all come in at the same time."

"We always walk back together," Magna lied. "You can check the sign in sheet if you want to."

One of the guards stuck his head in the office and addressed C.O. Barbie.

"We didn't find anything," he said.

"Did you check the bathrooms?" she asked.

"Yep," he said. His walkie-talkie suddenly erupted in static and he punched the button and spoke into it. Apparently whatever they had been looking for hadn't been found in the other dorm either.

"All right, ladies," he said. "A butcher knife is missing from the kitchen. This is very serious. If any of you know anything or if you took it, you need to fess up now. Otherwise you're all going to the box till we find it."

"You can't put us in the box if we haven't done anything," Curly said.

The guard stared at her and C.O. Barbie said, "Inmate, no one asked for your opinion. Now, did you take that knife?"

"Me?" Curly asked incredulously, "Hell, no."

"Do you know who took it?"

"No, ma'am, I don't," she said.

"Then shut up."

Sonya felt an amorphous guilt in her gut. She knew nothing about the knife but all her other crimes, the ones she had gotten away with, surfaced in her mind and swam in circles mocking her, and so she felt the guilt of crimes she did not commit as well.

"Well, I guess you ladies will be taking a little vacation," the guard said.

"Put me in the damn box," Panther said, defiantly. "I don't care. I'd rather be there than slaving in that hot-ass kitchen."

They weren't allowed to take anything with them.

"If you want to read the Bible, the chaplain will come and bring you one," the guard said as he sat in the main unit at a desk, filling out paperwork on each one of them. They had brought in the morning kitchen shift from the other dorm as well. Sonya didn't realize they had that many solitary confinement cells there, but apparently they did, and apparently other inmates were getting out of the box to make room for the kitchen workers.

"Who's going to make breakfast tomorrow?" Magna asked. "You?"

The guard looked up at her with slitted eyes.

"I don't give a damn whether one single woman on this compound ever eats again." With that, they were led to their individual cells. Sonya stared at the hard bunk. She was still damp from the shower and it was cold in the room. One small window at the top let in the light.

So this was prison. She'd been here all of six months and now she was finally finding out what it was all about.

Lights went off in the box at 8 o'clock. Sonya watched the outside light slowly leech out of the rectangular window at the top of the wall. When the window went dark, the whole room became black. If there were stars or a moon, she couldn't see them. She heard some of the other women yelling. Someone called out, "Don't be scared, y'all. Everyone gonna be okay."

She heard someone else sobbing, but it sounded far away. The thin scratchy blanket felt rough and unpleasant against her skin. There was no sheet covering the hard plastic mattress. She rubbed her feet together. Alice's words came to her: "I'm trying to imagine how I would feel if someone did that to my grandmother."

Sonya had never stopped to think how someone else might feel about what she did. She thought of herself as a teacher, showing people through experience how to guard themselves and their belongings. But there was a rending ache inside her. She had never before had to confront herself, never been completely alone, left with nothing but her thoughts. She searched her memory. Besides Tomas, had anything good ever happened to her? She had so few happy memories. And what about those old people she had conned? What did they feel? How easy it had been to gain their trust. They were like children, like babies.

She felt as if she were hovering at the edge of a canyon, and at any moment she would fall. But why should she care about them? She wasn't a bad person. She didn't beat them up. She only took what they were careless enough to let her take. Their carelessness and gullibility was their fault, not hers. You should take better care of your money, especially if you were old and it was all you had left to live on.

One year Maria had actually gotten a job at an old people's home. And Sonya had been the one to sneak into their little apartments while they slept, the television blaring to stave off their loneliness. That's what it was – a deep black hole of loneliness that they felt. And she had peered into that loneliness, been able to spot it miles away. Why? Because it called to the loneliness inside her. Like beckoning to like. And as the night wore on she began to understand the limitless unhappiness, the emptiness of her heart. She had fed off those old people like a vampire.

But now she could identify the ghost inside her. And she felt herself wailing as an infant, left alone while Dina went off to steal just as she had left Tomas to go steal. She remembered Dina shaking her and slapping her in the back seat of the car. She felt so utterly and completely abandoned.

And what could you do? Could you go and give those old people the dresses you bought from Burdines, the color TV you bought, those $250 leather boots you bought with their credit cards?

But of course, she wasn't thinking about the other one, about that man, with his dark eyes and smooth light brown skin. How she had whispered into his ear that she needed his help and when he had come in, he had looked disbelieving at her nakedness and then he had done what any man would do when a woman invites him into her bed, no strings attached. But how gentle he had been, trying to kiss her face and speak little sweet things in her ear. In Spanish, of course.

Closing her eyes, she felt a drifting sensation and then the sense that she was somewhere else. In another cell. Another prison. She heard the sounds of men's voices and smelled sweat and piss. A cross hung on her neck and she could feel the metal between her fingers. Fear slid a cold fist down her spine. Followed by a veil of despair. That's where he was. Locked up with those men.

She came back to the dark room with a start. How terrible. But what could she do about it now? Fate was almost always cruel.

Then she heard what sounded like music. Someone was singing. She wrapped the blanket around her and lay down in a huddle beside the door, her ear to the crack at the bottom. She could hear someone singing hymns. "And He walks with me and He talks with me and He tells me I am his own." It was Panther's voice. Sonya closed her eyes and fell asleep listening.

Saturday July 15

"Where are Curly and Sonya?" Lolly asked as she stood at the doorway of their classroom.

"They got sent to the box," Daffy answered. "A butcher knife went missing from the kitchen and so everyone on that shift got locked down."

"When will they get out?" Lolly asked.

"I don't know, but it better be soon because I am sick of eating peanut butter and jelly," Lucille remarked and pursed her lips.

"I heard that!" another one of the women exclaimed.

Lolly felt a knot of concern for Sonya and Curly. She wasn't sure what it meant to be "in the box" but it didn't sound good. She wished she could call up someone and insist that the women be let out if there was no proof they'd done anything wrong, but you didn't insist on anything in this place.

"Well, we'll have to work around them," Jen said, running a hand through her hair. "Let's do our warm ups and then we can start working on Lucille's eviction piece."

"Okay, and Nicole and Alice and I can talk about props and things we might need for the other pieces," Lolly said, and put a hand on Nicole's shoulder.

While Jen, Lucille, Daffy and the others worked out the blocking for Lucille's skit, Lolly took Nicole and Alice over to a corner table in the large room. They were seated next to a window overlooking the road between the classrooms and the library. Nicole nudged Alice.

"Look there, Indian," Nicole said. "Who's that girl? I saw her at chapel the other day. They must be taking her to the infirmary for something."

Lolly looked up and saw a tall, willowy, dark-haired woman walking next to a guard.

"That's Riley," Alice said. "I used to hang with her down in Broward before I got transferred here. She got out about three years ago. Shame to see her back in blue."

"She your friend?" Nicole asked.

"She was," Alice said.

"I see," Nicole said.

Then Alice laughed. "Not that kind of friend."

Lolly glanced down at her notes, trying not to pry. She wondered what it was like to live in this world. They had networks in here, just like in politics or the arts or anything. But when she was working with them, it was easy to forget they had other lives, that they were someone other than who they were in this room. Of course, they had no idea what her life was like, either.

"Okay," Lolly said. "I got a list of acceptable items to bring into the prison to use as props and costumes. Scarves are okay, and Jen and I have a bunch of them. Also beads for jewelry. Plastic, of course. The other thing we can do is use big sheets of butcher paper to paint some backdrops."

"Cool," Alice said in her characteristic gentle way.

"Lolly," Nicole blurted out. "If I come to work release in Tallahassee, will you come over and see me sometimes?"

"Work release?" Lolly asked. "Are you getting out soon?"

"In the fall if there's any spaces," Nicole said.

"Oh my God, yes, I'll come see you." Lolly was filled with a sudden joy. That was what she wanted: to see them free, to see them on the other side of the razor wire. "Yes, I'll definitely come see you."

Sunday July 16

Zack had called Saturday night, just to talk he said. Jen sat on her couch, drinking a beer as she found out about his work, and he found out about hers. She hadn't decided whether or not to go out to the bar that night.

"I saw you in a play once," he said. "Damn, you were really good."

"What play?"

"Something about a nun who got pregnant and claimed she was a virgin."

"*Agnes of God*. I can't believe you saw that. Did you like it?"

"It was weird, but you were great. You played a shrink. Man, I would come lie down on your couch anytime," he said with a laugh. Oh, he was stroking her ego, and she loved every minute of it. What actor didn't?

"Hey, I had fun riding around with you that night," she said. "Do they have one of those programs where they let civilians ride around with cops regularly? I'd like to do that. It would give me good material next time I have to play a criminal."

"We used to have a program like that, but we lost the civilians," he said in a somber voice.

"What?" She was lying in her bed, the telephone wedged between her ear and shoulder.

"Yeah, they were killed."

She paused for a moment and then said, "You are such a liar." And he burst out laughing. She went to bed early that night, thinking it might be wise to be functional when she saw him the next day.

Sunday morning, he knocked on her apartment door. She answered, wearing her jeans and a Florida State t-shirt. She hadn't seen him since that night they met and her memory of him was vague. Now here he was in living color. Her eyes traveled the length of his six foot two, maybe six three-inch frame and she felt a tingly magnetism. He had broad shoulders, and his grin was hitched up on one side of his face. But it was the eyes—the friendly gray eyes glimmering with amusement—that rang alarm bells up and down her spine. It took a moment to marshal her defenses, but she did.

"Breakfast first?" she asked.

"Depends. Whatcha got?"

"Fried cockroaches," she answered.

"Sounds delicious."

He followed her into the apartment and to the kitchen where she'd already made some pancake batter. A bowl of blueberries stood to the side.

"You like blueberries? I picked them myself," she said.

"I love them, but I know you didn't pick 'em," he said.

"Did too. They have a little garden behind the school where I'm working. So you want blueberry pancakes?"

"Okay, but only if you really picked the blueberries."

She poured the batter onto the skillet and sent him to the table in the other room with a couple of plates and a pitcher of warmed maple syrup. If she'd remembered that he was this good looking, she wouldn't have gone to so much effort. That one probably gets spoiled by every woman who knows him.

"Nice table," he said when she brought out the platter of pancakes. She sat down and handed him a napkin.

"Thanks. It's an antique that my mom left me—very valuable. How do you like the chairs? I found them on the side of the road."

"I like a woman who knows how to find a bargain," he said and took a bite of the pancakes. He leaned back, chewing appreciatively and then said, "You didn't pick these blueberries."

"So the kids picked them for me. They're fresh anyway." She grinned. She liked him. It was impossible not to, and that was somewhat frustrating.

"How's your prison class going?" he asked.

"Not bad. I mean, it's really a lot better than I thought it would be. My bleeding-heart sister's idea, but I'm getting paid for it, so I'm not complaining," she said.

"Not with taxpayer money, I hope," Zack said with a grin.

"Grant money, if you must know, but since tax payers pay you to put them in there in the first place, I don't see why they shouldn't pay me to make sure they get some kind of rehabilitation while they're there."

Zack looked down at his plate. "Most of the cops I work with pretty much think the people we have to deal with are scum and shouldn't get any kind of help. But I've seen some who just had bad circumstances. I think if you can turn even one of them around, you're probably making a difference."

Jen tasted the warm syrup on her lips and wondered what it would be like to kiss him.

After breakfast, she dumped the dishes in the sink and they went outside. The day was slightly overcast, and a nice breeze ruffled through the leaves of the heavy-limbed oak tree in front of her apartment building. His motorcycle was leaning on its kickstand. It was an impressive looking machine, the tank painted a deep maroon with a silver design, a maroon fender with the same silver design, a cushy black leather seat, slightly raised in the back for a passenger, and gleaming chrome reflecting her blue-jeaned legs.

"Wow," she said. He smiled proudly and handed her a helmet. His own helmet was as skimpy as it could legally be and looked like something a German soldier might have worn in World War II. She looked at the helmet in her hand. On the back in cursive yellow letters was written: "Birdie."

"Who's Birdie?" she asked.

"Yesterday's news," he said.

"Old girlfriend?"

"Just someone I've been fortunate enough not to see in close to two years," he said.

"But you kept the helmet," she said, slipping it on and tightening the strap. He reached over and pulled the strap snug.

"Well, I bought it, and I figured the day might come when I'd need it again. And it has."

Oh, now he was bullshitting her for sure. Like he hadn't taken anyone out in two years. He must be seriously wanting to get laid, she thought. He threw his leg over the seat and pushed the bike upright. She slid behind him and leaned her back on the sissy bar.

"Just lean with me," he said, "when we go around corners."

"Okay," she said, and thought it was a helluva way to get to know someone – with his hips tucked between her legs, and her crotch nuzzled against him.

The engine roared to life. They pulled out of the driveway and slowly took to the street. Jen looked around at the other cars as they pulled onto the main road. You are so exposed on one of these things, but she liked it, liked the sense of being completely unencumbered. She let her hands rest on the sides of his waist. She had on a light jean jacket because he said you didn't want bugs splatting on your arms and it wouldn't be hot when you were going seventy miles an hour. And soon she found he was right as they sped out of town and down the long country roads toward the coast.

They couldn't talk, of course, over the wind and the roar of the engine. Her eyes watered and the hard wind pushed at her face and ran its hands up under her jacket which filled like a balloon. The heat of the day disappeared, and she let her arms creep tighter around his waist as they seemed to fly along the road.

A sense of peace permeated her mind. It had seemed like a really lousy summer, her heart hurting over the break up with Daniel and memories of her marriage to Lyle now resurfacing and a sense of failure that dogged her no matter what things she managed to do well. Not to mention Lolly's cancer. Even the sad stories of the women in prison. All of that was momentarily blown away by the wind twisting through the strands of hair that hung from the back of the helmet. She promised herself she wouldn't mention her sister's cancer to him. She wanted to forget about that for today, and she didn't want pity any more than Lolly did. She wanted today to be an island in the sea of her troubled life, something pure and untouched by unhappiness.

It took a couple of hours to get to Apalachicola. As she pulled the helmet off her head, she felt more refreshed than she had in months.

"That was awesome," she said. He grinned and put an arm around her waist as they walked into Boss Oyster House. They got a table outside overlooking a canal and ordered a dozen raw oysters and a dozen steamed. The waitress brought a couple of bottled beers to their table and Zack leaned over to her and said, "Jennifer Johanssen. That's a nice name. It sounds like old money. Mine sounds like new poverty."

"I don't have any money," she said, "new or old. Just trying to make it day by day."

"Why Tallahassee?" he asked. "I would think if you wanted to be an actor you'd live in New York or L.A."

"Maybe I just don't have a lot of ambition. Maybe I'd rather be a big fish in a small pond. I do get to star in a lot of student films," she said and tipped the cold bottle up. The beer went down her throat smooth as spring water. The daylight had a pastel quality. She set the bottle down on the wooden plank table and said, "Besides, I kind of like teaching and directing. So that's why I came back to school. I was in a few movies, but after a certain age if you're not Meryl Streep, well, I decided it was better to reject them."

"Oh, you're one of those," he said.

"Yeah." The oysters came and he pulled a paper towel from the roll sitting on the table and handed it to her.

"Don't say I never took you anywhere fancy, okay?" he told her.

She laughed and said, "It's perfect."

"If you like oysters," he said.

"I love them."

He dunked one of the gray blobs into some cocktail sauce and said, "They sure are ugly but they taste good." Then he slurped it down. Jen's mind went straight to the gutter and his followed. Soon they were giggling and blushing as if they were teenagers and not people in their thirties with more than a few lousy relationships behind them.

As they got back on the bike for the long ride back to Tallahassee, Jen had misgivings about the day. He was too nice. Too good. Too easy to like. Once he knew about her, knew everything, then he wouldn't want her. She would have to be careful not to let herself fall for him.

On the way back to Tallahassee, he took a different route. They flew along a two-lane black top road through acres and acres of nothing but tall pine trees pointing their green fingers to the sky. It was scary how quickly her own body acclimated to the feel of him. *Stop it*, she told herself, not that it did any good.

They drove seventy miles an hour with the wind humming its tune in their ears. He slowed down as they came to a town called Sumatra. It was an odd name, she thought. The town itself consisted of a few blocks of pretty little houses, some with white picket fences, others with neat little yards behind chain link fences. A gas station. A brick post office with a flag flying in front. America, America. Of course, the yards were dotted with signs for George W. Bush. It was that sort of place, the kind of place that would infuriate Aunt Jewel. The two of them rumbled through the town like aliens skimming over the earth. A few bewildered glances from the inhabitants and then they were gone in a blur.

When they finally pulled up to her apartment, it was late

afternoon.

"I've got to work the night shift," he said, shutting off the engine. "What are your plans?"

"I'm going to my sister's house," she said, taking Birdie's helmet off her head.

"Are you two close?" Zack asked and removed his own helmet. His face was pink from the wind, his smile still cocked up on one side.

"We didn't use to be," Jen said and tried to smooth her hair. "But now, I guess we're closer. Listen, I had a good time today. Thanks."

"You want me to walk you upstairs?"

"No, I know how to get there," she said.

"Okay," he answered. Maybe he'd get the hint, she thought. Just enjoy the day for what it was and let it go. He put his helmet back on and straightened up the bike. Then he looked at her and said, "I'm off next Friday night. Why don't we go get some dinner and see a movie?"

No, she thought. *No, I don't want you to reject me.* She stared into his gray eyes and answered, "That sounds great."

"Good," he smiled. "I'll pick you up at seven."

Then he rolled away and she walked inside the building, shaking her head and wondering what she had gotten into this time.

Monday July 17

They were let out of the box bright and early Monday morning and sent directly to work. Not one word was said about the knife, but no one got extra punishment so Sonya surmised that it had not been found. That was not a good thing. She didn't like the idea that there was a loose butcher knife on the compound. Who knew what one of these crazy, murderous bitches would do?

"Lord have mercy, this kitchen never looked so good," Curly said, as they came into the bright fluorescent-lighted room and looked around at the big black stove and the giant sinks and the stacks of pots and the shelves of canned and boxed foods.

"I didn't mind being in the box," Magna sneered. "Nothing to do but lay on your ass."

Sonya shuddered. She had hated every moment of her time in the box. Panther looked at Sonya and said, "You handle that little bit of time okay?"

Sonya nodded her head. "I heard you singing. That was nice. I didn't know you could sing."

"Had to do something."

C.O. Dawkins waddled in and said, "Welcome back, ladies. Now, let's get breakfast going! You've got some mighty hungry inmates coming in here in a bit."

"How did y'all feed 'em all weekend?" Curly asked.

Dawkins smirked and said, "They had a lot of peanut butter and jelly."

When the doors opened for breakfast that morning, the inmates came charging to the steam tables.

"Hot food," one of them yelled. Some of the others smiled and said how glad they were to see the kitchen crew got out of the box. A few of them shouted insults at the guards who studiously ignored them. Mariposa was one of those who did not smile or have anything nice to say. She merely glared at Sonya, and Sonya felt her face redden with shame.

Alice was also in the line.

"Hey, girl, you're back!" she said.

Sonya grinned and gave her an extra helping of bacon. *It's gonna be okay*, she told herself. Ideas were forming in her head. New ideas. New ways of thinking. She looked again into Alice's dark, friendly eyes. Maybe. Maybe she could do something different. If she had the nerve.

That afternoon she ran into Alice at the canteen. Alice was buying some loose tobacco, and Sonya needed tampons. They walked back to the dorm together in the heat of the day.

"Alice, you think God put me and Mariposa in the same prison on purpose?"

Alice shrugged. "Truth is, it's a smaller world than you think it is. People are always running into their deadly enemies in a place like this. People whose lives are messed up, most of 'em wind up in a penitentiary or a nuthouse at one time or another. You and Mariposa just crossed paths at the same time."

"At first, I thought maybe she plotted to get in here same time as me."

"Oh, I'm sure she knew all about you before you came on the compound," Alice nodded. "And now she's got you where you can't run."

They walked along the smooth sidewalk under a cloudless slate of blue-white sky. It seemed that birds didn't even fly over the prison as if the fences extended invisibly into outer space.

"I'm not even gonna try to run," Sonya said, gazing at their shadows moving ahead of them on the walkway. "I'm gonna fix it."

Alice turned to look at her curiously, her dark hair lifting as they walked. Ahead of them Panther stood with her hands in her pockets, looking for all the world, like a statue made of onyx.

Thursday, July 20

Lolly had just finished eating a slice of cantaloupe. She had been told not to eat fresh fruit for some damn reason, but if this was going to be her last summer on the planet, she was not going to die without having one last crescent of sweet juicy cantaloupe. The sweet scent lingered even after she was done and stood over her sink. Then it blended with the lemon dishwashing detergent. She stared out the window as she slowly hand washed her plates and silver. The green outside was nearly overwhelming. She was glad she had planted the baby's breath by the window. It was hard for her to put in words how those colors, the multitude of greens and whites, affected her or how the scents washed over her. She was beset by calm. This life is good, these moments are good, she thought. They are why we come here. To experience this. And she couldn't think of anything sweeter or more delicious than this moment now. That thought was followed by a recognition that there was no point in hording life. It was like that melon. You had to taste it, enjoy it while it was ripe.

She turned off the water and heard the door open.

"Yoo hoo?"

"Come on in, Aunt Jewel," Lolly called, walking out of the kitchen and through the dining area toward the door. Aunt Jewel was bearing a sack from the local health food co-op.

"Whatcha got?" Lolly asked.

"Healing aromatherapeutic bath salts and ointments," Aunt Jewel said.

Lolly chuckled.

"Well, you never know what might work," Aunt Jewel said, raising her eyebrows.

"Thank you, sweet Auntie," Lolly said and hugged her. Aunt Jewel felt warm and solid in her arms. And she smelled like mint and rosemary.

"We're in for the fight of our lives," Aunt Jewel said.

Lolly was surprised at Aunt Jewel's bluntness, but then noticed the "Beat Back Bush" button on her cotton blouse. Nothing could distract the old woman from her politics.

"There are mighty powerful business interests in this country and they support this man. And let me tell you, he doesn't treat people very good. You know he joked about executing Karla Faye Tucker. Laughed about it. I don't care what that woman did, you don't elect a man president who laughs about killing another person."

"Well, that's why some of us are voting Green Party," Lolly said. She opened the door and stepped out onto the porch with Aunt Jewel following.

"But the Green Party doesn't stand a chance," Aunt Jewel cried. "Please, please don't tell me you're going to abandon the Democrats."

"So we should just go with the lesser of two evils?" Lolly asked, gingerly taking the steps from the porch to the moist ground. Her lantana plants – tiny little orange flowers clustered together – waved in a slight breeze.

"If that's what you want to call it. But Al Gore has always understood that without a healthy planet, nothing else really matters. He may be a politician, but he's got the sense to keep the earth alive. It's like the Cree Indians used to say—'you can't eat money.'"

Lolly didn't answer. There was no arguing with Aunt Jewel when it came to politics. She reached Aunt Jewel's pickup truck and looked in the bed. It was filled with political signs. She knew what was coming next.

"How about letting me put a sign in your yard?" Aunt Jewel asked in a low tone.

Lolly laughed. Lord, the woman was persistent. With Aunt Jewel behind him, Al Gore actually stood a chance against the mighty Republicans and their dump trucks full of money.

"Go ahead, Aunt Jewel," Lolly said.

Lolly leaned against the pickup truck as Aunt Jewel tried to find the most conspicuous place to put her sign. It wasn't easy with Lolly's garden overflowing with summer flowers. Lolly had always followed politics with her mother and Aunt Jewel. She had learned from them about how women had been jailed and beaten in their quest to become voters. She had gone out into the black neighborhoods in 1976 and then 1980 with her mom to register voters. She listened as her mother and her mother's cronies talked about how Ronald Reagan had undermined every good thing Jimmy Carter tried to do, how he thought ketchup was a vegetable, and how he invented a Cadillac-driving "welfare queen" to take food out of the mouths of poor women and children.

But now it was hard for her to become impassioned. It seemed every source of energy she had was directed toward survival.

Aunt Jewel had finally stuck the sign at the edge of the lawn. She came over to Lolly and slipped an arm around her waist. A mockingbird darted by, and a squirrel on Lolly's roof seemed to be watching her intently.

"Well, are you ready to go?" Aunt Jewel asked.

"No," Lolly answered. "But I guess I have to."

"Now, don't get discouraged, honey."

"I try not to, auntie. But that's pure poison they're putting into my body. Talk about toxic waste. I feel like a walking dump. And it makes me so damn tired." What she didn't mention is that according to the last blood test, her tumor markers had actually risen. "You better be careful when they cremate my body. It might explode."

"Don't talk like that. I don't want to hear that from you. You need to keep a positive attitude."

People always talked about having a positive attitude when you had cancer. If you didn't get better, they thought it was your fault for having a lousy attitude. What the hell did they know?

Aunt Jewel had brought a mason jar of jasmine tea in the truck with her. When they got to the hospital, she handed it to Lolly and said, "I thought you might get thirsty. This tea is loaded with antioxidants."

Lolly was thirsty, and she refrained from trotting out the old cliché about closing the barn door after the horse had already run away. They got on the elevator and pushed the floor for the chemo unit. Lolly opened the jar and drank deeply of the tea. At the second floor the elevator doors opened and a woman, accessorized in the gold and white standard of the southern rich, stepped in. She glanced down at Lolly's glass of tea and frowned. Lolly looked at it and noticed the light yellow color. She grinned and took a sip, then turned to Aunt Jewel and said, "They tell you not to drink it, but it's just so tasty and so warm."

Aunt Jewel turned her face to keep from laughing. The woman hurriedly got off at the next floor.

Friday, July 28

Jen stood at the back of the church and listened to the parents applaud their children. She'd spent three weeks directing the theater camp at the Lumina School Summer Camp. It was tough working with kids every day. They had a lot of energy, but she had enjoyed working with them more than she had expected. She didn't think she liked kids, quite honestly, but she was wrong. A ten-year-old girl with a mass of curly hair ran up and gave her a quick hug. Jen awkwardly hugged her back.

Lolly had come to watch the production. She had visited once or twice during rehearsals—just to pick up some tips, she'd told Jen. The kids seemed to gravitate toward Lolly naturally, and even now that the production was over, they were stopping by Lolly to hug her and look at her bald head and admire the henna tattoos. Lolly smiled and congratulated each child on a spectacular job. But she looked paler than usual and something about the way she held onto the chair in front of her for support made Jen's stomach tighten. She supposed she should go talk to her and see if she needed anything, but Lolly's illness wore her out.

The director of the school, a wiry woman with granny glasses, worked her way through the crowd of kids and parents and took Jen's arm.

"I'm so glad that Lolly recommended you to us. We had called up Amanda Hathaway at the university and asked her for a recommendation and she said she couldn't think of anyone for the job. Then one of the parents who knew Lolly asked her, and she said you would be perfect. She was so right," the woman said, smiling, oblivious to the stunned look on Jen's face.

"Lolly recommended me?" Jen asked.

"Sure. She said you were great with kids. Personally, I had my doubts. Nothing against you, of course, but your experience isn't with children," she said.

"No, it isn't," Jen said, recovering, "that's why I treated them like adults."

"Good idea." The woman nodded and then was pulled away by a tow-headed girl who had lost something.

Lolly never mentioned that she'd helped Jen get this job. It made Jen feel like shit. Her younger sister helping her stay afloat. Why had she moved to this crummy little town? And, of course, Amanda Hathaway hadn't been able to think of her. She looked around. Lolly was gone. She should probably go find her and thank her for the recommendation, but she felt sour inside.

After the kids had finally cleared out of the makeshift theater, Jen went outside and glanced around. Lolly's car was still in the parking lot, and Lolly was sitting in it. Jen walked over and knocked on Lolly's window. Instead of opening the window, Lolly opened the door and Jen looked in.

"Look at my belly," Lolly said. "It's huge. There's something wrong here."

Jen's breath was caught in her throat.

"Does it hurt?" she asked finally.

Lolly nodded. It was never ending, Jen thought, angrily. She wished someone would just give them a break. Let Lolly feel okay for a while—at least long enough so Jen could safely get mad at her once in a while.

"I'll take you to the hospital," Jen said. "Come on. Get in the passenger seat."

"I can't walk," Lolly said, plaintively.

"Yes, you can," Jen said and helped her out of the car. A few of the kids who were outside of the building watched curiously as Jen helped Lolly around to the other side of the car. Lolly's skin radiated fever, and Jen thought she herself might faint. The worst part was the guilt she felt for her own irritation. Jen closed the car door and noticed Lolly's fever-tinged face as she leaned against the headrest. Lolly closed her eyes and for a moment, Jen thought she saw the very life drain out of her. Then Lolly's eyes popped back open.

From the Journal of Nicole Parks

Saturday morning finally came. Summer is no time to be in prison. The mosquitoes will near about kill you. Of course where I grew up they were bad, too. The old folks used to talk about how the mosquitoes in the old days could cover up an entire cow so you couldn't see a speck of the beast. If you didn't get there quick enough to drag that cow into the creek, all you'd be left with was a bunch of bones in a leather bag.

At least in the free world there were lakes to swim in during the summer and lazy Sundays when Daddy would drag out the ice cream maker. How I miss that homemade peach ice cream. Nobody could make ice cream like my daddy.

But we don't have ice cream here in the North Florida Correctional Institution for Women—this dreadful place. This was the eighth meeting of our drama program, and I knew we were going to have to start practicing our material if we were going to put on an actual performance in September.

When Doc showed up alone again that day, I began to get suspicious. This was the second time Lolly had missed the class, and that wasn't like her. But Doc said she just had some kind of digestive disorder and would be back next week, so we couldn't really say anything. We had to be working on our production anyway.

I was waiting to see if we'd have any more drama from Mariposa and Gypsy, but they sat opposite from each other and didn't talk much.

"We need a few more skits or monologues," Doc said.

"Lucille, your eviction skit is coming along well. We've got Mariposa's skit and Curly's monolog. Nicole, you'll need to finish your two short plays and then figure out what order things should go in."

"I can do that," I told her.

"And you'll have to work with Alice and help her figure out different sets."

"I've got a skit I want to do about space aliens," Daffy said. Everyone laughed 'cause they knew if it was Daffy's idea then it would be hilarious.

"Is it a funny skit?" Doc asked.

"Oh yeah, it's very funny," Daffy said.

"A little comic relief wouldn't hurt," Doc said. I registered those words—comic relief. I liked having Doc around 'cause she introduced me to new ideas and new ways of saying things.

"I got one," Mariposa said. "Can I perform it for you?"

"Sure," Doc said, not even hesitating. She didn't seem to mind living a little dangerously.

We formed our little half-circle audience and Mariposa had a quick conference with Bonita. Then she went to the designated stage area. As she walked across the stage, she looked different, old and beaten down by life. She mimed taking off a hat and gloves. She slumped into a chair.

"They've taken my boy. Twenty-five years they gave him. In prison. My baby boy."

By this point, we all figured out who she was portraying, but nobody even looked over at Sonya.

"He was such a good boy. At twelve years old, he started working to help me pay the bills. He worked hard every day after school, doing any kind of work he could get—yard work, painting, washing dishes.

My Luis was a real money maker, and every week he gave me his money and said, 'Mama, buy some food for us.' Ah, me. He wasn't so great in school, but he finished and got his diploma because he said, 'Mama, they won't give me a good job if I don't have my diploma.' So he got a good job, working at a hotel and now . . . now, he's in prison for a crime he didn't commit. And I still got children to take care of and no one to help me."

Mariposa stood and walked over to a table. She picked up an imaginary stack of bills.

"They turned off the water yesterday. This here is an eviction notice. Daughter," she called out.

Bonita ran onto the stage.

"Daughter, you got to get us some money. I can't feed the other children. Go out and get a job."

"Here, Mama," Bonita said. "I got money. Look, I got a hundred dollars."

"Where did you get this money, Chica?"

"The men give it to me, Mama," Bonita said.

Mariposa then fake slapped Bonita, and Bonita ran crying from the room. Then Mariposa fell to her knees and wept loudly.

"Oh *mi Dios*, why have you taken my boy away? Now my daughter sells her body to help us live. Why? Why?"

She jumped up and looked frantically around. Then she pretended to open a cabinet. We were all watching, mesmerized, but I managed to slide my eyes over to the corner and spy out Sonya. She sat up ramrod straight with no expression on her face.

Mariposa mimed opening a medicine bottle and poured the contents down her throat. She fell to the floor and Bonita ran in crying, "Mama, please. Don't die. No, Mama, please."

But Mariposa just lay there. We all sat there not saying anything. Then Doc said, "Well, that's very powerful. We might be able to include that." Doc didn't seem to give a damn about any ramifications if it was what she called 'good theater.'

Mariposa got up and came back to her seat.

For the rest of the time Doc showed us how to move on stage and gave us pointers on projecting and that sort of thing.

When we walked back to the dorm I was behind Sonya. She was like some kind of zombie—no emotion whatsoever. I was glad I wasn't her.

Wednesday, August 2

Aunt Jewel had brought Lolly home from the hospital that morning. Lolly had no more energy in her body than a stone. She was tired and the heat was like a vacuum sucking the life force from her body. She sat down on the soft cushions on the old metal chair and stared out the porch screen. They had cut out her ovaries to stop the production of estrogen and told her she was now menopausal. So on top of chemo brain, she'd be mucking around in the foggy "change". So much to face—the chemo that might not work, missing work, the looks of pity and worry from her friends. Like a lava flow, it began descending on her.

On the metal table beside her were the shells that she often took to her poetry workshops to give the participants something concrete to write about. She picked up a lightning whelk that had been bleached white. It was about two and a half inches long, a small shell that fit neatly in her palm. It was curved smooth like a woman's breast. *So clean*, she thought, *washed and washed and washed, the tongue of the Atlantic sliding inside, deeper and further, spiraling inward*. She noticed a hole, a rip in the calcified fabric, fissure. So small. She wondered how that had happened. She ran her thumb along the ridges, feeling the texture. It felt good to hold something so solid, so beautiful.

Then the phone rang. She put the shell down, stepped inside the house, found the phone and brought it back out with her as she answered.

"This is a collect call from an inmate in the state prison system," a recorded voice said. Then she heard a human voice say: "Sonya Yakowski." The recording then resumed, "Will you accept the charges?"

"Yes," Lolly said. She couldn't imagine why Sonya would call her.

"Lolly, it's Sonya from the drama class."

"Hi, Sonya, is everything okay?"

"Oh, yeah. It's just that . . . I need some help and I didn't know who else to call."

"What is it? What's wrong?" Lolly asked.

"I want to tell the truth about Mariposa's brother. I don't want him to stay in prison any longer."

"Oh," Lolly said, stunned.

"I want him to be free."

The fog had lifted from Lolly's mind as she tried to sort out what should be done. There was no doubt she'd have to help, but she wasn't even sure where to begin.

"You'll probably have to go to court," Lolly said. "You may even get another charge. You're sure you're prepared to go through with this?"

"I can't sleep. I can't eat. I've lost seven pounds just this week. I keep seeing his face and hearing Mariposa's voice. I'm a mother, you know. I know what it's like to lose a son."

"What about your family?"

"They've ruled me my whole life. I'm tired of it. And it's not like they'll lose the money. That money is long gone. Besides, the hotel settled out of court. They can't do anything."

"Okay. I'm not sure what the first step is. I guess I'll have to find an attorney and ask them what to do. What about you? Do you have a lawyer? I think you'll need one."

"Just the family lawyer and he's not going to help me unless they pay which they won't, believe me."

Lolly looked up at the tall pine trees looming over her flowered yard. Jen's gray Blazer had pulled into the driveway and Jen was getting out of the truck.

"Well, I'll see about getting someone, a public defender or someone who will work pro bono. Don't worry, Sonya. I think you're doing the right thing."

Jen opened the screen door just as Lolly hung up. She was carrying two plastic sacks of groceries.

"What's this all about?" Lolly asked.

"I thought I'd make dinner," Jen said. Jen wore a pair of blue jean shorts and her golden brown hair was pulled back into a ponytail. She looked all of twenty years old.

"Dinner? Can you actually cook?"

"I can make spaghetti," she answered. She set down the bags and pulled out a jar of tomato sauce with Paul Newman's handsome face on the front. "And Paul makes the best sauce in the world. Besides, he's one of your do-gooders. We'll be supporting a good cause, right?"

Jen picked up the bags and headed into the house. Lolly followed her.

"That sounds good," Lolly said. The fatigue crept back on her. No sense in questioning Jen's sudden kindness. She sat down at the dining table where she could watch Jen in the kitchen. "I just had an interesting phone call. Sonya called. Collect. From prison."

Jen wheeled toward her, holding a box of angel hair pasta.

"What did she want?"

"She wants to come clean about the 'rape' in the hotel."

Jen came to the doorway and leaned against the white wood molding.

"It was Mariposa's skit last week," Jen said. "She showed what happened after a man went to prison for a crime he didn't commit. The family fell apart. The mother attempted suicide and the sister turned to prostitution to pay the legal fees. Honestly, she had most of us in tears."

Lolly nodded, "I'm not exactly sure what to do, how to help her."

Jen pondered the dilemma.

"I could ask Zack what he thinks she ought to do," she said.

"Zack?"

"That cop I told you about."

Lolly began to chuckle and soon she was laughing uncontrollably.

"What's so funny?" Jen asked.

"I just had this big discussion yesterday with my oncologist about miracles. I told him I'd never seen one, but now here you are, cooking dinner and . . . and dating a cop. Dating a cop! Do you realize how insane that sounds? I used to call you the 'agent of chaos' you were such a troublemaker. I mean, Jen, I can remember when you and that kid down the street stole a car. And that's not even going into the Miami years. God only knows what you and Lyle got into."

Jen turned back to the kitchen without speaking and noisily filled a pot with water and put it on the burner. Then she said over her shoulder, "That was a long time ago. Since then I've managed to go to college and get not one degree, but two degrees-almost three. Now I'm a teacher. I'm hardly one of your hardened criminals."

She opened the jar of Paul Newman's and poured it into a sauce pan.

"What about the DUI? When was that? Last week?"

Jen banged a spoon on the counter and came back to the doorway.

"Okay, so my drinking is maybe a little out of control sometimes. I've been dumped by my lover and I can't get a real job. Drinking isn't illegal."

"When are you going to stop making excuses for yourself?" Lolly asked.

Jen stared at her for a moment. Lolly felt a pillar of anger burning inside her. Jen had everything—looks, talent, and even charm if you weren't related to her. But still she found ways to pity herself.

"You know, I didn't come here to be abused tonight. I don't have to fix this dinner. I just thought I should thank you for helping me get through this summer—financially, I mean."

Jen's hand was on her hip and in that instant she reminded Lolly so much of a little girl with hurt feelings, threatening to run away from home. *That's it*, Lolly thought. She's still a little girl, needing love and attention, and no one has given enough to her. Lolly had gone about it wrong all these years, ignoring yet envying her sister.

"No, you don't have to fix me dinner. You can walk out of here and go get pissy drunk if you want to. I love you anyway," she said. "I love you no matter what you do."

Jen's brown eyes widened and her lips parted.

"Well, that's nice to know," she said. Jen turned back to the boiling water and broke the pasta in two before dropping it in. She probably wanted a reward for doing something good. *It was just another role,* Lolly thought. *Another opportunity for applause.*

Thursday, August 3

Tallahassee was just the kind of place where you always knew someone who worked with someone who was married to a man you once slept with. That wasn't exactly true for Lolly, as she had gone away for college and was not one to rove from relationship to relationship, but it was true for just about everyone she knew. With all the incestuous connections, Lolly figured she had to know an attorney but she could only think of a friend from her mother's church who was assistant counsel for the Department of Insurance. Not exactly helpful for a wrongful rape accusation.

She knelt in the dirt of her garden by the basil and mint herbs, yanking out weeds. She loved being surrounded by the smell of her garden. She didn't have to go in to work since she'd only just gotten out of the hospital, though she was trying to hang on to the job with its benefits for as long as she could. Not only that, she hated to relinquish the semblance of normal life. They had been letting her take Thursdays and Fridays off for chemotherapy, but she tried to make up the work on the weekends when she felt a little better.

A couple of squirrels yammered at a neighbor's cat prowling through her yard. Lord, it was hot. Probably a hundred degrees, but she had to be outside. The dirt felt good in her hands, velvety smooth. She sat back on her bottom and gazed up at the pine trees in the yard next door. Where would she find a good attorney for Sonya? She figured she'd have to do some calling around and see who knew someone. She stood up and dusted herself off, and as she did so, a name formed in her mind: Jeremy Erwin. She straightened up, the sheer genius of the thought igniting a spark of hope in her chest.

Jeremy Erwin was a boy she had known in high school. Well, she hadn't really known him. She'd merely admired him from afar. He was a few years older than she, worked for the school newspaper and had then gone on to Florida State where he'd made a name for himself writing firebrand editorials for the *Florida Flambeau*, a now-defunct student newspaper that battled the fraternities and all things sexist, racist or simply stupid. Now, his name cropped up with regularity in the newspaper as he worked the last-ditch efforts to save death-row inmates.

Would he know her if she called? Perhaps she should mention she was the sister of Jen Johanssen. He surely would remember Jen. He was male, after all. She went inside the house and picked up the phone, hesitating. Would he make time for her? Then she sighed and decided to do the deed before her proverbial iron got cold and she needed to go to bed.

A receptionist asked her name and if Mr. Erwin would know what this was in reference to.

"Uh, it's about a case. A woman I know in prison. Could I leave my number?"

"Certainly," the woman said, and Lolly got the feeling the little pink "while you were out" slip would wind up in the waste basket, but she gave her the information anyway.

She hung up the phone and felt odd and a little hollow inside. High school associations always did that to her. But Jeremy had been a bit of an outsider himself. His parents had plenty of money, but his mother was Jewish and from Miami, and perhaps that had been enough to give him an edge that the other rich kids didn't have. He refused to belong to any particular crowd. He wasn't the cutest guy or even the smartest but he was the person who seemed to have the most integrity, and in the only conversation she'd ever had with him, she remembered that he was funny and kind—something she hadn't expected at all.

The phone rang not fifteen minutes later as she was sorting through the bottles of medicine she'd brought home from the hospital.

"Hi Lolly. Jeremy Erwin. How the hell are you?"

"I'm just the hell fine," she said. She couldn't help adding, "You know who I am?"

"The fire that burnt the sky to black will char my heart with its hot tongue."

"Oh no. That must have been my Sylvia Plath phase," she said and cringed. "Where did you read that?"

"I went to one of your readings a few years ago at the Warehouse, and I bought one of your chapbooks."

"Now I'm mortified," she said.

"You shouldn't be," he said. "You were good. And very cute up there, I might add."

"Are you flirting with me?" she asked.

"I'm a married man. It's safe," he said.

"Drat."

He chuckled. "So what can I do for you besides quote poetry at you?"

Lolly fiddled with her medicine bottles and said, "I teach a class, an arts class, out at the women's prison. And one of the women has a problem."

"Only one of them?" he asked.

"Well, this one has a legal problem that I promised I would try to help her with," Lolly explained. "She accused a man of raping her. He's doing time for the rape, but now she says he didn't really rape her and she wants to set the record straight."

"Oh," Jeremy said and was silent for a moment. Lolly was silent, too, holding the cordless phone between her shoulder and ear as she tapped the bottles on the table. When he spoke again, his voice was more businesslike. "Why don't I stop by after work and you can fill me in on the details?"

Lolly gave him directions to her house. She was surprised at his immediate interest and hopeful. It was hard to think of Mariposa's brother locked up for a crime he didn't commit.

Aunt Jewel stopped by with some take out Chinese food. She was in a foul mood, having just spent the last three days watching the Republican convention. Lolly was glad she left early. She didn't want Aunt Jewel interrogating Jeremy about his politics when he came over.

It was almost seven when Jeremy showed up in her doorway. The door was open and he peered inside.

"Knock, knock?" he called.

"Come in," she said. She was sitting on the couch where she'd been trying to read a magazine. She found it so difficult to concentrate anymore.

Jeremy entered and sat down on the sofa with her. He gazed at her for a moment, and she gazed back. She realized she'd seen him several times around town and not even known who he was. He looked different than he had in high school. He was more solid, with a beard, and he was a little shorter than she remembered. Even in the dim light of the fading day she could tell his eyes were green like her own.

"How are you?" he asked, a note of concern in his voice. She had grown so used to walking around with her bald head bared she sometimes forgot that it was a dead giveaway. At some point, she had stopped trying to hide the truth.

"I have cancer," she said.

"What's your prognosis?" he asked.

"I have stage four breast cancer. That means it has metastasized in assorted other places. There's not much they can do except throw a whole lot of chemo at it, and so far it hasn't done much. But I'm still alive."

"I can see that," he said in his gentle voice. The light in the room was dim though the sun had yet to go down on this summer evening.

"I've seen you around," Lolly said. "There was a party for some visiting artist or something. And you were there with Jocelyn Nightingale."

He nodded. "Yes, Jocelyn is my wife."

"Oh," Lolly said. Jocelyn was a tall, flamboyant dancer and choreographer with cascading red hair. She was one of the bigger fish in the small pond, and she carried herself as if she were royalty. The only problem was that she was quite often drunk and had been known to cause her share of embarrassing scenes. She was far worse than Jen who managed to create her trouble away from the mainstream artistic set. Jocelyn wasn't Lolly's favorite person, but Lolly didn't dislike her either, and she had to admire the woman's work. It was brilliant. Lolly felt a little sorry for Jeremy.

"You'll have to forgive me," she said. "The chemo makes me feel like someone poured glue on my brain."

"That's okay," he said. "So tell me about this woman. You said she's in prison?"

Lolly told him Sonya's story and mentioned Mariposa as well. She said she believed that Sonya was telling the truth and had only accused the man as a plot to extort money from the hotel where the supposed rape occurred. "Apparently, she belongs to one of those families of traveling criminals. I did some research on the Internet about them. They're con artists. Very clannish. Don't get caught all that often."

Jeremy had heard of them. He said he would look into the case. It wouldn't be hard to find the records. He had Sonya Yakowski's name as well Mariposa's last name. And the county where the crime supposedly occurred. Once he had the facts, he would go down and depose Sonya.

"I don't want her to get into trouble for this," Lolly said. "She's already doing time, and she's got a little boy. I know what she did was wrong, but ..."

Jeremy patted her hand. "Well, they could charge her with perjury but we can probably make a deal for immunity, I think. The State's Attorney won't have any interest in keeping this guy locked up.

It may be a little complicated but it's doable."

"Jeremy," Lolly said. "She won't have any money to pay you."

"It's my job to make sure that innocent people don't get shafted by the justice system," Jeremy said. "Sounds like this man, Luis? Sounds like he fits the bill."

Lolly felt a wave of relief. She wasn't sure why she cared so much, but she did. It was her curse.

Jeremy stood up, and Lolly stood up with him. An odd moment passed between them.

"Is there anything I can do for you?" he asked.

Lolly smiled and shook her head. Then she thought for a moment. One of the gifts of cancer was that you got to say what was really on your mind so she spoke up, "Well, you can come visit me sometime and talk about poetry or tell me about your cases or anything."

It was a bold move. She was a bald-headed, one-breasted, one-legged, menopausal 30-year-old woman, and he was married to a gorgeous redhead with a dancer's physique and who was famous in some circles. She wasn't expecting that anything would happen romantically, but it would be nice just to waste a little time in the company of a man like him, someone with whom she felt so immediately comfortable. *That wouldn't be wrong*, she told herself.

"I'd like that," he said. His cheeks rose with his smile, and his eyes crinkled. A summer terminator breeze brought an end to the day.

From the Journal of Nicole Parks

It was weird that we decided on the theme of death. I could tell that Doc expected us to come up with something different from that. Lolly was surprised, too. She'd had us doing writing exercises on freedom, love and passion. But somehow "death" seemed right. Mariposa had the suicide story that I helped her develop into a skit. I turned my Antwan story into a 21st century style Romeo and Juliet. And Curly, Lord, Curly had the scariest daggone voice you ever heard. We all near about died of shock when that chubby little blond got that maniacal look on her face and that creepy voice: "I am death." That was perfect for the dance number we put together at the beginning. The thing I hadn't come up with yet was Viola's exorcism.

Curly also had a monologue that I thought we should put in there. There she is wearing her Star of David and then she stands up and tells this story in a West Virginia ying-yang hillbilly voice. Too bad she's got at least twenty years to do, I swear that girl has some talent. And I wonder what she did to warrant such a high number. She looks so sweet. But when she tells that story, in her mama's voice, the story of the daddy who molested her and how she couldn't love anybody proper after that even though that nice Jewish man married her and took her down to Miami. Well, it's just a heartbreaking story when she talks about leaving her two girls and at the end when she says one of them is doing twenty years in prison and you realize that Curly is the daughter. I had some big old alligator tears at the end of that one.

I'm for the death theme, too. If I could, I would be murdering a certain someone named Antwan G. See, a girl who used to deal for him showed up on the compound last week, talking about Antwan got a new Shorty and how fine she is. It wasn't like I hadn't noticed that my mailbox has been empty for a month; same with my bank account. The worst thing in the world is not to have any money in this place. 'Cause what you get if you can't buy from the canteen is: one tube of nasty generic toothpaste, one stubby toothbrush, one razor if you trade your old one in, one bag of pads, ten tampons, and one bar of state soap, which will destroy your skin. Sometimes the chaplain gives you some shampoo.

Now Antwan has dumped me and I can't help but think what a fool I was. Lord, I promise if I ever get out of this place I will never make that mistake again. Never. How did I wind up here? I never even stole anything in my whole life. OK, I just got to breathe here and think about this play we're putting together.

As I sit here in the dayroom and look over all our stuff I think we have at least four good skits and about seven monologs. We aren't going to use either of the rape monologs. That got us into enough trouble. I'm still scared that Mariposa is gonna go off on Gypsy and then everything'll get cancelled and the shit-eaters will put a stop to Lolly's visits. You have to be so careful. You cannot imagine.

That Sunday afternoon, for the first time in the seventeen months I had been locked up, my name was called for visitation. I hurried to the visitor's park, my hands fluttering like butterflies. I burst in and saw the tiny little old lady sitting at a table.

"Well, you proud, stubborn thing," Granny Hazel said, standing up to her full four feet ten inches. She pulled me into her arms like she always had and then stepped back to give me the once over. Usually, she would nag me about being too skinny, but this time she said, "What have you gone and got yourself into, child?"

"Just foolishness, Granny Hazel," I said, trying to downplay my situation.. We sat down and then I remembered my manners. "You want something to eat from the vending machines?"

I had to borrow some of her money to get us some snacks, but she didn't mind. She even promised to leave something with the guards for my bank. While I was sitting there with Granny Hazel, catching up on all the family gossip, Viola came over to my table with a handsome redbone man.

"Nicole, this is my brother, Junebug," she said.

I gazed into his nice dark brown eyes and he grinned at me. I couldn't help but wonder what was wrong with him if he was snaking on a locked-up chick, but my female instincts took over and I gave him as sexy a smile as I could with my granny sitting there.

"Viola never said how pretty you are," he said.

I introduced him to Granny Hazel and she immediately started the inquisition. Where was he from? How old was he and then finally, "And what do you do for a livin'?"

"I'm in sanitation, ma'am," he answered.

Now, Granny Hazel didn't have but an eighth grade education but I knew she didn't think some garbage man was good enough for her granddaughter, nevermind that granddaughter was sitting there wearing a prison number on her chest.

Junebug had a certain appealing sweetness, but you've got to understand I had been the number one lady of one of Miami's biggest ballers, so I just wasn't all that interested.

"Nice meeting both of you," Junebug said as Viola led him back to her table.

Granny Hazel pursed her lips and raised that famous eyebrow of hers. Then she dismissed Junebug with a wave of her hand.

"You do know that your momma and daddy got back together," Granny Hazel said.

"What?"

"Oh, yeah. They been together for a while now. Started seeing each other soon after you went away to school, but they didn't want you kids to know and get disappointed if it didn't work out. Guess it is working out. Nelson never loved anybody like he loved Brenda."

I was stunned. I had never dared hope they would get back together, but then while I was locked up, it happened. Then as sudden as one of those Florida thunderstorms that I could hear rumbling outside, I felt tears ambush my eyes.

"How come Momma doesn't write to me?"

"You write her?" Granny Hazel asked.

I shook my head.

"Like mother, like daughter. She's hurt and she's stubborn like you. You the one who done wrong. You the one who's got to make the first move," Granny Hazel said, leaning in toward me, her little chin jutting forward and her fingers clutching my hand.

"I know," I said. "It's just hard. I'm so ashamed, Granny."

"Well, we all make mistakes," she said and then looked around. "Course we don't all wind up in the penitentiary."

I saw Viola hug Junebug good-bye. He glanced over and waved at me.

I smiled but not too big. I didn't want to be too encouraging, but as I watched him walk out the door I couldn't help but admire his body, which was muscular but not fat. Then I noticed Viola and remembered why I had wanted Granny Hazel to visit me in the first place.

"Granny, you remember when you had those ghosts in your house down by the lake? 'Member when you did that exorcism?"

"Oh yeah, I'm surprised you remember. You were just a little thing."

"I would never forget it. But I don't remember how you did it. Weren't there some special Bible verses and didn't you burn something?"

Granny Hazel nodded.

"Sure, but what you need to know that for?"

"See that girl, Viola? She's being haunted."

Granny Hazel narrowed her eyes and watched Viola as she left the visitor's park.

"She surely is. There's a shadow following her." Then Granny Hazel turned her piercing eyes to me and said, "Killed him, didn't she?"

"How did you know?"

"Don't worry about how I know. But I'll tell you what to do to get rid of that demon because that's surely what he is and what he was. Now, listen closely."

Then Granny Hazel began to spill her secrets.

Tuesday, August 8

Sonya sat in the office with two lawyers and a stenographer.

"So you're saying Luis Rodriguez did not rape you? You admit the sex was consensual," asked the assistant district attorney, a large, well dressed woman with a barely disguised scowl on her face.

Sonya nodded.

"Yes or no, please?"

"Yes, I had sex with him but he did not rape me." Sonya said heavily.

"Was this for the purpose of bringing a lawsuit at Resort Suites, for financial gain?"

Sonya glanced at Jeremy who had helped her work out a deal with the state attorney's office.

He spoke up, "You don't have to answer that, Sonya." He turned to the other attorney. "The purpose of this deposition is merely to clear Mr. Rodriguez only. Ms. Yakowski admits to nothing else."

Sonya blurted out, "I was cheating on my boyfriend and my brother caught us. That's why I said it was a rape." She thought that sounded plausible. The assistant state attorney shook her head and tsk, tsked.

"You're lucky that your suit never went to court, or we'd have you on fraud, perjury and God knows what else. As it is, I will be seeking indictments against the other members of your family. You can rest assured of that." She stood up, picked up her briefcase and walked out the door. The stenographer followed.

Sonya looked at the attorney.

"Will this get him out of prison? Will it clear his name?"

Jeremy grimaced and said, "The wheels of justice move slowly, but he'll get out. Now we just have to keep you from staying in any longer than you already have to. If she presses charges against your family members, will you be willing to testify?"

Sonya felt a wave of fear prickling along the back of her neck.

"They'll never find them," she said. "They'll leave the country. They aren't fools."

"But they'll make a mistake, Sonya. People always do."

"Not my family," she said.

The lawyer shrugged and said good-bye. Sonya was left to wait for a guard to release her and send her back to the dorm. *What had she done*, she wondered. What had she done?

As she came out of the administration building and was led back down to the dorm by the guard, she saw Mariposa walking along the sidewalk. Mariposa was a heavyset woman with a pretty face. She didn't look like someone who belonged in prison. Luck, Sonya's mother had said, was a son of a bitch who would steal up on you and cold cock you just for the thrill of seeing you fall.

Friday, August 18

Jen looked at Lolly, her bald head reminding Jen of a bird, a sick, helpless bird like the kind they used to find in the spring time, baby birds that had somehow fallen out of the nest prematurely, left there to be tortured and devoured by the cats, the remains carted off by ants.

Jen helped Lolly out of the car and led her into the house.

"Are you okay?" Jen asked.

"I feel like shit," Lolly answered. "I just need to go to bed."

Usually the effects weren't that bad till the next day, but this time Lolly had vomited by the side of the road. Jen hated all of this. She and Lolly went inside and Lolly went straight to the bed where she settled down as if she were rock that would never be budged again. Jen couldn't get over the sight of that needle going into Lolly's port. She closed her eyes but there it was, poking through that delicate skin just below her collar bone. Lolly was pleased to get the port. It would save her veins, save her from the punctures of tired nurses, but the way the round thing about the size of a quarter could be seen just under Lolly's skin gave Jen the shivers. A normal body was bad enough with its mucus and blood and feces. But a cancerous body was like a cesspool.

"I need a drink," Jen said, as she brought in a pitcher of ice water and a cup.

Lolly looked at her with dull eyes.

"You always need a drink," she said and reached for the water.

"Are you leaving now? Already?"

Jen sighed. What more did Lolly want? She had stayed there in the horrible room with all those sick, unhappy people in their chairs taking their doses. It was time for her to get out, to get away.

"I've got a date," Jen lied.

"With the cop?" Lolly asked.

"Yeah," Jen said. Another lie. The last person Jen wanted to see was Zack. She just wanted to feel brash and wild. She wanted to go home with somebody who did not know her, someone she could fuck and forget. Not Zack. Mostly, she just wanted to get away from her wasted sister. Lolly groaned. The doorbell rang, and Jen felt a tremor of joy at the prospect of escape.

It was Lolly's friend, Sue, who had offered to come care for Lolly that evening.

"Thank God," Jen said, opening the door.

"Is she doing okay?" Sue asked.

"Not really," Jen said. "Her appointment with Mengele wasn't fun. Thanks for coming over. I really appreciate it."

"Hey, Jen, don't worry about it. Lolly has a lot of people in this town who love her."

"Yeah, but she doesn't want them to see her like this," Jen said.

Sue grimaced and skirted past Jen to go into Lolly's room.

"Hey, lady," she said to Lolly as Jen grabbed her keys and headed out the door.

She hopped up into her Blazer, and gunned the engine in her hurry to get out. The tires even squealed as she turned out of the neighborhood onto the bigger road. Damn, she needed a drink bad. She was glad it was summertime and most of the students were gone.

It was seven o'clock—a little early, but that was okay. She turned onto Monroe and headed downtown. The bar she wanted to go to had opened about a year earlier. It was a narrow place without much in the way of ventilation and the smoke was suffocating, but who cared tonight? She whipped into a parking spot. Still daylight as she headed inside to the cool dark bar. The walls were blue, and the ceiling a maze of pipes. This was usually a popular place with the local hiperati, and she wouldn't mind chatting it up with whomever happened to be there, but the place was nearly deserted. That was fine. She could settle there for a while. People would straggle in, and perhaps there would be some decent music.

Sam, the bartender, a guy with a long thick mustache, lounged behind the bar with his arms crossed, watching her as she came in. It seemed he had served her drinks in nearly every bar in town.

"Hey, Jen," he said with a smile. "Haven't seen you since you tore out of here with that young stud a while back."

"Oh God, don't remind me," she said with a laugh, barely remembering the night she had left here with young Gary in tow. *Where was he now*, she wondered. Oh yeah, gone back to Tampa for the summer.

"What's your poison?"

"A shot of Cuervo Gold, please," she said, sliding onto the bar stool like a fighter pilot sliding into the cockpit of an F-16. He poured her a generous shot and dropped a few lime slices on a small plate for her.

"Salt?" he asked.

She shook her head and downed the shot, then quickly sucked the flesh of the lime. The tequila rang all the right bells and whistles like a perfect pinball shot. "Better?" Sam asked. "How about a cold one to chase it?"

"Sure. Whatever you've got on tap," she said.

"Michelob? Or something fancier?"

"Mich is fine."

He poured the beer into a frosted glass and leaned on the bar.

"So what's up?" he asked.

"My sister has cancer. Again."

"That sucks." Sam's eyes grew dark. He was a nice guy. A really nice guy. That's why he made such a great bartender.

"Yeah, it does. Our mom died a few years back and so it's up to me to take care of her. Can you imagine me taking care of anybody? I can barely take care of my cat, and a cat is easy."

Sam shrugged.

"You know, the Buddhists refer to hard work like that, you know the kind of stuff no one wants to do, they call that 'polishing the Golden Buddha.'"

Jen nearly choked on her beer. "The Golden Buddha?"

"Yeah, like when a monk has to scrub the toilet, he's polishing the Buddha."

"What does that mean? Is that like your reward is in heaven? Isn't that some shit they feed to poor people who have to dig ditches?"

"I don't think they believe in heaven, not like we think of it anyway," he said. "But you can look at it like a spiritual task."

"So when I'm cleaning up Lolly's vomit, I'm supposed to think of it as polishing the Buddha?"

"You can," Sam said with a smile. "If it helps." Another customer came in, and Sam went over to take his order. Jen took a sip of her cold beer. *Now this is polishing the Golden Buddha*, she thought.

Jen drank slowly but steadily, and the bar began to fill with people – the theater critic from the newspaper stopped by and talked to her for a while, an artist she knew was there, a professor from the economics department came in and bought her a beer. This could be a really good town as long as you were careful not to sleep with everybody. And though Jen had her moments, she tried to steer clear of anyone she might run into on a regular basis.

About ten o'clock a local musician named Hank took the small stage at the front and began to play. He was really good and had a following around town. Jen found a little table near the front so she could listen to him and get away from the conversation at the bar. She didn't mind sitting alone. With the music ringing in her brain pan and the smell of smoke and beer wafting past her and the jostling of people laughing and talking loudly, she felt completely at home. The only other time she felt like this was on a stage. And the beer made her feel like she was filled with neon light. This drunken happiness was temporary but oh so sweet.

Someone sat down at her table. She looked up into the face of a very handsome man. She knew him. Of course. It was Zack.

"Hi!" she said, broadly and swayed in her chair. "Here you are," she exclaimed as if she'd been waiting for him all night.

"I thought you were taking care of your sister," he leaned over and yelled into her ear over the music and noise.

"She can take care of her damn self," Jen said.

"You planning on driving home?" Zack asked.

"No, officer," she said. "I'm gonna get one of these cute boys to give me a ride."

Zack looked at her, his mouth set in a tight line.

"How about I take you home right now before you get any more shit-faced than you already are?"

Jen chuckled and then said, "Not only no, but hell no."

She turned back to watching Hank wail on his guitar. After a few minutes she looked back at Zack, but he was gone. Oh well. She wandered back to the bar where some people were having a heated discussion about politics. A rather loud woman with enormous black hair was expounding on the sins of Big Sugar and how the bastards were rapidly destroying the Everglades. Jen suddenly remembered something she had read and inserted herself into the conversation, "You know I heard that Clinton was on the phone with someone from Big Sugar when he was giving Monica a pelvic exam with the cigar."

At this comment, a couple of the men burst into laughter and the loud woman flashed her eyes and said, "That's right. You can't even trust the damned Democrats."

Jen felt proud of that little score and headed to the bathroom. On her way, she noticed her reflection in the mirror behind the bar. She looked blowsy and old. *What the hell was she doing here*, she wondered. Then she noticed someone else in the reflection—a gorgeous young woman with short spikey blond hair and a dozen earrings. The man standing with her was Gary. For an awful second their eyes met in the mirror. Both of them looked aghast. *So much for not pissing in your own drinking water,* Jen thought and hurried into the bathroom. If she stayed there long enough, maybe he would be gone when she got out.

He wasn't gone, but he had his back to her and there was a nice healthy crowd to keep as a buffer between them. It was time to leave. She stumbled out of the place and fished for her keys in her purse. Her wallet was there, hairbrush, lipstick, a bunch of old receipts but no keys. Damn, she'd have to go back inside.

"Sam," she yelled over the music. "My keys are gone."

"I think that guy who was sitting with you earlier took them. He gave me some money and told me to call you a cab when you were ready to leave."

"Really?" Jen asked, confused.

"I already called the cab when I saw you walk out the door. Give them about five more minutes," Sam said and handed her a ten.

"Thanks."

She walked outside and leaned against the Blazer as she waited for the cab. The summer night air was warm as bath water and the sky above was heavy with the orange haze of the city lights. A crescent moon glimmered far away. Jen sighed. The orange cab pulled up and honked. She got in the back seat and closed her eyes as she let the driver take her home.

"Here you go, Ma'am," the cab driver said. She hated it when people called her ma'am, made her feel old. She sat up and looked out the window.

"This isn't where I live," she said.

"This is the address you gave me, and I brought you here. Fare is eleven dollars even."

Jen dug in her purse and grabbed a wad of bills. She threw it into the front seat and stumbled out of the cab onto the front lawn of

Lolly's house. The cab driver wasted no time getting away.

Why the hell did I tell him to bring me here, she wondered. She walked along the gravel driveway past the jungle that looked grey in the light of the sliver of moon that obliviously orbited above. Opening the screen door, she had no idea what to do. The porch was cluttered with Lolly's gardening implements and some outdoor furniture. An elaborate metal bird cage occupied one corner. Jen sat down in one of the chairs. It had cushions on it, and the night air was warm. Once she was in the chair, she had no inclination to move.

The night felt like a heavy curtain over her life. For some reason she couldn't fathom, she began shaking. Fear as big as a bear settled next to her. What was she so afraid of? Death? But she wasn't the one dying. She remembered a moment when Lolly was just about three years old and Jen must have been four or five. They had gone to a party at the house of some friend of the family. Jen couldn't remember much. Just that Lolly was standing beside a swimming pool and it had seemed so easy to shove her over the edge. Jen was little and had not known what to expect. What was weird was how quietly it happened. Lolly just sank without a whimper. Jen had stood at the edge of the pool waiting for Lolly to do something, but she didn't. Then Jen had turned and screamed, "Mom!" The funniest thing was how she had gotten credit for saving her sister's life.

Jen let her head fall back. She wished she could cry, but she couldn't. She merely felt a strange, nameless terror closing in on her as if now she had fallen into a black pool and there was no one to save her. The screen door opened and shut. Jen looked up. There was no one there. And no breeze. But she smelled something like cinnamon. It was the scent of her mother.

Everything was preternaturally quiet. Even the crickets had stopped. She held her breath and imagined her mother, standing there, waiting, waiting as she always had for an apology that Jen had never made. She wondered if it was too late.

"I'm sorry for everything, Mama," she said out loud. "I'm sorry for being so damned sorry."

A cricket started a high-pitched beat. She would have to change. She would have to stop drinking. She would have to take care of her sister this time. That was all there was to it. She remembered Vivien Leigh as Scarlet O'Hara holding a clump of dirt in her hands and swearing she'd never go hungry again. It was one of her favorite scenes of all time. The one that made you respect Scarlet in spite of all her nefarious deeds. But Scarlet came to a bad end. Scarlet was a lousy role model.

Jen stood up and went to the metal bird cage. She opened the door with a creak and fished around till her fingers found the spare key to the house. She wasn't sure what she was going to do, but she felt suddenly quite sober.

Inside a light shined from the hallway, but otherwise it was dark. She opened Lolly's door and stood in the doorway silently watching her sister sleep, the light from a streetlamp glowing through the window. She and Lolly had slept together until Jen turned seven. How comforting it had been, nestled in the big bed with her sister's warmth next to her.

"Jen?" Lolly asked.

"Sorry. I didn't mean to wake you," Jen said.

"What the hell are you doing?"

Jen came into the room and sat down on the bed.

"You know those Miami years you mentioned a while back?"

"What are you talking about?"

"When you said, god knows what Lyle and I got into. I'll tell you what we got in to. Cocaine and porn movies. I was in some porn flicks, Lolly. I never told you. I was too embarrassed."

Lolly turned on the small bedside lamp. She wore a thin cotton gown and the flatness of half her chest was obvious and made Jen want to cry.

"Damn, Jen, we all do stupid stuff."

"Yeah, but we don't all do it so publicly," Jen said.

Lolly had sat up in the bed. She reached over and took Jen's hand. "I don't care what you did. I really don't."

Jen looked into those large green eyes and understood why the women at the prison adored her. When it really mattered, Lolly simply didn't judge a person. Jen laid her head on Lolly's ruined chest and Lolly put her arms around her. They slept together in the same bed for the first time since they were children. And Jen dreamed she was floating in a wide lake with mallard ducks swimming by, creating ripples with their wake.

From the Journal of Nicole Parks

My job function at the prison is in keypunch where about thirty of us work, doing data entry for the State of Florida. Nothing like free labor. For some damn reason I have put myself into the same situation as my ancestors who were forced to be slaves. Not that I'm picking cotton, but I am damn sure not earning any money for the work I do. I guess the free lovely accommodations and the highly palatable cuisine are my payment, not to mention the company!

Okay, so I don't have much to say about the work. It's work. Sometimes we are crazy busy and other times there's a lull. I don't like the lulls because I have too much time to think. And these days I'm not really missing Antwan anymore. Funny thing about that. Now I think about Sunday dinners with my family. Momma would make a big old ham and some greens and cornbread—all that good southern stuff. And I was the pie maker. In summers, I made blackberry pie that was so good people used to beg me for my recipe. My secret ingredient was Cointreau, an orange flavored liqueur. But the best part of making blackberry pie was going out and picking the blackberries that grew wild in our backyard. Every summer I would watch as the red berries started turning black overnight. You can tell which will be good ones. Each one of those little sac fills up with juice. I only picked the juicy ones, left the others for the birds. I used to get thorns all in my fingers and sometimes it'd be so hot you felt like you would faint. They don't have any blackberries here on the prison grounds. Nothing but grass and concrete. No trees, even. I miss trees. I miss Sunday dinners. I miss my momma.

Finally I broke down and wrote my momma a letter.

Here's what it said.

Dear Momma,

I am writing to you to beg for your forgiveness. I know that after you and Daddy divorced things were not easy for you. And I know how you always made sure me and the boys had everything we needed—clothes, food, and beds of our own in a clean house.

I have no excuse to be where I am. You were so happy when I got my scholarship. I shouldn't have thrown away that opportunity the way I did. You always told me I had so much potential and to always count my blessings. I see now that you were right. I feel so bad for some of these women in here, Momma. They've had terrible things happen to them. Rape, abuse, poverty. I can see why they wound up here. Many of them never had a chance out there.

Momma, I've been taking a writing class here. This lady named Lolly has been encouraging me a lot. She's going to help me get back into school when I get out and also maybe find a part-time job. I want to earn your love back.

Granny Hazel came to see me and said you and Daddy have got back together. That makes me so happy. There's no way I can explain to either of you how I messed up so bad but I hope you will let me make it up to you someday.

Love,

Nicole

And what's more I even put that dang thing in an envelope and mailed it.

Monday, August 21

Aunt Jewel arrived at 9:30 to take Lolly to the doctor's office.

"What's wrong with your arm, child?" Aunt Jewel said.

"I don't know, I woke up and it was all swole up, Aunt Jewel," Lolly said. "I called into work. I hope they don't wind up firing me. Then what will I do?" Lolly's arm felt hot and heavy from her armpit on down. It was red and puffy.

"Did you take your pain medication?"

"Yes, ma'am, I did. But my leg and back still *hurt* and I just feel so *damn* weak," Lolly said. She hated to complain all the time, but this crap was getting old, real old. Today she was due for PET scans and blood work, checking for tumors and tumor markers. It was early for them to be checking but since she felt so bad, the doctor said they needed to find out if the chemo was working at all or if they needed to switch drugs.

As Aunt Jewel drove to the hospital for the tests, Lolly found herself dozing off. It was only a short drive, but she couldn't stay awake for some reason. Under the purr of the engine Lolly dreamt that a white-haired man had cut off her other leg and was running it up the flagpole of the hospital. She came awake with a jolt.

"We're here," Aunt Jewel said and pulled up in front of the entrance. "Wait for me to go park and wheel you around."

"That's okay, Auntie. I can walk," Lolly said. She wanted to use her body, wanted to experience it while she still had it.

At the doctor's office later that day, Lolly waited in the examination room for him to come in with her results. She was playing a game with herself to see if she could read the results by the expression on his face. No need to get too hopeful, she thought.

He was a youngish man about her own age, and she often thought that he seemed frightened of her. Maybe he was a mind reader.

When he came in, the oncology nurse, a woman named Luanne who looked like she should be in charge of a concentration camp, came with him.

The doctor shook his head and that was all she needed to see. "Your tumor markers are up from 78 to 125."

"That's not good," Lolly said.

"Well, markers are often unreliable, but what really concerns me is that your PET scans show intense hypermetabolic activity in the brain, liver, sternum and pleural wall."

Lolly had expected bad news, but the actuality sounded so much worse.

"We can try a different course of chemo. Or radiation."

"Will they work? Is this terminal? What about the lesions that the MRI showed?"

The doctor looked up at the ceiling as he spoke. Lolly wondered if he thought he was talking to God.

"Your situation is not curable, Lolly. It is treatable though."

Lolly lay down on the examination table and let her arms fall.

"I don't want any more chemo. I'm sick of all this. Just help me feel okay, okay?"

The doctor came closer to her and looked down at her face.

"I can give you some steroids. They'll make you feel like wonder woman for a few weeks. And Luanne here will show you how to wrap your arm to get the fluid moving."

Lolly took a deep breath and blew out. There was the drama production to consider. She had to be well enough to get through that.

She couldn't let the women know she was dying. Not yet anyway. She sat up.

"Okay, wrap my arm, give me the steroids and plenty of pain killers. No more chemo."

The doctor took out his pad from the pocket of his white coat and began to scribble.

Thursday, September 7

Sonya gripped the phone receiver so tightly her fingers had turned white.

"Ma, please, please tell me what's going on," she begged. Through the window she could see Magna and Daffy in the line waiting for their turn to use the phone. She turned away so they couldn't see her face.

"I don't know," Dina replied. "My heart's no good. I can't go chasing Ziggy all over the damned state. I'm worried sick. If Duke finds him, he'll kill him."

"What about Tasha? Has anyone seen her?"

"Someone heard she was telling fortunes in Palm Beach, but she says she ain't seen Ziggy. You know if he don't want to be found, he won't be," Dina said.

"Ma, is he going to sell my baby?"

"Who knows what the crazy lunatic is gonna do? Stop harassing me." Dina then sobbed and said, "I'm sorry, baby. I didn't know he would do this. They just said they wanted to take care of him for a while. Duke was off in Toronto. He's talking about going into business for real. Can you imagine?"

"Ma! Listen to me, you've gotta find Ziggy. Get Tomas back. Please, Ma."

"We're trying to, damn it. What else you want us to do? Go to the cops?"

After Sonya hung up, she headed toward the bathroom so she could cry, but there were too many women in there, so she went looking for Alice. She desperately needed someone to talk to right now. She peeked into the day room and saw her sitting on one of the plastic and metal couches with that new chick, Riley, the one who had done time with her years before. Maybe they had been lovers back then, Sonya wasn't sure. She only knew she didn't like Riley, didn't like her big straight teeth and her eyes hard as quarters and her puffy hair. Mostly she didn't like Riley's smirk. They were leaning close to each other, engaged in some deep conversation and Alice's thick black hair hung down like a curtain so Sonya could not see her face. No, she couldn't go in there. Her heart felt like an engine choking. She couldn't talk to Alice now.

"Hey, Sonya. Girl, you feeling okay?" It was Nicole, looking at her with a concerned expression on her pretty brown face. She was carrying her towel and toiletries bag so she must have been heading to the shower. Lots of people talked to Nicole about their problems. She knew that much. And it was because Nicole never gossiped about anyone. She just kept that notebook full. That didn't bother Sonya, but still she didn't feel like she could say anything to Nicole so she just shook her head, and Nicole continued on to the bathroom.

Sonya went inside the dorm and lay on her bunk. She took Tomas's picture from her drawers and clasped it to her chest, remembering the night he was born, how they had cut her open because the birth took so long but she was awake the whole time and then they put this wiggly little body in her arms. And she remembered the way he yawned and snuggled close to her and it felt as if she were flooded with love. She kissed the top of his head and he smelled like a little puppy. Where was he now? What had Ziggy done to him? As those questions gnawed inside her, she felt as if she were slowly sinking in the middle of a gigantic lake.

"Girl, get up off that bed and come down to the dayroom." Panther stood in the aisle watching her. Something in Panther's voice was like a life saver. She felt it pulling her, tugging her to shore. She gathered her fractured emotions back into herself and sat up. Her eyes met Panther's.

"Come on," Panther said. "Whatever's bothering you is probably something you can't do nothing about."

Sonya came to the aisle and blurted out, "I'm worried about my baby. My brother has kidnapped him."

Panther sighed and reached a hand out to touch her, just quickly brushing her arm, careful not to get caught in physical contact. "You know, I heard that worry is just another kind of prayer. A bad kind. Like you trying to do God's job. Just let God take care of your baby, girl. He'll be okay."

"I try," Sonya said though in fact she had never even considered God in all this.

She'd never been in a church in her life.

"Try and cry, my godmother always said," Panther said.

Sonya wasn't sure what that meant, but at least she didn't feel as if she were drowning anymore. She walked with Panther down the wide aisle and slowly breathed. The truth that she had never admitted to herself was that something about Panther frightened her—all that cocksureness all the time. Not like her, who only put on confidence as an act when she needed to take someone's money. Panther seemed totally unafraid of anything or anyone. She was the sort of person that you couldn't help think should have been doing something with her life other than wasting it in prison. But here she was and sometimes it seemed as if there were too much of her in spite of her wiry body. But now that too-muchness felt like a solid place to hang on and catch her breath. Besides, it seemed that something had gone wrong with her friendship with Alice. Something named Riley.

Panther walked into the dayroom and Bertie, who had the most enormous butt on top of the skinniest legs, decided to pull out the headphone of her radio so the music came blaring out of the speakers. They weren't allowed to play music like that except in the rec room and Sonya glanced through the windows towards the C.O.'s office. The C.O. was apparently somewhere else in the dorm. The song that was playing was an old disco hit, "Funkytown." The music snared Panther, who loved to dance. She bent over and slid a few feet, then turned and brought her arms out in front of her. Everyone watched her. She moved her sinewy body in ways that seemed to defy the laws of physics.

"Get it on, girl," Lucille called. And Panther responded.

Sonya was mesmerized. She had seen Panther cut it up a few times in the rec room or in the kitchen, but she had never really stopped to watch her. Looking at her now—the twisting neck, the jerking arms, the legs moving all over the place, Sonya felt a door open in her heart and damned if Panther didn't come dancing right in. The feeling caught Sonya by surprise. It was so different from anything she'd ever felt before. She glanced at Alice and Riley and saw that Alice was watching Panther and smiling in admiration. Sonya suddenly felt proud.

Then someone yelled, "Turn it off." And they looked up to see the C.O. heading straight toward the dayroom. Bertie quickly stuck the headphones back in the jack and the sound disappeared. The C.O. threw open the door and stepped inside. Panther smiled at her.

"Well, how you doin'? Come to hang out with us?"

The C.O. pursed her lips at Panther and put her hands on her hips.

"Y'all try to stay out of trouble," she said. She was one of the more tolerant C.O.s, especially of Panther. She turned and walked out of the room. Bertie muttered something but did not turn the music back on.

"You know how to play spades?" Panther asked Sonya.

Sonya shook her head.

"Well, we're gonna teach you."

So Panther, Lucille and Bertie taught Sonya how to play spades that evening before lights out. Sonya caught on to the game quickly.

She was especially good at bluffing the person next to her into laying down their biggest trump cards, and she and Panther won the game by eighty points. The sharp pain in her chest had become a dull ache that intermittently dissolved in the wake of Panther's laughter.

Saturday, September 9

Jen and Lolly had divided the women into two groups so they could work with the different skits. Mariposa had stopped her constant glowering at Sonya. All Jen could figure was that Mariposa had learned about Sonya's confession. Mariposa had decided that Viola would be an angel in her skit, and she would come in and stop the mother from committing suicide.

As they watched the new version, Jen resisted the urge to say it was too sentimental. This was their material, and they could do it however they wanted to do it. Daffy showed the women how to make costumes out of large black trash bags. She made one for herself that looked like a streetwalker's leather miniskirt.

"Girl, you need to quit," Nicole said.

Lolly seemed to be feeling so much better and laughed along with the rest of the women. *She seems so easy around them*, Jen thought. On the day that Lolly had not come, Nicole and Lucille and a couple of the others who had taken other classes with Lolly told the rest of them about how Lolly had inspired them.

"Lolly has been through fire," Alice said.

"Oh go on, Indian," Daffy retorted. "I swear, girl, I expect you to start doing a Pow Wow. Talking 'bout walking on fire."

"I didn't say she walked on fire," Alice laughed, "Just that she's like one of the elders. Even though she isn't old."

Jen had listened to them that day, and realized that Alice was an elder herself. So maybe she knew some things.

About halfway through the session, Lolly and Jen gave the women a break to go outside or go to the restroom. Sonya approached her. Of all the women, Sonya was the one that Jen believed had the most acting talent.

"You know, if you wanted to go into acting when you get out, you could probably have a career," Jen said to her. "I mean it's a tough business and I've never encouraged anyone in my life to do it, but you really have talent. The question is whether you have the desire to go along with it."

Sonya's façade immediately dropped.

"I can't think about that now, Doc. I'm worried to death. My little boy. My mother was taking care of him, but when I called her last night she said my brother Ziggy and his wife had him and they took him to West Palm Beach. You don't know how angry Ziggy is with me. I got this letter from him yesterday. He threatened to make sure I would never see my child again, and now he has him."

Jen took the letter from Sonya and began to peruse it. It was hand-written on legal-sized yellow paper, a document full of invective and threats.

"I need help," Sonya said, gazing at her. Jen searched those eyes. She knew Sonya was a con artist. Was Sonya conning her now? But what could she possibly gain? Money? That was one thing Jen didn't have.

"How can I help?"

Sonya's voice grew dead.

"I don't know," Sonya said. "He's going to sell my baby. I know it." She hesitated. "It wouldn't be the first."

It took a moment for Jen to comprehend what Sonya had just told her. This man had kidnapped babies and sold them? Outside, thunder roared, and she saw a streak of lightning through the windows. The other women began filing back into the room.

Alice came up to them and showed Jen a sketch she'd made of a back drop for one of the skits.

"Wow, this is good," Jen said. She glanced up again and Sonya had walked away. Jen looked over at Lolly, who was going over some dialogue with Nicole. Damn it. Why had Sonya injected this information into her and then walked away?

Nicole had written a street version of *Antigone*, and Sonya had the lead. For the rest of the rehearsal, Sonya seemed distracted. As soon as it was time for her to say her part, she was completely focused, but otherwise she was somewhere else. Jen was equally distracted. When four o'clock came and it was time for the women to leave the classroom, Jen slid a hand around Sonya's wrist.

"Wait, just a moment," she said. "I want to give you some pointers for your lines, Sonya."

They would only have a moment when the room was empty. Lolly walked out with the rest of them and waited under the overhang to stay dry.

"How old is your baby?" Jen asked.

"He was fifteen months old yesterday," Sonya answered, her lips quivering.

"Where would I find them? Where in West Palm?"

"You can never find my people," Sonya said. "They find you." Then she looked away and seemed to think of something. "Tasha, Ziggy's wife, sometimes tells fortunes on the strip in West Palm. Maybe you could find her there. But I don't know what good it would do."

Jen grimaced and said, "Honey, the easiest person to con is a con artist."

Sonya shook her head as tears filled her eyes. Then she turned to walk out of the room into the downpour.

Monday, September 11

Jen stopped at Hopkins Eatery for a salad to go on the way home from class. As she paid for her dinner, the young woman at the cash register handed her the change and asked, "How is Lolly doing?"

"Oh, she's feeling better. Thanks," Jen said.

"I'm so glad. Let us know if there's anything we can ever do to help, okay?"

Jen assured that she would and walked out into the warm evening air. There was nowhere you could go in this town where people weren't wondering how Lolly was doing. It was true that she was doing better. She'd been back at work fulltime and if you didn't know that she had cancer you wouldn't guess she was sick. And yet Jen felt a nagging fear that any moment she'd get a call and it wouldn't be good news. She'd even gotten a cell phone just in case, which started toodling just as she got in the Blazer

Lolly wanted to know if she'd put together her guest list for the performance Friday night.

"Yes," Jen answered, starting the ignition of the truck. "I asked a couple of people from the theater department, but they were all suddenly busy. But my friend, Joel, from the newspaper said he'd come with his partner. And I also invited Eden and her husband from the Shakespeare Series."

"What about Zack?" Lolly asked.

Jen hesitated. She was sitting in the parking lot by the dumpster.

"I don't know," Jen answered.

"Well, I'll put him on the list anyway. What's his last name?"

"Holtz."

When she got to her apartment, Jen sat down at the table and pushed aside a stack of books. She looked down at the salad and decided she needed to make the call first. You'd think it would be easy to talk to a person at the police station but she had to wade through a series of recordings before she finally got to a live person.

"I'm trying to get in touch with Officer Zack Holtz," she said.

"You mean Detective Holtz?"

"I don't know. He was in a patrol car and wearing a uniform when I met him."

"Well, Officer Holtz was promoted to detective about three weeks ago. So it's probably Detective Holtz you're wanting. Is this in connection with a crime?"

"Uh, no," Jen said. Slipping into her "spokesperson" voice, she said, "This is about a department of corrections event that we would like to invite him to." well, if I'm going to get killed I may as well get it over with. she thought.

"All right. He's not here now, but I can connect you to his voice mail."

She heard his recorded voice in the standard message. In a way, she was glad. It would be a lot easier this way.

"Hi, Zack. It's Jennifer Johanssen. Um, this Friday night we're having the performance at the women's prison. Anyway, we're allowed to bring in a few outside guests and I thought you might be interested in seeing what we managed to accomplish out there. So, I've put you on the guest list. Call me if you have any questions. . . I hope you can . . ."

She was cut off by a recording, telling her that her message had been saved.

"Oh screw you," she said to the robotic female voice and hung up the phone.

She leaned back in her chair. Her salad sat in front of her uneaten. She stabbed her fork into the bowl of greens and forced herself to take a bite. *Enough with the self-loathing*, she thought. She'd made mistakes her whole damn life. Time to get over it. Either he'd call her back or he wouldn't.

He didn't.

Friday, September 15

Lolly drove along Route 90 out to the prison with Jen in the passenger seat. The two sisters were quiet as they passed through the small town of Monticello, past the old antebellum courthouse and the big old wooden houses lining the road near the center of town. Lolly thought of all the trips she had taken down this road to the prison. She gazed at the sky ahead of her and noticed the clouds scuttling across. She wished the performance wasn't today. She wished she had more weeks to be with these women, to work with them, to feel as if she had some purpose.

"I'm feeling a little nervous," Jen said.

"You?" Lolly asked.

"Yeah. I'm always nervous when I'm not the one on stage. Once they go out, you no longer have control."

Lolly glanced over at her. Jen's chin was so firm. She reminded Lolly of their mother sometimes.

"Well, the first performance will be like a dress rehearsal anyway. Just the staff members and the superintendent."

"I never dreamed working with these women would be like this," Jen said. "I'm sorry I gave you a hard time at first."

"It's okay. I knew you'd come around."

"How did you know?" Jen asked.

"You're my sister. How could you not?" Lolly grinned.

The first show went well enough. It was all quite tame for the staff. Daffy did not wear her trash bag mini-skirt quite so provocatively. They didn't burn the sage for Viola's exorcism. The staff clapped politely except for one blond woman whose smile was the most patently false thing Lolly had ever seen. *That must be C.O. Barbie*, she thought.

"Excellent job," the superintendent said, shaking Lolly's hand. The other staff members politely echoed the superintendent, but Lolly could tell they didn't get the whole thing. But they did appreciate the fact that programs like this kept the women distracted and made their jobs easier.

After the staff left, Lolly and Jen and the women stood on the stage and went over final notes for the performance that night.

Daffy was laughing.

"Y'all, that wasn't nothing. We did the boring version today."

Lolly and Jen glanced at each other. Jen was grinning, and Lolly knew they were going to pull out all the stops tonight.

"Okay, go get your dinners and try to get back here by 6:30," Lolly said.

The women were in high spirits as they headed out the door. But Lolly noticed that Sonya had dark bags under her eyes and a crease between her eyebrows as if she were dogged by worry. Sonya stopped briefly to talk to Jen, but Lolly didn't hear what she said.

"She okay?" Lolly asked Jen after all the women were gone. They were sitting in the pews of the chapel, eating some crackers and peanut butter that Lolly had thought to bring.

"Her brother has kidnapped her little boy," Jen said.

"Oh shit," Lolly said.

"She wants me to help her," Jen continued.

Lolly settled back and tried to think. She wondered if she should have brought Jen into this place. What if her sister got into trouble? Jen wasn't always the most realistic person in the world.

"Jen, you don't have to help her. We already got a lawyer for her. Please don't put yourself in any danger. I don't know what I'd do if you wound up in a place like this," Lolly said and looked around. "Imagine seeing the same places day after day, never going to a restaurant, never going to the park, never having someone make love to you. Why . . . the bars in Tallahassee might go out of business."

Jen ignored the last comment and said, "I'm not going to get in trouble. I swear."

Lolly rubbed a hand along Jen's forearm. "You seem sad these days."

"I am, I guess," Jen said. "I blew it with that cop. And I'm worried about you. And I'm worried about Sonya and her baby."

"Promise me, you'll tell me before you do anything to help her, won't you?"

The doors opened then, and a guard came in to say there were some guests up at the control room and could Lolly come down and help check them in.

At 6:30 the women came back and gathered in a side room next to the stage area; Jen went over notes for the next show while Lolly doled out the plastic beads and the scarves she had brought for costumes. Street clothes were forbidden, of course, but the scarves had been acceptable.

"How many inmates will be here?" Jen asked.

"About 400," Lolly answered.

"I'm so excited," Nicole said.

"Would someone help me with this damn scarf?" Lucille asked in an irritated voice.

"We got our own scarves to worry about," Mariposa answered. She was looking in a hand mirror and applying lipstick.

Curly caught a case of the giggles.

"Breathe, everyone," Lolly said. "You'll be fine."

A guard came into the room and said all the inmates were in. The crowd murmur swelled behind him.

"Now, Lolly, you know we're gonna need to be able to burn this sage for the performance. And I'm gonna be quoting from the Bible."

"Honey, it's y'all's show now," Lolly grinned and then looked at her watch. "It's time. Y'all ready?"

She looked around at the women. They all had on their costumes and stood quietly looking at Jen and Lolly. They could hear a raucous audience.

"We're ready," Alice said.

Lolly went out onto the stage to introduce the show. As she stood there she looked out at the filled chapel. Folding chairs lined the back of the room. She stood before them—this group of incarcerated women, these convicted felons, these women who were not wanted in the world. And she felt a vibration deep inside her.

"Welcome to our drama production," she began.

Jen came through the door to the chapel as Lolly introduced the plays and looked out at the audience. In many ways they fit the stereotypes in her head. They looked tough as leather, muscled up women, tattooed and scarred, black women in elaborate hair styles, white women with three-inch long black roots in their yellow hair, mousy women, women who looked just like men and then a few plain as dirt women. Though a few were somewhat pretty, they were not by and large a beautiful bunch, but Jen suddenly felt as if she could see them through Lolly's eyes. They were exquisite in their own rambunctious way. Maybe it was their unapologetic stance. Something was there in their look that Jen admired. These were real women, so completely different from the air brushed paper dolls that television and magazines portrayed. Survivors with the battle scars to prove it.

She glanced over at the front row on the other side of the chapel. She saw Joel and his partner, Eden and her husband, some of Lolly's friends and there on the end was Zack Holtz wearing a polo shirt and khaki pants. She couldn't believe he had come.

Then the show began. It was as outrageous and wonderful a show as she had ever seen. The first skit was "The Exorcism of a Haunted

Woman" written by Nicole Parks. Viola ran onto the stage and twirled as if she were being chased and pinched by invisible demons. Jen had been most nervous about this skit because Nicole had been so vague about what actually was supposed to happen. But now Nicole seemed sure of herself. She began reciting the 23rd Psalm while Alice used dual flashlights to create effects. When Curly started dancing around Viola and waving the burning sage, all the women in the whole place, led by Nicole, began to chant: "Leave her be. Leave her be." Jen noticed chills on her arms, and as she looked around the room an eerie quiet suddenly descended. Then Viola fainted, which looked real enough, but it was all apparently part of Nicole's script.

Sonya brought the house down as Antigone, a woman whose brother was killed in a street brawl. Instead of Creon the King, the antagonist was the Mayor of Miami. The plot was a stretch, but no one in the audience knew the original, and Sonya's stage intuition was pitch-perfect. When Sonya whirled across the stage with a fiery look on her face and declared she would avenge her family, Jen figured the passion was genuine.

Curly's monologue about a West Virginia woman who abandoned her daughters brought tears to Jen's eyes, or maybe she was just in need of shedding a few tears. She heard sniffles around the audience, and there was a stunned silence at the end of the monologue, followed by loud whistles, stomping and applause. Then Daffy's skit about the aliens from the planet of the dead caused hoots and hollers. Mariposa's skit was beautiful. Somehow the sentimentality that Jen had feared had been wrought into something that felt honest.

The show ended with Lucille's skit about the eviction. At the end when she began to sing "Papa was a Rolling Stone," every woman in the entire place seemed to know it by heart. Jen and Lolly glanced at each other and over at their guests as suddenly four hundred women were singing in unison: "wherever he laid his hat was his home." Their voices rocked Jen's body. It was like no performance she'd ever been to. It was like standing in a hurricane or watching a volcano erupt. It was just that powerful.

Then the show was over. Lolly and Jen stood up in a daze and went to the stage where the women beckoned them. Alice presented them with two plaques that she had made. And then there were hugs, in spite of the guards. And it didn't seem like a prison until a buzzer sounded, and everyone slowly filed out.

Sonya gave Jen one last hug and surreptitiously handed her an envelope. Then Sonya followed the rest of them out of the door. Jen glanced in the envelope. Inside were pictures of Sonya's family. Jen looked up and noticed a tall very pretty woman with long dark hair watching her curiously. Most of the inmates had left, but this one lingered near the door. She smiled when she noticed Jen looking at her.

"That was a good show," she said, but Jen got a strange feeling as if the woman had meant something else entirely. Alice had just finished wrapping up the sheets she'd painted for the set and came down from the stage holding the sheets.

"Here ya go, Doc. Hey, Riley," she said. "Did you like the show?"

"Yeah, no wonder you're so happy here," the woman named Riley said and turned insolently away. Alice just shrugged.

"You can't please everybody," she said.

Lolly came running over and hugged Alice quickly.

"Thank you!"

Alice nodded and hurried out the door. She was the last one.

When Jen and Lolly came through the prison gates, they found Zack standing there in the dark, nearly empty parking lot.

Lolly walked over and extended her hand to him.

"I'm glad you could make it. You must be Zack," she said.

"I'm glad I made it, too," Zack said with a grin to match Lolly's. "You gals did a good job." He turned toward Jen. "Can I give you a lift home?"

"Sure," Jen said. "Lolly, you don't mind, do you?"

"No, go have fun. I'm kind of tuckered out," Lolly said.

"I bet you are," Jen said, and then with a pang of guilt, asked,

"You gonna be okay driving home by yourself?"

"Of course, I am," Lolly said.

Jen got in Zack's car—a black 1973 Monte Carlo.

"I haven't been in a car like this since high school," she said with a laugh.

"I just bought it last week. I'm not much into cars with computers. I want something I can fix myself."

They rode in silence. They'd only been on a few "dates" before Jen had ruined things at the bar that night. And none of those dates had ended up in bed. Now, she wondered what he expected from her. Perhaps he no longer entertained the idea of a real relationship.

"I trust you got your keys back?" Zack said.

"Yeah, found them in the envelope by my door," she said, "Very thoughtful of you. Where are we going?"

"I don't know. Just driving, I guess."

They turned down a canopy road, the headlights carving into the dark, the windows open, the sound of the air humming past.

"I'm glad you came tonight," she said.

"Well, I wasn't sure I should," he answered.

"I'm glad you did anyway."

He paused and then said, "Me, too."

"They were really good, weren't they?"

"Amazing," he said. "I don't know. I see those people at their worst. It colors your perception of humanity sometimes."

"Are you a forgiving person, Zack?" Jen asked.

"I can be," he said. "I can give people a second chance. I mean I don't intend to let someone make a fool out of me, but ..."

He didn't finish the sentence. They sat back and silently let the night unravel around them.

Eventually they wound up at a fish camp on the north end of town. Zack bought them a couple of beers and they wandered down to the boat slip. It was warm out and the moonlight fell bright and white over the lake water. As they sat down on a bench, Zack slipped an arm around her shoulders. She turned to him and let him kiss her. She felt a window swing open inside her. His breath was sweet and his tongue soft and warm. She pulled closer to him and kissed him back. What she felt for him was a yearning that she'd never experienced with Lyle or Daniel. But she wouldn't give in to it. Not yet. Maybe never, she realized.

An hour or so later, he pulled up into the parking lot behind her apartment and turned off the engine. He turned and reached over to push the hair off her face.

"Look, I probably shouldn't have called you," she said.

"Why? You gonna blow me off again next time I find you in your favorite watering hole?" he asked, leaning back against the seat and gazing forward.

Jen wiggled her foot and said, "No, more likely you'll blow me off when you know some things about me."

Zack glanced sideways at her. "Oh? You got some deep dark secret past I should know about?"

Jen shrugged. "You could call it that."

"How far back in the past are we talking?"

"'Bout twelve years, I guess. That's when I left my husband." She had leaned her head against the window and was gazing at the wisteria vines on the fence.

"Twelve years?" Zack laughed. "I don't care about what happened twelve years ago."

"You might. And I don't want to get my tender little heart chewed up any worse than it is, so I'm afraid I'm going to have to ask you to wait right here while I go inside and get something."

"I'm not going anywhere 'til you say so," Zack crossed his arms.

Jen got out of the car. The heat had dissipated and the air had a soft silky feel to it, but she barely noticed it. She climbed the stairs to her apartment, feeling disgusted with herself. She should have left things alone. But what difference would it make now? Her life had sucked before she met him, and she was used to it. She always had the theater, her one true love.

She unlocked the door and went inside. Manny meowed at her from his perch on top of the couch.

"Hey, cat," she said. She went into her bedroom and opened the closet door. The shoe box was shoved into a corner under a pair of old Reeboks. She pulled it out and opened it. Still there. The only copies she had of her bare naked ass on video. The top one was "The Color Pink." It was all soft-core stuff, but still it was humiliating. She tapped the video on her hand. She shouldn't do this. She should just tell him. But she couldn't make herself say it. And the truth was, if he was going to dump her, which of course he would, she wanted there to be no mistakes, no second thoughts. Get your heart hammered once and then move on, she told herself. She trusted him enough to believe that he wouldn't show the video to anyone else. Seeing this would answer his questions better than she ever could. She took the tape outside.

Zack sat in the car with his radio playing "Money for Nothing" and his fingers tapping the steering wheel. When he saw her, he turned down the music. She handed him the video. As he stared at it, she tried to read his expression, but he didn't give any sign.

"This is a sample of the kind of acting I used to do," she said in a monotone voice. "Good night." She turned and walked back into the building.

"Hey, I'll call you this weekend," he said.

Over her shoulder she answered, "I'll be out of town."

On the stairs, she heard the engine come to life and the tires of his car as they rolled across the gravel.

From the Journal of Nicole Parks

The Saturday after the show Lolly came to see us without Doc. It was our "wrap up" session. We were not prepared for this wrap up, though I guess we should have seen it coming.

Lolly came into the room and we all sat in our usual circle. First she had us write down how we felt about our class and what we had learned from doing the drama production. Everyone had positive things to say. Viola say she was freer than she had been in years, and I explained that the exorcism we had done in the production was real. Lolly didn't seem to mind.

After everyone spoke, Lolly took off the little cap that we had gotten used to seeing her wear. Tiny hairs were sprouting on her head, and I wondered why she had cut it so short.

"I have cancer," she told us, looking around the room. I felt my heart crumble.

"No!" Lucille said.

"Yes, it's true. I didn't want to say anything before the production because I didn't want you to be distracted."

"Oh my God, why did we choose death as a theme?" Daffy cried out. Those were my sentiments as well, but I wouldn't have just blurted it out.

"How bad is it?" I asked Lolly.

"It's pretty bad, Nicole," she said. "I might not live that much longer. I could say I'm okay with that, but I'm not really. On the other hand, I don't have much choice, and so what I'm trying to do is to enjoy every second of my life. And I want to tell all of you that you have really helped make that possible. The show last night was wonderful. It made me so happy to see you and all of your talent. You worked so hard. You gave me a great gift."

We were all silent for a few minutes or maybe for a lot of minutes. No one knew what to say.

Bonita let a few tears fall and she said that Lolly had given us the gift. Finally Lolly said, "Look, I don't want to be all sad if it's okay with you. I felt I should tell you the truth because you have been so honest with me. But if you don't mind, I'd like to end on a happier note."

Daffy spoke up. "I could tell some jokes."

"That would be good."

Then Daffy proceeded to tell some of the dumbest jokes you ever heard, but for some reason we all laughed anyway. And then other people started telling funny stories. And our last class ended with hugs. We didn't care if the damn guards saw us or not.

Fortunately for me, this would not be the last time that I was to see Lolly Johanssen. My mind had been so occupied with the production that I hadn't even noticed the time slipping away, but come Monday my classification officer called me in her office and said that there was an opening in the Tallahassee work release center and I could have it if I wanted it. Like I wouldn't want it? Was she crazy?

So just like that, it was two days and a wake up, then one day and a wake up and finally it was the night before my "wake up." I went into the dayroom about 8 o'clock with Daffy following me. She kept brushing the tears back. You'd a thought someone had died.

"Ima miss you, girl," she said.

"Well, I'm gonna miss you, too, but I won't miss this place," I said. We sat down in that corner area where my girls all liked to hang and pretty soon they were all there—even Indian and Gypsy. I was like the star because I was going into the free world the next day. It felt like my birthday.

"You nervous?" Lucille asked.

"Just a little. Mostly, I'm excited."

"She's gonna get some dick," Daffy said.

I slapped her on the arm and saw Indian grin at me.

Panther sauntered in and sat next to Gypsy. I noticed Gypsy didn't move away. Maybe Panther stood a chance after all. Panther was all full of advice, of course: "Don't let them trip you up in that work release center. Those so-called counselors are treacherous. I seen many a girl come back with even more charges stacked up on 'em."

"Aw, Nic is way too smart to get caught up in that shit," Daffy said.

"For real," Sonya agreed. Sonya had told me about her little boy being taken and I knew it was chewing a hole in her heart.

"Girl, I made you a card," Daffy said and handed me the nicest card talking about how I would be a famous writer some day and that I had full permission to turn her life story into an academy-award winning movie. Lucille brought out a tin of cookies she'd scrounged up from somewhere, and Sonya offered to buy everyone drinks from the vending machine. Then Alice gave me a portrait she had drawn of me in a frame made of cardboard. You would have sworn that frame cost money and the picture was incredible. That girl could draw like no one's business.

I noticed that Riley wasn't hanging around Alice, and I was glad. That chick gave me the heebies. She had those cold lizard eyes. I knew that Alice didn't have a thing for her. Alice was just nice to everyone, and she'd of course be nice to someone who had done time with her earlier.

Viola came in the dayroom, swiveling her head every which way till she saw me and the gang. She came straight for us and grabbed my hand.

"Thank heavens," she said with that trace of Haiti in her voice.

Daffy, ever the street girl, rolled her eyes.

"Is your ghost back messing wit' you, Viola?" Daffy asked.

"No," Viola said adamantly, her eyebrows arched up. "That man will never come back. I am free, thanks to my good friend Nicole."

Then she looked at me with her dark self and smiled like she could be in one of those "come to Jamaica" commercials. She pulled a card from the pocket of her dress and handed it to me.

"I wanted you to have this," she said.

It was the 23rd Psalm, all decorated with flowers and birds. "The Lord is my Shepherd," I read aloud. I was touched. I glanced at the windows quickly to make sure there wasn't a C.O. around and gave her a brief hug. She practically fell out.

"Can Junebug come see you at work release?" she asked.

"That's not a good idea, Viola," I said. "I don't want to take any chances and break any rules. I know he wouldn't mean to get me in trouble, but you never know. I better wait to see him after I get out of there. I won't be there but a couple months."

Viola nodded. "Then I'll make him promise to leave you alone 'til you say it's okay."

I didn't know if that day would ever come, but no need to tell that to Viola.

And so that was it—my last night at the state prison. I had survived it. No one had beat me up or tried to rape me or any of that. While I was doing my time, I had thought it would never end, but once I got to the end, the whole ordeal wasn't as bad as I had expected. In fact, I was a stronger person now. And if I hadn't gone to prison, I never would have written a play and seen it performed, never would have written all that poetry, or this memoir, never would have met Lolly Johanssen.

After the C.O. ran us out of the dayroom, saying it was time to clean up and get ready for count, I took my gifts to my locker to store them for the night. I also figured I better throw some of my old junk in there away.

As I stood at my locker I noticed Riley, the supermodel herself, cozied up with Magna. Not like lovers. More like conspirators, if you know what I mean. They were whispering and glancing sideways and passing looks back and forth. They were up to no good. I knew that much, but for once I wasn't curious. I decided just to mind my own business and get out while the getting was good.

The next day I was gone in a white Department of Corrections van. It felt crazy good to be away from that place, the smells and the noises. I took my work release in Tallahassee where Doc and Lolly lived. I hoped I would see them. In fact, the first Saturday that I was there, Lolly came by with two bags of clothing that I could wear to work. Granny Hazel knew of a Muslim dude who ran a little weekly Muslim newspaper in town, and he hired me to come to his office every morning and answer the phone and file stuff for him. Once you're convicted, it's hard to get a decent job. The Muslim dude said he had to give "a sister a chance." I liked it because he wasn't trying to get in my pants, and after my burn with Antwan I planned to take my time before getting caught up with a man again. He even helped me learn how to do layout. The only problem with the job was that he closed the office at one o'clock in the afternoon because he had another job, which meant I had to go back to the work release house and do nothing except clean the place. I didn't care for that at all. I was going to have to find a second job soon.

Those damn women who ran the work release center made C.O. Barbie look like Mother Theresa. Panther was right: it was their greatest pleasure in life to send women back to the joint instead of out onto the street.

Tuesday, September 19

As the two of them walked slowly around Lake Ella, Lolly wanted to ask Jen about the policeman, but Jen just shook her head when Lolly tried to bring it up. So she tried another topic. Lolly had noticed a change in Jen over the past month. She hadn't gone out and gotten drunk once, and she made a point of calling or coming over to the house every evening and checking on Lolly. It seemed as if for the first time in her life they weren't just sisters by accident. It seemed as if they were friends.

"Are you going to be in any of the Community Theater shows this fall? I heard they're doing Pinter, seems very risky material for them," Lolly said.

"Actually, they asked me to direct it," Jen said. "But I told them no."

"No? Why? They'd have to pay you if you directed, wouldn't they?"

Jen didn't answer, and Lolly realized why she had turned them down.

"You did that because of me, didn't you?" she asked.

"Lolly, someone needs to be around to take care of you. I mean, I know you're not on the chemo anymore and I'm sorry I wasn't helpful this summer, but directing a show will take up all the time I have when I'm not teaching or acting in state videos. All of it. I can't do that."

"Shit. So now I'm ruining your life once again."

Jen stopped and pulled Lolly's arm. A woman with a golden retriever jogged past them.

"Lolly, you are my sister, and I know I've probably never said this before, but I love you and I want to take care of you if you need it. Do you hear me? I'm not going to let anything take that away from me. I was just a kid last time, an angry kid, but I'm not that kid anymore."

A slow smile crept across Lolly's face.

Jen glanced at the sidewalk and said, "We better get moving before the friggin' violins start playing."

They walked on slowly in an easy silence. They passed the large tree where as kids they had clambered along the low sprawling branches. Lolly felt strangely at peace. She had lost all hope in the doctors. She was glad that Jen was accepting of her decision not to fight this thing anymore.

As they passed close to the street, a man in an old BMW pulled up and called to her.

"Lolly!" He parked the car and came over toward them. It was Jeremy.

"Who is that?" Jen asked her.

"Jeremy Erwin, you remember him from high school, right?"

"I think so," Jen said.

Jeremy sailed over to them.

"Hey, there. I just drove by your house," he said to Lolly. "Hi, Jen, you're looking wonderful."

"Thanks," she said.

Then he turned his gaze to Lolly.

"How about me? Am I looking wonderful?" she asked. Her hair had begun to grow back; it was a curly black that was quite different from the hair she used to have.

"Better than wonderful," he answered with a smile. "Listen, Lolly, I've been doing some research on your cancer."

Lolly felt a jolt of surprise. Why had he done that?

He continued, "There's a program in North Carolina. A doctor up there is doing stem cell research on stage four breast cancer. It's experimental, of course, but I really think you should check it out. Here, I brought you all the materials. It sounds very promising, Lolly. Very promising."

Jeremy handed her a folder. Her face flushed.

"This is very sweet, Jeremy," she said. "But my insurance won't cover anything experimental, and I know stem cell transplants aren't free."

Jen interrupted. "So what, Lolly? If there's any possibility that this could save you, we have to try it."

Jeremy cleared his throat and said, "You're right. It's not free. The cost is about thirty thousand."

"Dammit," Jen said.

Jeremy leaned forward. "A lot of people in this city love you, Lolly. We could come up with the money."

"I couldn't ask anyone..." Lolly began.

Jen was staring across the lake at the American Legion Hall.

"We'll have a benefit," Jen interrupted. "We'll have a benefit on your birthday—Friday, October 13. That gives us enough time."

"That's plenty of time," Jeremy agreed.

"We can pull this together," Jen said thoughtfully. Lolly looked from one to the other. A benefit? The idea had never occurred to her. Would people actually come?

"I don't know," she said weakly. She felt overwhelmed. Jeremy put an arm around her and she whispered, "Okay. We can try it."

An enormous gray goose waddled up to them and honked as if they were in its way.

Friday, September 22

Sonya went to the library to look for Alice but as usual found Riley in there. Only this time Alice looked up at her and immediately left Riley and came over to talk to her. They wandered into an aisle between book shelves so the library lady wouldn't spy them. Riley sat at the table, pretending to read a magazine, but her lizard eyes shot daggers down at the two of them.

"Hey, Sonya," Alice said. "Panther told me about your son. Are you okay?"

"No. But there's not much I can do. I told Doc about it, and she said she'd help. Do you think she will?"

Alice thought for a moment and then nodded her head. "I believe she will if she can. I know it's hard for you."

"I'm just so worried about him. My brother Ziggy used to torture me when I was little. I mean, really torture me. He would pretend it was a game, but a couple of times, it got serious. He would burn me and make me swear not to tell anyone. He'd make me let snakes and bugs crawl across me. If I flinched, he beat me up. And this is the man who has my son. I can't breathe when I think about it."

Alice moved closer to her and said, "I wish there was something I could do to help you. Please, come talk to me anytime. I know it seems like maybe I haven't been there for you, but I want you to know I am here if you need me."

Sonya looked at Alice. She finally felt that she understood her.

Alice was like a holy person. Sonya, who had never been to church, realized this for the first time. Alice Jaybird, the woman who had shot to death a man she didn't know, loved people and it had nothing to do with sex or what she could get from them. She had not turned away from Sonya. She had simply allowed Riley into her life as well.

Sonya noticed Riley standing at the end of the aisle.

"I'm going now, Indian," she said in a loud voice.

Alice turned to her and said calmly, "Okay, see you later."

Riley tried to smile, but it was a sneer. Then she turned and walked away.

"She seems mad," Sonya said.

"She is," Alice answered. "When we were both down in Broward, I wasn't like this. I was into all kinds of shit. I was even dealing drugs on the compound. She expects me to still be like that."

"What changed you, Alice?" Sonya asked.

Alice smiled and looked at the books on the shelf in front of her. She absently stroked the spine of a novel.

"I don't know exactly," Alice said. "But when they transferred me up here a couple years ago, I saw that I had a chance to change. I fasted for about a week, didn't sleep at nights. My mother was real sick, and I was worried about her. Then one morning just before dawn, I was wide awake and I was remembering my childhood and I could hear the songs my mother used to sing—the Indian songs. And I remembered how she used to sit for hours doing beadwork, so intricate, so beautiful. Something just lifted off me. Something I didn't even know had been there. When they brought me here, I was a different person. I don't like being in prison, but I sometimes think we're always in prison. We just don't always know it."

Sonya stared at Alice who was now looking at her with her dark eyes. She felt completely accepted by Alice, something she could never in her life remember feeling.

The buzzer rang and it was time to go to the cafeteria. They walked together across the compound.

Alice had her hands in the pockets of her state work pants.

"Since I got here, I started reading different books, holy books from different religions. One morning before anyone else was up, I got this crystal feeling as if my ancestors were there with me, and I was this empty vessel into which they kept pouring and pouring their love. I swear I felt like I was shooting light from my insides."

Sonya listened in amazement.

"The feeling faded after a while, but I never forgot it. Never forgot the vision of my ancestors there with me all around my bunk. All the scheming and lying and plotting I'd done in the past, it all seemed pointless. I just want to be happy. And I can be happy if I choose to be. I'm trying to help Riley see that. She's got a lot of time now, and I'd like to help her. But she always wants to get into something."

"Like what?" Sonya asked, but Alice didn't have a chance to answer.

Lucille and Daffy came up behind them.

"Hey, y'all," Daffy said. "Sonya, where's your friend?"

"What friend?"

"Panther," Daffy said with a grin.

"I don't know but if you see her, Daffy, tell her I'm looking for her," Sonya said and smiled.

That night Sonya figured out at least one of the things Riley was trying to get into. A bunch of the women from the other side of the dorm were acting sly and knowing. Then the C.O. came into the dayroom and started yelling at them about some hooch she found in the laundry room. Nobody fessed up, but it was pretty clear that Riley and a few of the others were feeling no pain. She wished she had something to ease her own pain, but nothing could make her forget her missing child.

Saturday, September 23

Hadn't Irv been surprised to hear from Jen.

"Jenny, Jenny! Honey, it's good to hear your voice," Irv had said when he got her call. "I'd never forget you or your pretty pink ass."

Pink? Well, he should know right? He'd seen it magnified and in close up.

"It's good to hear your voice, too, Irv," Jenny said with a sardonic undertone. "I called because I'm coming down to Miami for a couple of days and ..."

He interrupted her.

"You need a place to stay? Sweetheart, there's always room in my bed for you," Irv said.

"That's nice. I think Elayne might not feel the same way. How about your guest room?" Jen was sitting in her office in the theater building. A student passed and waved at her.

"Oh all right, be that way. You're too old for my tastes anyway. Over thirty aren't you?"

"Thirty-two."

"Oh, Lordy. That's old for a woman," Irv said sadly.

"And what are you? Seventy?" Jen asked.

"Sixty-nine, sweet cheeks. Always and forever, sixty-nine. My favorite number," Irv answered.

"God, you haven't changed a bit. Anyway, I've got kind of a gig. I'll explain it to you when I get there," she said and then continued in a low voice, "but Irv, I need to portray a filthy rich bitch. Which by the way I'm not. Not rich anyway."

"We can fix you up, hon. It'll be like the old days," Irv said.

Jen had lied to Lolly and said she had an audition, then left out some extra food for Manny, and the next day Jen got in the Blazer with a couple of tailored dresses she'd bought back when money flowed like milk and honey. They were nearly ten years old, but they still fit and they still looked stylish.

Irv actually produced a few legit videos every once in a while, but porn had made him a rich man. For all his blatantly sexist jargon, Jen felt perfectly safe with him. For one thing, Elayne kept a pretty tight rein on him. How her feminist colleagues would shudder at the mere existence of someone like Irv, but she understood him at a certain level. He was crude and vulgar and looked at women as commodities, but he was what he was and never pretended to be anything but that. And there was some substratum of society that needed the Irvs of the world. Besides, he was generous at heart. He was obsessed with sex but he saw it as something natural. He didn't understand all the stigma attached to soft porn. It was a good healthy outlet, he said, better than violence.

As Jen drove down Highway 27 through horse country, she thought about her flight from Miami nine years earlier. Her heart had been shattered and her self-image dirtied. Irv had given her ten grand for her last film and she packed everything she owned in the car, including the little kitten that had come crying up to her the day after the abortion. On that day she had just walked out of the wine shop with two bottles of Pinot Grigio determined to get obliterated when the small orange tabby kitten came up and rubbed against her legs. When she picked up the kitten, it clung with its sharp little claws to her shoulder. Lyle hated cats and so she had never been able to have one. Well, the hell with Lyle, she had thought.

A woman stood outside of an apartment next to the wine shop.

"You want him?" she asked. "I got six of 'em in here."

Jen felt the tiny claws gripping her.

"I think he wants me," she said.

"Well, take him with you," the woman said. "I got to get rid of them."

Jen had taken the cat home with her and packed up the car. The cat didn't seem to mind riding in the car. Twelve hours later they were in Atlanta where Jen found an apartment, got a job waitressing and signed up for college classes. She'd always been a fairly decent student and school seemed the thing to do while she regrouped. A couple of years later she had a BFA in theater arts.

After college she landed some minor roles in independent films, but moviemaking had turned sour on her. The self-importance of the producers and directors, the "above-the-line" men (usually), and then the looks and rumors that followed her. Too many of them knew Lyle and Irv and knew about her former work. She was sure some of them had seen it though they refused to admit it. The lewd comments that one crew guy or another might make, the gropings when no one was looking. One insufferably pretentious young director who held nightly viewings of "The Last Picture Show" had berated her talent, her intelligence and even her looks, calling her a "stupid cow." But this had only happened after she declined his offer to suck his dick one night after the screening.

When she went home for her mother's funeral, she felt completely washed up. It seemed easier to stay.

Her mother had left the house to Lolly, but there was a little money so Jen had gotten an apartment and enrolled in school again, returning to her first love: the stage. And audiences were appreciative. Maybe it was a small town, but it was a college town and they had a taste for good theater. She felt at home and had slipped into this easy, though by no means profitable, life. Lots of local acting, some teaching, a few directing gigs.

She wondered as she pulled onto Interstate 75 what happened to old porn stars. She didn't think many of them had taken her route. Maybe they married rich, maybe they got jobs in strip clubs and finally died off from drug abuse or killed themselves in car crashes like Linda Lovelace.

Finally she had turned onto that hellbound lane known as the Florida Turnpike and late that afternoon, she hit North Miami. The traffic in the city was nightmarish. It had been bad when she left nine years ago, now it was gladiatorial -- or rather, it was like being a bee in an angry swarm. Good luck pulling out of the swarm. Taking her life into her hands, she swerved out of the rush of cars into the neighborhood where Irv said he still lived. It was easy to find his house in spite of the construction on the main road. He had that ostentatious fountain in the front and the big black gates that opened onto the circular drive.

By Miami standards it was not a big house, but Irv wasn't hurting in the financial department. He just didn't pour it all into his house.

Jen lifted the big door knocker and let it drop and in a moment Elayne opened the door and ushered her into the cool house. The house was typical nouveau riche with lots of glass and leather. A pool gleamed sapphire blue just beyond the glass doors.

"So good to see you, dear," Elayne said. Jen wondered if Elayne remembered her, but Elayne continued. "We're so proud of you. Saw you in some bank commercials, and Irv says you're a college professor now."

Jen shook her head, "I'm not a professor yet. I'm an adjunct. I haven't finished my doctorate. Anyway, I still act whenever I can. Theatre, mostly."

"That's nice, dear. Very nice." Jen was thankful that Elayne didn't mention Lyle. She wasn't sure what had happened to him, and she didn't want to know. Later Irv was only too happy to talk about it.

"He married some little tart and moved to North Carolina where I hear that he's a pig farmer."

"A pig farmer?" Jen asked in shock as they sat by the pool, having after dinner cocktails.

"That's right. A pig farmer. Soo-eee," Irv called and Jen burst into laughter.

"So tell me about this gig you've got, Jenny. Sounds mysterious."

Jen explained the situation to Irv.

"I don't get it," Irv said. "If the family knows that this man's wife is telling fortunes in West Palm Beach, why don't they go have a little chat with her?" Irv asked, rubbing his round protruding belly.

"Sonya says her husband tried to talk to her. But the woman claims she doesn't know where this Ziggy character is. She's also the only one without any warrants against her, so she can call the cops on them if they harass her too much."

Irv took a sip of his bloody mary and asked, "Are you going up to West Palm tonight?"

"I'd like to, but, Irv, I need to fool these people into thinking I'm wealthy," Jen said.

"Not a problem," Irv said. "Elayne, come here! Bring the crown jewels with you."

That night Jen was back on the highway, but this time in a mint condition Austin Healey and wearing a large cubic zirconium rock on her left hand, some Versace sunglasses propped on her head and Elayne's genuine "paste" tennis bracelet. Irv had tried to convince Elayne to hand over some real jewels, but Jen said the fakes would fool anyone. It was knowing how to inhabit a role that did the trick.

With the velvety South Florida air blowing through the windows of the car as she tooled up I-95, she had a moment of wishing she'd never left. She had loved living down here. Loved the constant stream of people, the noise, the jostling of cultures. But like a fool she'd gotten caught up in it like a fish caught in a net and whisked into the air, unable to breathe.

It was only a little more than an hour to get to the West Palm exits. Irv had told her that West Palm had gotten a new look and there was a thriving night life there with live music in the park and people strolling along the downtown strip. That's where she'd find any fortune tellers that happened to be lurking about.

Graceful palm trees lined the roads as she drove down the main drag. Irv was right. Well heeled pedestrians were loitering in front of shops, tourists tripped along and families carried ice cream cones and packages. She saw a magazine shop and bookstore, restaurants, and art galleries. It had that South Florida flavor without the Miami edge.

Cruising up and down the street, Jen didn't see any fortune tellers set up, but there was a sign that said "Psychic Advisor" over a large hand in front of a doorway between two stores. Jen had gotten the idea that Tasha's business was more or less just an outside booth somewhere, but she could give it a try. She parked the car and found her way back through the drifting crowds of tourists to the sign. The door was open, and so she went inside a small room with a desk and some new-agey posters of dolphins leaping above waves on the wall. A woman with layers of makeup – bright blue eye shadow, thick false eyelashes, and a solid quarter-inch of base sat behind the desk, a cell phone to her ear. As soon as she heard the voice, Jen realized she wasn't a woman at all. She grinned and thought it was good to be back in South Florida.

"Can I help you, honey?" she asked.

"I want to see the psychic," Jen said hesitantly.

"He's not in right now. But he'll back in about half an hour. He just went to get some dinner. Go do some shopping and come back. He'll be expecting you. He probably already knows you're here." Then she laughed and went back to her cell phone conversation.

Jen turned around. She was pretty sure that Tasha wasn't impersonating a man so this was obviously the wrong place. Outside she wandered along the strip. Maybe it would be better if she couldn't find Tasha. She stopped and stared in a window at some clothes. Wouldn't it be nice not to be broke all the time? *Forget it*, she thought. When she'd had money she had only blown it. If there were such a thing as

God, he or she or it probably figured there was no sense in wasting any more on her.

She could afford some chocolate, however, and she stepped inside a confectioner's shop.

"Are there any fortune tellers around here?" she asked the guy behind the counter. "Besides the psychic advisor down the street? My friend said she had her fortune told by some woman around here and it was really good."

The guy looked up toward the ceiling as he thought about Jen's question. "You know there was a woman used to set up a table right along the strip there, but they ran her off. I'm thinking she might have gone down closer to the beach. There's some kind of Italian restaurant down there and a couple shops. Go about three blocks east and then make a right. You might find her down there. If she's still around."

Jen got in her car and followed the man's directions, and there she was—a woman sitting beside a small table with the sign "Fortunes—cards or palm reading" propped up in front of it. Jen wanted to park nearby, wanted the woman to spot her car. She found a spot near the corner and whipped the sports car into it. It would be better if she had someone with her, but she'd have to figure out a way to pull it off.

She walked through the crowds and passed the fortune teller without giving her a second glance. She pretended to walk purposefully. She was not a mere tourist. The art gallery. Yes. That would do. She walked in. What was the largest thing she could buy without spending too much money?. Everything was tacky and expensive. Then she noticed some prints against the wall.

"May I see one of those?" A young woman was more than happy to let her look.

Jen looked at the price. She could afford it. She bought it quickly and asked the young woman to wrap it for her.

Carrying the large wrapped poster out of the gallery, Jen stood aside to let someone pass just as she got to the fortune tellers' table. Their eyes met.

"Would you like your fortune told, ma'am?" the fortune teller asked. She was very pretty with long eyelashes and a sharp nose and high cheekbones. She smiled at Jen and Jen allowed herself to be charmed.

"How much do you charge?"

The woman glanced at her diamond tennis bracelet and said, "Fifty dollars."

"Oh, that's way too much," Jen said.

"I can give you a short reading for twenty-five," the woman said.

Jen considered it and then placed the package against the wall. She sat down in the chair by the table.

"Cards?" the woman asked.

"That will be fine."

The fortune teller told Jen to shuffle the deck of cards. They were larger than regular playing cards and the deck was thicker. Jen awkwardly shuffled them.

"Now cut them with your left hand," the fortune teller said.

The fortune teller took the cards from her and smiled without showing any teeth.

"So," she said. "What sort of advice are you looking for? Love problems? Money problems?"

"No," Jen said in a slightly haughty tone. "I don't have money problems." *One had to have money to have problems with it*, she thought ruefully.

The fortune teller turned over a card. It showed a woman in a black cape staring down at some toppled goblets, water spilling on the ground. The woman appeared to be crying. Behind her were several goblets still upright.

"The seven of cups," she said. "You have lost something."

Jen inhaled slowly and felt the woman surreptitiously studying her reactions.

"Yes," Jen said.

"Not something. Someone," the fortune teller added with more confidence.

"That's right," Jen said. And she thought of Lolly, lying in the hospital bed after her latest round of surgery' how thin, how attenuated her spirit seemed.

The fortune teller turned over three more cards in succession.

"The King of Swords, the Five of Pentacles and the three of Cups," the woman said.

Jen looked at the last card—a picture of two children picking flowers outside a house—and let her face twitch slightly.

"A child?" the fortune teller asked softly. "You lost a child?"

Jen nodded. Her lungs felt cloudy, arms tight, stomach squeezing. She had lost a child, not that she thought about it much, not that she thought about it ever. But like a tumor it was there inside her, waiting to be exposed.

Now the fortune teller seemed to be on solid ground as she turned over more cards, placing them in some kind of pattern that Jen didn't understand.

"You have experienced great sorrow. You are searching for something, an anchor, a purpose, I think?"

Jen raised her eyebrows and shrugged. Maybe.

The fortune teller turned over another card. She smiled now with all her teeth. The card said "Death" and Jen felt a shiver of horror.

"This is a good card," the fortune teller said.

"It looks terrible," Jen said with a catch in her voice. She realized she had all the right emotions to play this scene so close to the surface.

"No, it means this sorrow will come to an end."

"Really?" Jen felt the woman exerting her charm on her. This woman was a pro.

She turned over one last card. It was a picture of The Sun—a joyful looking card. Jen wondered how she had managed that. The fortune teller herself looked relieved that the cards were on message.

Now she leaned closer to Jen and tapped the card with a red fingernail.

"This is it. A new day. New life. You will have another child. Not from your own womb perhaps. A child who needs a good home. Are you planning on adopting?"

Jen pulled her lips in and wondered what to say.

"No," she said. Then it came to her why not. "You know how the people in this state feel about lesbian parents. The child I lost was my girlfriend's child. A little boy. He was born with birth defects ..." She stopped talking.

The fortune teller's eyes roved over the cards.

"Such a pity. And yet there are so many healthy children who need homes."

"Tell that to the bastards who run this state," Jen said, picking up one of the cards—the King of Swords—and realizing she would never know what sex the child she had aborted would have been. Or see the color of its eyes.

"What are you feeling so guilty about?" the fortune teller asked. "Guilt serves no purpose. What's done is done."

"What do you mean?" Jen asked.

"I don't know. It's not my guilt."

Jen stared at her for a moment, her thin exotic face, her large brown eyes, her long neck. The black hair falling like foam around her head and down past her shoulders.

"I could help you," the woman said.

"How?" Jen asked with a note of suspicion in her voice.

"I know of a child. An orphan. He needs a good home," she said.

Jen was silent.

"I don't know," she said. "Is it legal?"

"Who is to say he is not your child? Papers can easily be arranged. But of course if you are not interested," the fortune teller watched a young couple passing by.

"How old?" Jen asked.

"Not very old. Not even two years old yet. Still a baby."

"Why not give him up to the state?" Jen asked. "If he's really orphaned. Surely there are many couples who would adopt him."

"The state asks too many questions, the state has too many forms to fill out, the state gives nothing for all the time and expense you have invested in the child."

Jen leaned forward and said in a low voice. "It sounds illegal."

"You can call it what you like, but what is worse? To let a child grow up abandoned, neglected, shoved from one foster home to another? Or a happy boy growing up, loved and cherished by a devoted mother? A good mother. Someone like you."

"And what makes you think I'm a good mother?"

The fortune teller laughed. "I can see it in your face. You don't have to be psychic to know someone's heart. You act like you're tough, but you have a soft heart. I know that much." And she said it with such conviction that Jen felt a little spooked.

"How much would the adoption fees for such a baby cost?" Jen asked.

"Not much. Maybe thirty thousand dollars. Not much more than going overseas for a baby, and no questions asked."

Jen fished in her purse for a pen and some paper. "What is your name? How can I contact you?"

The woman smiled and shook her head. "My name is not important. Give me your number and someone will call you."

Jen wrote down her cell phone number and the name Jane Barkley on the slip of paper. Jen handed the woman the slip of paper and dropped the pen back in her purse

She felt the woman's eyes on her as she carried her package back to the Austin Healey, got in the car and drove away.

Wednesday, October 4

This was too much. Too damned much. Where was the air? Outside it was beautiful. Summer's heat had finally broken, letting the October balm sweep across the landscape. And yet Lolly couldn't get there from where she was – a terrible, terrible place.

She tried to sit up but it was as if a pair of strong arms kept pushing her back down. *Air*, she thought, *please God, just give me some air.* Her skin felt prickly, her tongue thick as a wad of tissue, her eyes felt like two stones in her head. Was there any part of her body that cancer was not ravaging, ransacking, plundering? If she'd had any breath, she would have screamed. *Okay*, she thought. She'd have to get help. Now. She wanted more time, just a little more time. Wasn't there a song like that? She inhaled sharply, fighting for air.

She reached for the phone. It was easy. She could just dial 911, but the phone slipped from her fingers. Damn. She wanted to cry but didn't think she had the breath for it. Then she looked up and saw Jen standing in the doorway, staring at her, frightened and wary. *Death ain't pretty, babe*, Lolly thought.

"I can't breathe," she gasped.

Jen seemed to wake up. She swept in and pulled Lolly to a sitting position. Jen's hand felt so cool on her brow.

"Is that better, Sissy?" Jen asked. Lolly nodded as air trickled into her chest. Jen hadn't called her Sissy in probably 25 years.

"Okay, I'm going to take you to the hospital right now," Jen said.

"You hear me? We'll take your car so it'll be easy for you to get in."

"Clothes," Lolly said, pulling off her sleep-T. Jen pulled a large loose dress from the closet and brought it to Lolly. Lolly saw Jen's eyes register the empty space where a breast should have been, the hard fold of tissue like a closed enveloped. Then Jen slipped the dress over Lolly's head and down over her body.

"Can you stand up?"

Lolly nodded.

"Do you want your leg?" Jen asked.

Lolly shook her head and pointed toward the crutches. Jen snatched them from the wall and helped Lolly get them under her armpits.

Jen helped Lolly into the car and then flew to the emergency room. Lolly sagged against the window of the car.

"Are you doing okay?" Jen asked.

"Better," Lolly whispered.

The emergency room was one of those separate realities where nothing anyone did was related to the real world. Time passed like water. The pain in Lolly's chest was like a strobe light—off on off on sharp and bright. She heard Jen's voice, strong and authoritative, as if she were the star of a daytime drama. "Look, I need someone to see my sister immediately. This cannot wait. She has cancer. And she can't breathe. We need to see a doctor now. Right now. No, I'm not going anywhere. Get a doctor out here now. Now."

Lolly felt a moment of utter gratitude for Jen's acting lessons. Within minutes she was being wheeled into the back room and people were hovering over her, listening to her chest. And the fluorescent lights were blazing like thin strands of starlight. Hands touched her body, prodded. The pain sang its song like a baby crying.

"Her lungs are filled with fluid."

"We have to operate."

"Will she be all right?"

"We can relieve the pressure."

The rest of the day blurred into a foggy night when she woke up sore but able to breathe.

Thursday, October 5

Jen walked out of the classroom with her books in a satchel. Teaching two classes at the university didn't exactly fill her days or her bank account, but she was busy enough planning Lolly's benefit. She'd need to give Jeremy a call and see what progress had been made in getting a sound system donated, preferably with someone to run it. And in the back of her mind was the nagging worry about what to do about Sonya's baby.

Oh God, she thought; there was Amanda Hathaway, the queen of the stage, standing in front of the bulletin board where Jen had posted a flyer announcing the benefit. Amanda stood tall and elegant, doing her best Joan Crawford imitation. Sometimes Jen was overfriendly to Amanda just to drive her crazy, but today she didn't feel like bothering. She had too much on her mind. She walked past her and headed toward her office to call the hospital and see how Lolly was doing.

Her office was small, and she shared it with an adjunct from the dance department. She pulled the phone from her office-mate's desk and sat down, looking up at the poster from a made-for-TV movie where she'd played a dead woman. She only appeared in flashbacks. The poster showed her falling off a cliff. Students for some reason really got a kick out of that.

She was half-way through dialing the number when she felt a presence in the doorway. She glanced up and saw Amanda Hathaway, gazing down her long nose.

"I thought I detected the presence of royalty," Jen said.

Amanda attempted a smile. She wore a thick gold braided chain around her neck and a lavender silk blouse with dark gray pants.

"I saw the flyer about your sister," Amanda said in her arch tone. "I didn't realize she had cancer again."

Jen didn't respond.

"I won't be able to come to the benefit," Amanda continued, "but I would like to donate something to the cause. I hope you will offer her my sympathy."

With that Amanda stepped into the office, something that had never happened before, and dropped a check onto Jen's desk.

Jen stared up at Amanda. "Thank you," she said.

"Well, everyone knows your sister is a wonderful poet and a ... a good person," Amanda said. Jen seriously doubted that Amanda knew much at all about Lolly, but perhaps some of Lolly's admirers in the English department – one of them was some sort of semi-famous playwright, after all – had given Amanda a little background. She also knew that Amanda's message was clear. This truce between the two of them was temporary, but Jen appreciated it all the same.

"As I said, Amanda, thank you very much."

Jen couldn't get through to anyone in Lolly's hospital room, so she drove over. This place was becoming familiar to her, and she wished it wasn't. The endless hallways with their shiny floors, the signs that directed you here and there, the doors that swooshed open and the stream of people who wandered about with their faces full of worry and fear.

Jen found Lolly in her room talking to a nurse. The nurse left and Lolly looked up at Jen. Her face was pale, but she seemed to be breathing all right.

"What did they say?" Jen asked, sitting in the plastic chair beside the bed.

"I had fluid in my lungs. They drained it out and I can breathe okay, but they don't tell me what they can do to make sure it doesn't happen again. They just look at me like I'm crazy for even asking. What is wrong with them, Jen?" Lolly's eyes began to tear up.

"I don't know. Listen, we've got appointments in North Carolina with those other doctors. Maybe they can help. It's not that far off," Jen said.

Lolly sniffled and pulled herself together. She wore a flowered hospital robe that looked hideous on her. Jen couldn't wait to get her out of this place. Hospitals teemed with infections and death. Lolly would be lucky not to pick up something else while she was in here.

"How's the benefit coming?" Lolly asked.

"Good, I think," Jen said. "I've got Hank and his blue grass buddies signed up. And Paulie said he'd come sell beer and wine. I was at a sandwich shop a while back and they asked about you. So I called them up and they offered to cater the event. And another friend of yours, Rusty, is going to be playing with his band."

Lolly nodded but didn't seem to be listening.

"Jen, I need someone to help take care of me at the house. That scared me when I couldn't breathe. What if you hadn't come?"

"We can get one of those home nurses," Jen said.

"No, I was thinking of hiring Nicole. I talked to her at the work release center. She only works in the morning at that newspaper. She needs to get out of that place before she goes crazy. We'll have to do it through an agency, but we can specifically request that they hire her. I've got the numbers here. Will you do this for me?" Lolly reached for a slip of paper on the roll-away table by her bed.

Jen took the paper.

"I'm coming home tomorrow. If she could start right away, that would be best," Lolly said. "I don't think I'll be going back to work for a while."

"Okay," Jen said.

They were silent for a moment and then Lolly asked, "Say, what happened with that audition you had in South Florida? Did they call you yet?"

"Audition?" Jen asked.

"Yeah, you said you had an audition the other day in Miami or Orlando or something," Lolly said and reached for the big plastic hospital cup on the tray.

"Oh, yeah," Jen answered. She glanced out the window and noticed a tree in the distance, its leaves already brown. She felt as if a stake were lodged in her chest. She had probably gotten herself in too deep with this whole baby thing. She glanced over at Lolly who was watching her thoughfully. She wondered what Lolly had ever done to make her not trust her. If anyone would understand this, it would be her sister.

"I didn't have an audition. I lied," she said. Lolly looked confused. "I went down to try to find Sonya's sister-in-law, and I did. They have Sonya's baby and they're willing to sell him."

"What?" Lolly almost screamed. The hospital cup rolled to the floor with a clatter.

"Yeah, they want thirty grand. I pretended to be some rich bitch in need of a baby. So now I have to come up with the money or else..."

Lolly shook her head.

"You have to call the police," she said.

"But if Ziggy or Tasha get suspicious, they'll disappear. They might even kill that kid, Lolly," Jen said.

"Then get in touch with Sonya's parents. Get the money from them," Lolly said.

"I'm afraid," Jen admitted. Lolly looked at her sympathetically.

"I know you are. I would be, too," she said. "On the other hand, I'm proud of you for trying to do something. Not everyone would get involved."

"Thanks," Jen said, rising from the chair. She didn't want to stay any longer. She was fighting the urge to go have a couple shots of Cuervo. She kissed Lolly on the cheek and left.

When Jen got back to her apartment, she saw she had a message on her cell phone.

"This is the person who's got that merchandise you were looking for. I'm gonna be in your area in about a week. I'll give you a call when I'm in town, and we can see if you're still interested in making that purchase."

Manny jumped into her lap, and she ran a hand over his head and along his soft back. So Ziggy had bitten. Now she had to figure out how to get in contact with Sonya's husband. What if they wouldn't come up with the money? She stared out the window at the darkening sky.

Wednesday October 11

Cancer had given Lolly the opportunity to experience all of the stages of life in about six months. She had middle age spread, aches and pains and memory loss. She sighed. She had been out of the hospital for several days now and was ensconced in her bed at home, wearing a prayer scarf that a friend had brought from Iran. He said the scarf contained his grandmother's tears. She held it to her face. Her eyebrows and eyelashes had begun to grow back and she rubbed the scarf over the tiny crooked hairs.

How odd it was to know you could be looking at the last days of your life. Some days she felt so lousy she didn't care. Other days, well, those days she just tried to enjoy. You only have now, that's what the mystics say. And there was something freeing about not worrying about the future. No need to wake up one day like the woman in that old cartoon and gasp, "Oh, I forgot to get married."

She heard the front door open. Relief at last from the parade of thoughts that staggered through her mind like drunken sailors. She gazed down the hallway which led to the living room and saw Nicole bearing flowers. They were wildflowers.

"There's a vase in here, Nicole," Lolly called to her. "We can throw out these dead daffodils."

"Jen and I stopped and picked these from the side of the road. She said you would love them better than store bought flowers. And we didn't want to take any from the yard," Nicole said. She stood in the doorway to the bedroom holding the spray of yellow flowers and blue bells. Her black hair hung in many small braids with beads at the bottom of each braid. Her makeup was impeccable and her eyes bright. But it was always Nicole's big warm smile that lit up something inside Lolly. That time in prison hadn't seemed to dim her sparkle at all. But maybe that was just wishful thinking. Lolly looked closer.

"How are things?" she asked.

"Oh, I'm nervous," Nicole said. "I want to go home when I get out of work release, but I still haven't talked to my momma. I got a letter from her, but she didn't say anything about my coming down there. I'm scared she won't want me to come back."

"All you can do is try," Lolly said. "Show up at the door and say, here I am."

"Yeah," Nicole said, taking the vase with the dead flowers into the kitchen to empty it and replace the water. She came back in carrying the vase with the new flowers in it. "So what do you need me to do for you today?"

Lolly blinked slowly and said, "Well, I gotta pee really bad and I feel so unsteady today. Will you hand me my crutches and just stay nearby?"

Nicole handed her the crutches. They were painted in green and purple designs.

"You have the most colorful life, Ms. Lolly," Nicole said.

"Please, don't call me 'Ms.' anymore, Nicole. I didn't like doing that at the prison. Makes me feel old. Of course, I am old now. Seventy-five in cancer years," Lolly said. "Sorry. I need to stop wallowing in self pity. I'm going to suck the marrow from the bones of life today, ya hear?"

"I heard that," Nicole said.

Lolly went into the bathroom. After she finished peeing, she wavered in front of the sink. She'd been negotiating through life on crutches for a good part of the past seventeen years, but she had a completely different body now and she had to learn how to balance all over again. Funny what changes. Ovaries gone, but a big hard belly to make up for them. The perennial stork, she said with a laugh. Maybe she'd come back as a bird—a heron, a crane or the ever-popular stork, standing on one leg peering into the shallows for dinner.

The trip to North Carolina was supposed to be next week. What if they did manage to save what was left of her? What if they gave her a few more years of life? Perhaps she should start planning.

Nicole was changing the sheets of her bed when she came back out.

"Thank you, sweetie," she said. How fortunate she was that Nicole had come to work release in Tallahassee. Lolly had plenty of friends who would be happy to come take care of her, but it felt better to pay someone to do it. And Nicole was so pleasant to be around. Nicole had her own problems, which gave them something else to talk about beside Lolly's declining health. "Let's sit on the back porch for a while. I want to hear all about the classes you're taking in January. You did get registered right?"

Lolly hoped like hell she wasn't repeating herself. Was this information that Nicole had already given her? She was turning into her Aunt Jewel, probably the only person left who was a suitable companion since neither of them could remember anything from one day to the next. Lolly found herself forgetting things that were such a standard part of her knowledge base. Like actor's names. Not obscure actors but famous ones. The woman who played Sophie in *Sophie's Choice*. The man who played Hans Solo in *Star Wars*. It was like forgetting where you lived. Once she went to boil some water and forgot to put water in the pan. Damn near burned the house down.

After Nicole made the bed, she cooked up some waffles from the freezer, thawed some frozen strawberries and mixed them with syrup the way Lolly liked. Lolly missed fresh fruit. She wasn't even sure why she wasn't supposed to eat fresh foods anymore. Lolly was hungry, starving in fact. The new drugs gave her the appetite of a giantess. She'd lost ten pounds while taking chemo that summer, but since she'd quit the chemo which was doing nothing but making whatever life she had left not worth living, she had gained back the ten plus another fifteen.

Nicole cleared off Lolly's plate. Lolly felt a pang of guilt being waited on like this.

"Nicole, I hope...," Lolly began. She didn't know how to put this but she tried, "I hope you don't feel like a servant or something. I'm sure you could get a better job, maybe work more hours at the newspaper. You're so much smarter than this."

"You don't want me helping you out?" Nicole asked in a hurt voice.

"Yes, I do. It means a lot to me. I guess I've just watched *Driving Miss Daisy* too many times."

"Driving who?"

Lolly smiled and shook her head. "Never mind. Just know that your friendship means as much to me as anything else you do."

"I know that, girl. You're my mentor. The first and only one I've ever had. It's a privilege for me to be taking care of you now that you need it. And I bet you'd do the same for me."

"I would," Lolly said.

"I'll tell you something else. All those other females at that work release center are working as maids in motels, cleaning up other people's nasty shit. Stranger's shit. At least I know you. And you are not a nasty person. Besides, when you're sleeping I have been reading your books, girlfriend. That Zora Neale Hurston is something else. I want to write like her."

"You write like Nicole Parks. Nobody else," Lolly said.

"Okay. Maybe I could be the Danielle Steel of the ghetto like one of those hip hop writers." Nicole said. "What do you think about that?"

"My only advice is not to let college corrupt you," Lolly said with a laugh.

"I won't. I just need to get some of that grammar under my belt, but my style will still be my own."

A breeze swept over the porch and some leaves rustled. A smattering of acorns dropped on the wood deck. Autumn was finally sneaking in. Lolly closed her eyes and it seemed as if that leaden feeling was lifting momentarily.

"Nicole, I want you to promise me something," Lolly said.

"What, Lolly?"

"Promise me you won't forget the women you left behind." She opened her eyes and stared at Nicole, who had sat down in the plastic lounge chair across from her. "Don't forget them."

"Oh, I won't," Nicole said. "I'll never forget that damn place as long as I live."

"Not just the place, the women," Lolly insisted, leaning forward. "Promise me someday—not in the next year or even in the next ten years—but someday you'll go back there and give something back to them."

Nicole absorbed this thought. It had never occurred to her. She tilted her head and her eyes lingered on Lolly's eyes.

"I promise," she said. "I'll go back someday and I'll do what you did. I'll teach them that they have something to say. I'll be there to listen to them."

Lolly smiled and closed her eyes again. The sun felt so good, so indescribably sweet as it melted over her skin. And the tangy smell of autumn was like an intoxicating perfume. *This beautiful life*, she thought. This beautiful life.

From the Journal of Nicole Parks

I was so happy when Lolly hired me to help take care of her. I mean, I was sad that she needed so much care, but happy that it got to be me, and even happier to get out of that work release center which wasn't really all that much better than prison if you ask me. Except, of course, that you could leave. And boy did I love being outside where there were trees and where you could actually see men. Not that I got to do much interacting with the opposite sex, but sometimes on my way to work in the white van I would see those college boys and my heart would feel thick and full.

I tried to make friends with the women at the work release center, but it wasn't easy. Some of them were here from the county. They hadn't gone to "da big house." My room-mate was a squirrel faced stud who worked at McDonald's and wore a du-rag like a guy. She said she thought it made her like an Arabian sheik.

"And like I got me a harem of beautiful women with long black hair, wearing them *I Dream of Jeannie* outfits," she said. "Shit. I am not going to be working at McDonald's all my life. I don't care what them people at school saying, talking about learning disabilities and shit. Man, I can do more than blow trash off a damn hot tar parking lot."

"Yeah," I told her, "you could be managing McDonald's and then you'd have a harem of young women all wearing their red and gold polo shirts and their black slacks."

"That's right, sister," she answered. "Like my girl Wanda. She looks so appetizing when she slips them French fries into her pretty mouth."

I felt like I was living some kind of schizo life between my roommate at the center, the Muslim dude who ran his newspaper and then Lolly and her flowers and birds. But Lolly said I should write down the stories of everyone I meet so that what's I did.

Taking care of Lolly wasn't that hard in the beginning. She could get around and was even doing some work from her computer at home. My main job the first week was to help plan for the benefit, and that was just fun. I had to call different businesses and see if they'd donate stuff, refreshments and things like that. I was surprised at how generous people were.

Lolly's Aunt Jewel would show up every day and she'd have more suggestions, some of which were pretty odd. She wanted to make tomato sandwiches for refreshments, which didn't sound like a good idea to me, but I didn't say anything. We didn't get any hard liquor for the party but plenty of places donated cases of wine or beer. I wasn't planning on drinking a drop. Those drill sergeants at the work release center would just love me to screw up like that.

Lolly's sister Jen was another matter. I liked her, but I could tell she was up to something and it wasn't just the benefit. She was worried about something. One evening when she came to pick me and take me back to the work release center, she holed up in Lolly's room with her for awhile. When she came back out, she tried to pretend like nothing was going on, but I could tell she had troubles. She was all tight around the mouth, and had bags under her eyes. I'm naturally curious, but I couldn't get much out of her except that she wanted to get in touch with Sonya back at the prison. When I told her that I write to Daffy and I could send a message, she said to ask Sonya to call her or Lolly, but she didn't say why. What that lady could be wanting with a con artist like Gypsy I sure couldn't figure out.

I was also enjoying my work at the little weekly newspaper. I was learning how to edit copy and do layout design. At the center, I always complained about my jobs so the others wouldn't get jealous. Last thing you need in an environment like that is a bunch of jealous females trying to ensnare you.

Friday, October 13

It was amazing, Jen thought as she stood at the doorway collecting money, how they had managed to pull this together in three and a half weeks. By 8 p.m. the hall was packed with people. Sue was taking checks at the door, and Jen knew a lot of people were dropping more than the requested ten dollars. They had lined up three local bands, a juggler, a face painter for kids and one knock-out jazz singer for the night, not to mention all the poets who had to get up and read their tributes to Lolly. One of Jen's former poetry teachers had a table selling books, all proceeds earmarked for Lolly's treatment. She tried to estimate how many people had showed up, and already it looked like more than two hundred were there. *How on earth did Lolly know so many people*, she wondered.

Jen had been glad to have the distraction of planning for the party. It helped her not think about Sonya's baby or how she was going to rescue the child. She had spoken to Ziggy and managed to put him off while she "got the money together." Then she had tried to contact Duke and Dina but hadn't heard back from either one. Maybe Ziggy had changed his mind or found someone else. And if he did call her, she still didn't have the money. Jen and Lolly agreed that she'd have to tell the police as soon as she heard from Ziggy if they didn't have word from Sonya's mother or husband. But thinking about the police made her think about Zack and the fact that she had lost him. That was another thing she wasn't in the mood to think about.

Nicole stepped up to the microphone.

"Excuse me, ladies and gentleman. My name is Nicole Parks, and I have some very special poems that were written for Miss Lolly from the women inmates at North Florida Correctional Institution for women. When I told them about the benefit, they all wanted to take part so they mailed me poems that they'd like me to dedicate to her."

Jen glanced over at Lolly. She looked much better than she had coming out of the hospital a week ago. Her hair was short and curly. Her smile big as ever. *We can beat this*, Jen thought. *Beat this damn cancer and get on with our lives.* Jeremy sat at the table next to Lolly. His wife had come with him but she was busy roving around with a drink in her hand. Jen wouldn't have minded a beer herself, but she figured she should stay sober and make sure everything went smoothly.

The crowd listened appreciatively to Nicole read the poetry. Jen leaned back against a pole and in between poems felt a tap on her shoulder. She turned around expecting it to be one of the musicians wanting to find out the order of appearances. But instead she was confronted with a wide chest.

She looked up into Zack's face.

"Wow," she blurted out in surprise. Every cell in her body had gone on red alert. Just the smell of him so close to her, sweet and musky and soapy made her feel slightly dizzy.

"So you're here," she said stupidly. "How did you hear about this?"

"Are you kidding? You aired it on all the radio stations. Even the cops know about it. A couple of my buddies volunteered to direct traffic."

"I'm speechless," Jen said.

"Well, we're not the enemy," Zack said, sounding offended.

"I didn't say you were. I'm just surprised. That's all. It's very kind."

The poetry reading had ended, and Hank got up on the stage with his mandolin. A banjo player joined him and bluegrass picking filled the air.

"You want to get some fresh air?" Zack asked.

Jen nodded. They wended their way through the crowd and cut through the coffee shop next door. Stepping out on the back deck, Jen realized that the heat had finally broken and there was a cool breeze shuffling over the lake and whispering in the oak leaves. They took the steps down to the ground and found a bench near the lake. An awkward silence hung between them. She wondered why he had come and why they were out there now.

"Sorry I didn't call you. I knew you were out of town and then we had a pretty serious case come up. A robbery of an armored car. We had FBI agents swarming all over the place."

"I think I read about that in the paper," she said.

"We only got three of the guys. The fourth is still at large."

They sat and another silence ensued.

"So, did you look at it?" she asked.

A bright orange moon spilled a thread of gold over the lake.

"Yeah," Zack said. "You were hot." He let an arm settle behind her on the bench.

Jen's head whipped toward him.

"You know what?" she said in a clipped voice. "I need to get back in there." She rose and turned to walk away, but he reached for her wrist and held on.

Standing, he looked into her eyes and said, "I didn't look at it, crazy. Why the hell would I need to?"

"You didn't? Really?" she asked.

"Really."

She stopped and took a breath. The wet smell of mud and soft smell of the autumn breeze melded together.

"Sit down for a minute," he said gently. Jen sat back down. "There's an old Zen story about two monks who are traveling in the countryside."

"Wait," she interrupted. "Are you and Sam the bartender in the same Buddhist cult or something?"

"We take a martial arts class together. But I'm not exactly a

Buddhist. I just know a few stories and this is one of them. You want to hear it or not?"

"Sure," she said.

"Okay. The two monks come to a stream and there's a prostitute there. She's afraid of crossing the stream. It's not all that deep but she doesn't like water. Anyway, the younger monk says, 'Climb on my back and I'll take you over the stream.' So she does and the two monks cross the stream. The one carrying the prostitute on his back sets her down and she goes on her way. The two monks go the other way. They walk and walk. The whole time the older monk is very sulky. He won't even speak to the younger monk. Finally, they stop for the night and the older monk turns to the younger one and says, 'How could you carry that sinful woman across the stream? It's a disgrace!' and the young monk looks at him in surprise and says 'I only carried her across the stream. You've been carrying her ever since.'"

Jen stared at him blankly.

"Don't you get it?" he asked. "You're like the old monk. You've been carrying that little videotape around with you for years like it says something about you. Maybe you think it does say something about you, but, lady, it doesn't mean anything to me. I'm just a guy who's met a woman that he'd like to be with, but for some damn reason she doesn't seem to think that's a good idea."

Jen crossed her legs and absorbed this information. Finally, she said, "I think it's a good idea. It's... it's certainly not a bad idea. Not to me anyway."

Zack didn't say anything for a few moments. She turned to look at him and for a moment they just stared at each other. Words didn't seem to be necessary. At some level something was being decided, independent of anything else. He leaned forward to kiss her, and as he did so, Jen's cell phone began to chirp.

Zack waited while she answered it.

"Have you got the money?" the man asked.

"Uh...Yes," Jen said, looking into Zack's gray eyes.

"Okay. Tomorrow night. Eight o'clock. I'll call you from the hotel."

He hung up. Jen took a deep breath.

"I need your help," she said to Zack.

Saturday, October 14

Zack and Jen sat at Cabo's Tacos under the eight-foot surfboard that, according to the laminated card, the owner had purchased in 1978 and surfed in Puerto Rico.

Jen took a big bite of her burrito supreme.

"Are you nervous?" Zack asked.

"A little," she said.

"You haven't lost your appetite," he said.

"I learned a long time ago that you don't want your stomach growling in the middle of a performance," she said.

Zack tapped his fork on the table and ignored his food.

"Why are you so worried?" Jen asked.

"Why do you think?" he responded. "I don't want anything to happen to you."

"I'm not worried about me. I'm worried about that 15-month old baby," Jen said.

"Me too, Jen, but if anything is weird at all, you get out. We'll worry about the kid."

"Look, you said these people live on 'the con' not on violence."

"That's true, but Ziggy is different from the rest of his family. He's got a record of assaults. And you should see the pictures of Sonya after the supposed rape. She looked like hell."

"You've done a lot of work since last night," she said.

"Yeah, you didn't give me much time on this," he answered.

"Well, I guess you've got a point," Jen admitted. "Anyone who would sell a baby to a total stranger is seriously disconnected from his own humanity. It's not like the guy is starving."

"No, he's doing this to get revenge on his sister. Like being in prison isn't enough."

Jeremy and Lolly suddenly appeared at their table.

"Hey," Lolly said.

Jeremy dropped his keys in front of Jen and said, "She's all spruced up. She may be old but she is a Beamer."

"Thanks," Jen said with a smile. "Sit down with us, okay?"

Lolly sat next to Jen and squeezed her hand. "Please, please be careful."

"Don't worry, Lolly," Zack interjected. "We won't let anything happen to her."

Jen grinned with wry amusement that Mr. Worrywart was suddenly consoling her sister. For some reason, the fear and worry that had chewed away at her ever since she'd first found Ziggy's wife had evaporated.

Jeremy shook hands with Zack as he sat down.

"Congratulations on that armored car bust," Jeremy said.

"Don't tell me you're gonna be defending the scumbags," Zack said.

Jeremy shook his head. "Nope. That's not my type of case. Is the fourth guy still loose?"

"We'll get him," Zack said, leaning back.

"I'm sure you will," Jeremy said. A businesslike waitress with rings hanging from her eyebrows came up and took Jeremy's order for a beer. Lolly said she didn't want anything. The waitress scooped up Jen's empty plate and briskly strode away.

"So what happens next?" Jeremy asked.

"We've got people watching all the hotels on the strip here," Zack said. "As soon as he checks in somewhere, we get a nice couple to take the room next to his. And we wait for him to call Jen."

Jen glanced at Lolly, resting her chin on her fists.

"I'm glad you came," Jen said.

"I've never missed any of your performances," Lolly said. "And this is a big one."

At 8:15, Jen parked Jeremy's BMW and walked to the outside staircase at the end of the parking lot. Carrying a small satchel filled with confiscated drug money, she climbed up the metal stairs, mentally embodying the role. She was a wealthy woman about to receive the baby she was willing to buy. She stopped and whispered, "All right, I'm about to go in."

She stopped at the door at the end of the hallway and knocked. The door opened and there was the infamous Ziggy. David Bowie's song, which had been traipsing through her mind, suddenly went sharply out of tune and disappeared. This Ziggy was about five feet nine inches tall and somewhere around two hundred and fifty pounds. He wore a white button down shirt with a grease stain on the front, brown trousers and Converse sneakers. He needed a shave, and his eyes shifted away from hers.

"Took you long enough," he said. People skills were obviously not one of his strengths.

Jen looked at her watch and replied, "Actually, I'm quite punctual."

She stepped into the room and thought, *well, if I'm going to get killed I may as well get it over with.*

Then she saw him—the child, lying on his stomach asleep on the bed farthest from the window, his little legs bowed out, his small fists closed. She went over to him, drawn as if by some magnet and put her hand on his warm back.

"I can't believe this," she said softly.

"What?" Ziggy asked defensively. "You think there's something wrong with him? He's healthy. Nothing wrong with that kid."

Jen realized she had slipped out of character, something she had never done before. She turned to him with a cold look and said, "I can't believe that I am finally getting my child."

"You gonna keep it for yourself?" Ziggy asked.

"Yes, I am. But don't try to find us."

"Lady, you give me the money and you'll never hear or see me again. I'll be a ghost."

Jen tossed the bag onto the other bed.

"Don't pick him up 'til I count the money," Ziggy said, and greedily opened the bag. Jen stood stock still, looking down at the sleeping baby. Just a few more minutes, she thought, watching his deep even breaths. He grunted and moved his feet. They were bare and she noticed a rash down his thighs. He wore a big diaper that looked wet. And a t-shirt. Didn't he come with anything else? Any clothes? Well, it was still warm outside, it wouldn't matter. She would go get clothes for him right away.

"All right," Ziggy said. "Nice doing business with you. Enjoy your baby. Look, I'm going to leave first. After I've been gone for ten minutes, you can leave, okay?"

"I don't remember any such arrangement," Jen said.

"You want the baby, you do it my way."

He picked up the satchel of cash and started to walk out the door when a cell phone began ringing. Ziggy reached in his pocket and pulled out the phone.

"Yeah?" he said. Then a look of consternation crossed his face, and he glared at Jen. Within seconds he threw down the bag and had grabbed her by the throat. "Tasha says there's cops outside. What the fuck you trying to pull, bitch?"

Jen could smell his breath, hot and sour like moldy bread. She twisted out of his grip and gasped for air. Then she saw the gun. It was black and large, and Ziggy's eyes narrowed as he pointed it at the baby.

"It's not you that we want," she said in a shaky voice.

"Who's we?"

"F.B.I.," she said. Her mind was racing as she began to concoct her story. She had to offer him hope, a way out of prison.

"Look, we're after Duke."

"Duke? How do you know about Duke?"

Jen panted and prayed for words. It was one thing to act, another to write your own script.

"The armored car robbery. He planned it. He's still got the money. We don't want you, I promise. We just wanted to get the baby as a way to lure Duke out in the open."

"How do you know this is Duke's baby?" Ziggy screamed. The baby stirred on the bed, and Jen began to shake. Please don't kill the child, she thought. Then her brain kicked in.

"One of the guys we got snitched him out," she said.

"So why are there cops here?"

"Just for the baby. We don't want to bust you. We only want the baby. You're free to take the money and go. That money is nothing. Your brother-in-law has half a million dollars that doesn't belong to him."

"I'm free to go?" Ziggy asked. Jen held his gaze and nodded.

"As long as you don't hurt the baby," she said. "If the baby gets hurt, then we've got nothing to get Duke with, and you'll wind up growing old in Raiford."

She saw Ziggy registering her words. He would have to know about the armored car hold up; it had been all over the news. It was probably pissing him off no end that he hadn't just ransomed the baby back to Duke.

"You come out with me," Ziggy said. "Leave the baby here."

Jen glanced at the baby.

"Don't worry. He's had some strong cough syrup. That baby ain't gonna wake up for a while."

Jen wanted to kick Ziggy in the nuts, but as long as he held the gun she would do what he wanted. Ziggy opened the door and motioned for her to leave. He walked out behind her, nudging the gun in her back. They were on the second floor. They walked slowly down the walkway.

"You stay in front of me. Anyone fucks with me and you'll have a hole right through your gut, lady."

Jen felt her bowels nervously loosening. In the movies, the heroine would jab the guy with her elbow and grab the gun. She now realized how insane that was.

A bright light suddenly came on and Jen saw Tasha standing in front of a white SUV. In the shadows behind the SUV, there were figures standing. Were they police? Ziggy was going to kill her for sure, she thought. Her breath rippled out of her lungs.

"Give it up, Ziggy," a voice said close behind them.

"Shit," Ziggy said. He stood still for a moment, and Jen thought he was weighing his options.

"Now, motherfucker," the voice yelled. She knew it was Zack's voice but could never have imagined the ferocity in it.

Jen felt Ziggy's gun drop from her back. She turned quickly and saw Zack behind Ziggy. He took the gun from Ziggy as two uniformed cops came up the stairs.

"I thought it was Duke you wanted," Ziggy said. "She said you wanted Duke not me."

Zack shook his head.

"Guess you were the sucker, huh?"

Ziggy turned in rage toward Jen, but the uniforms were already there and in minutes he was handcuffed and listening to one of them recite his rights. Jen pushed past Ziggy and Zack and ran back to the motel room.

She picked up the baby and held him in her arms. He stirred and then woke up and looked around. She expected him to cry, but he didn't. He just gazed into her face in surprise. He had dark hair and round eyes, and he was beautiful.

"Hi," she said, softly. He looked down shyly but did not try to wriggle out of her arms.

Zack entered the room.

"Social services will be here in a minute for the baby."

Jen felt the weight of the child in her arms, his warm little body as his legs kicked.

"He needs some clean diapers, Zack. And some clothes."

Zack came closer to her and put a hand on the baby's head.

"They'll have all that stuff, sweetheart. Don't worry about him."

Zack slipped an arm around her shoulder, and she swallowed hard.

Sunday, October 15

Jen lay fully dressed in her bed with Zack's arms wrapped around her. It was 3:09 according to the digital numbers on her alarm clock. Zack was snoring softly. His arms felt warm and protective, but she couldn't sleep. She could only think about that child and wonder what would happen to him now.

She must have slept eventually because in the morning Zack woke her with a kiss. The kiss became longer. His body felt solid and strong, his hands gentle as they held her head. She had never made love to him before but that morning it felt as if she'd never made love to anyone else. To feel his skin against hers. To have him close. To swallow him. She felt something waking up inside. Had she ever felt this way before? Had she ever wanted anything so badly? And then they were naked and she was no longer thinking about Sonya's baby or anything else. All thought was gone. The only thing left was the two of them, their bodies and something she didn't yet have a name for.

A few hours later, Jen sat down at the little breakfast table beside the front window overlooking Franklin Street. A median ran down the middle of the street with purple crepe myrtles and dogwoods. Zack wandered in, scratching his belly. She was reading the *Democrat* and drinking her coffee. She smiled up at him. It occurred to her that this is what she'd been seeking for a long time. This incredible level of complete comfort. He sat down across from her.

She took a sip of coffee and asked him, "What's going to happen to the baby?"

Zack frowned and got up without answering. This was a bad sign, she thought. He went into the kitchen and came back out carrying a mug of coffee and a banana.

"It's complicated," he said without sitting down. "He could get stuck in the foster system for years. And then if Sonya gets out and they decide she isn't a fit mother, he may be stuck there."

"What about his father? Why can't his father keep him? Or the grandmother?"

"There's warrants out on all those people," Zack said.

"Zack, kids in the foster care system—especially here in Florida— they fall through the cracks all the time. You know that. You've seen what happens."

Zack agreed. It gave him a sick feeling to think about some of the things he had witnessed. He sat down and stared out the window.

"I mean there's no stability," Jen continued. "No one loves them. Even a family of criminals is better than no family."

"Some foster homes are okay."

"I know that, but I can't stand the thought of it," she said. Zack took a bite of his banana and gazed at her thoughtfully.

"Well, what can you do?" he asked. "You can't save the whole world."

She'd certainly tried to convince Lolly of that. But this wasn't the whole world. This was one little boy. And con artists or not, his father and his grandmother loved him and would take care of him. They weren't the ones who tried to sell him.

Monday, October 16

Jen and Lolly got up at 5:30 and drove to the airport. Lolly wore a surgical mask to keep her from catching germs. She had decorated the mask to look like a tiger's face, and when people saw it they smiled. On the jet to Raleigh, she slept most of the way.

When they arrived, they rented a car and followed the directions to the hospital. Jen kept glancing away from the highway to the pink-clouded sky and the red and gold leaves on the trees. As they passed a lake, a billowy silver cloud hung above the black water, and the rising sun probed the mist with shards of pink light.

Once they found the medical center, they parked on level three of the garage and descended in the elevator. Inside, the place looked like some kind of museum with glass and chrome and huge slabs of decorative granite making up the floor.

They waited in one small room after another. Lolly had lingering bronchitis from her recent stint in the hospital when they operated on her lung lining. A picture of blue trees hung in the small exam room, and Lolly looked at it intrigued.

"I love the colors in this," she said. "They're so tranquil."

When the doctor came in, he shook their hands and smiled. His lower jaw protruded somewhat, his eyes were serious. He looked more like a hockey player than a renowned specialist. He talked to Lolly, and Jen took notes as Lolly asked her to do. Lolly also talked. She had plenty to say.

"They fucked me up in the hospital," she said. Jen decided not to write that down.

"The doctors think I'm going to die," Lolly says, her usual smile replaced by tight angry lips. "They don't care about me. I have cancer in my other breast but they don't want to remove it and cancer in the scar from my mastectomy."

"I understand you had some cancer in the lining of your lung," the doctor said.

"Yes, I was in the hospital a couple of weeks ago. They cut me open and put talc in the lining of my lungs. Then they gave me a damn infection, and I had a fever. They tell me they don't know what to do anymore. That is, when I can get through to them," Lolly said. "Only four oncologists in the whole region. They wanted to wait six months before even seeing me about the first lump. I'd be dead by now."

Jen realized she hadn't been listening to Lolly before now. Not really. Hadn't heard the rage simmering in her voice.

The doctor nodded his head as Lolly gave him her history. He had looked at her records. He agreed that her cancer may have been caused by the radiation she received when she was 14. The two of them traded terms that Jen couldn't even spell.

"I've got an idea for you. We'll add Femara to the hormone therapy and give you some new chemo. One gives you constipation and the other gives you diarrhea. They balance each other out nicely," he said with a grin. He had downward slanting eyes, and he reminded Jen of a sad-faced clown entertaining children with his misfortunes.

"If the chemo slows the cancer down, then I recommend a stem-cell transplant. Only 25 people have done this, but so far no one has died," he said.

Jen heard good news. She heard a distant song of hope. But that didn't seem to be what Lolly heard.

"That's not very many people—25," she said. Her hand continued to manipulate her ear lobe nervously. "Are you going to put me through hell and then I die anyway?"

"Whenever you don't want to continue, let us know," he said. "Everyone has to make that decision for themselves. When you're through fighting, then you call up hospice. It's their job to make it as painless as possible."

Jen realized what he was saying in his matter-of-fact voice, and she felt her breath jerk. She wanted to snatch Lolly's hand away from her ear, wanted to squeeze that bony wrist in an iron grip and scream, *don't you dare call them up.*

The doctor lead them down the hall to a room where pictures of the insides of Lolly's body hung over a lighted board. The three of them examined the black and white and gray pictures. After hours of talking to first one person and then another, looking at scans and getting chest x-rays and giving blood and stool samples, Lolly said she was starving. They purchased some Indian food from a cart in the hospital's chilly lobby. The food was warm and they hadn't eaten in a long time and they both started to feel better as they ate.

Lolly chewed a piece of doughy nan.

"You know what? I've learned to let people love me, to quit trying to control everything. I've learned that I'm brave as hell. People always told me that before but now I know it. I'm brave as hell."

"Yes, that's right. You are," Jen said. She remembered an earlier visit to a different doctor when Lolly was getting chemo, and how Lolly brought popsicles for all the other patients. She thought about the way the nurses smiled when they saw Lolly, and how she asked about their families.

"Let us eat cheesecake!" Lolly said with a grin.

Next, they had to go see another doctor about some fluid in Lolly's left lung before they could go home. They would have to drive to another building, taking Lolly's leather artist portfolio now full of scans and chest x-rays. Jen got in the car and picked up Lolly from the front of the hospital.

Jen drove four or five blocks away to another granite building, dropped off Lolly and parked in another parking garage. The walk to the lung clinic took her down long endless hallways. *Kafka must have been the architect*, she thought. She hoped she wouldn't stumble across Lolly passed out against a wall somewhere. She finally found her sister standing at a counter in the pulmonary clinic. Lolly's eyes were glazed with fatigue.

"Go sit down," Jen said. "I'll check you in."

This doctor was handsome with a square face, a golden beard and eyes so deep set they almost looked Neanderthal. Like the first doctor, he projected a certain sincerity and compassion commingled with detachment. He asked Lolly a series of questions about her recent operation. Jen tried to take notes but she couldn't keep up. The doctor took his stethoscope and listened to Lolly's breathing. His hands roved around her rib cage, checking for points of pain. He stopped and looked clinically at the scars from her operation. He checked the pulse in her leg and then tried to check it in her other leg. A brief barely perceptible confusion crossed his golden features.

"That's my prosthesis," Lolly said.

"The fluid in your lung is to be expected," he explained. "This procedure is never completely successful, but partial success is not bad. It should keep the lung from filling up again."

"Why can't they remove the cancer from my lung lining?" Lolly wanted to know. "Why can't they help me?"

The doctor explicated further, but he wasn't really answering her question which is, "Why is this happening to me—again?"

Jen saw the look in the doctor's fathom-deep eyes. He had no answers.

"We gotta go," she said to Lolly. While Jen stopped in the bathroom, Lolly went to find a wheelchair.

"They said it'll be twenty minutes before someone can bring us a wheelchair," Lolly said when Jen entered the clinic lobby. An authoritative blond woman stood by. "There's one over there, but they say we'd have to bring it back."

"I'll bring it back," Jen said firmly and didn't leave the blond woman any time to dispute the matter. Lolly got in the chair and Jen pushed her out of the clinic and down the hall, turning a corner, down another hall, wheeling down the long hallways.

Jen laughed.

"The hell with them," she said.

Jen pushed the wheelchair past the elevators and around the rotunda and then over the long glass-enclosed walkway that looked down on the street below. With her foot, she pressed the automatic door opener and wheeled Lolly out into the parking lot, past a row of cars to the aisle on the other side and planted her at the door of the car. Then she took the wheelchair back inside and tried to assuage her guilt by pushing it as far back as the elevators, but she couldn't face those hallways. It was time to go home.

Tuesday, November 7

Lolly's stomach bulged like a pregnant woman's. It was full of fluid. Tomorrow the doctors would drain it again. Keeping her comfortable. She'd been on the new chemo treatment for three weeks now, and the doctor was right, it wasn't as debilitating as the last round. Give it six weeks, he'd said, hopefully. If it helped, then she would go back to North Carolina for stem cell treatments. Jen had offered to be her donor.

"What are you doing to your leg?" Aunt Jewel asked in astonishment as she walked in the door. Lolly was at the table with the leg on the table and she was administering bright red feathers to the toes. Nicole came in from the kitchen where she'd been cleaning out Lolly's paint brushes.

"She's making a work of art, can't you tell?" Nicole said.

"Well, I never," Aunt Jewel said.

"Don't worry. It's one of my old legs," Lolly said. "They're going to display it at the health care wall next month."

"Oh yeah. I heard about that," Aunt Jewel said. "Good for you. Glad to see you got your old spirit back. What it's called?"

Lolly smiled at her and said, "Hope is the thing with feathers."

"Did you vote, young lady?" Aunt Jewel asked Nicole.

"No, ma'am," Nicole said.

Just then Jen opened the door.

"Hey, I'm here to take Nicole home."

"Why didn't you vote?" Aunt Jewel was now zeroing in on Nicole.

"I don't have my civil rights back yet," Nicole said. "Or else I would surely have voted. My parents raised me to vote. Though I'm not sure it does any good."

"Don't say that, young lady. Don't say that," Aunt Jewel said.

Jen was fully in the room by now. She had come over to the table and was looking at the leg, which Lolly had painted and covered with glitter, slogans and feathers.

"It's beautiful," Jen said.

She and Lolly exchanged a glance. Lolly had always been the one to admire Jen. How strange it felt to suddenly have Jen's admiration after all these years.

Nicole left with Jen around seven o'clock. Lolly set up camp in the recliner in front of the television, and Aunt Jewel plopped down on the couch and stuck her feet up on the ottoman. She had a pitcher of weak screwdrivers by her side and a bag of corn chips.

"The only night I let myself get drunk," Aunt Jewel commented. "You don't mind if I sleep here on the couch?"

"Of course not," Lolly said. "It's good to have you here." She had never told anyone how she dreaded being alone at night, feared dying all by herself.

Election night wore on with various pundits and anchors making their prognostications. Aunt Jewel had a grim look on her face. Finally she turned to Lolly and said, "Tell me you didn't vote for Nader. On your mother's grave, please tell me."

"I did not vote for Nader," Lolly said, truthfully. What she didn't mention is that as she stood in the voting booth, she had blacked out momentarily. She hadn't fallen or fainted but she'd gotten so light-headed, she wasn't quite sure what happened. Everything went black for several seconds and then she stumbled out of the booth. A man caught her and helped her stay upright. She staggered back outside where a friend was waiting to drive her back home. It was one thing to have your body betray you the way hers had, but now she was worried about what was happening inside her head. And yet what was the point of telling anyone? They couldn't do anything. She had to let the chemo have time and hope.

"I sure hope Al wins," Aunt Jewel said. Then she looked over at Lolly with her watery blue eyes. Lines creased Jewel's face and she had a light downy mustache. *We're growing old together,* Lolly thought.

"You know you were born in the midst of the greatest period of social activism this country has seen since the Civil War."

"Yes, I know. I remember the stories of Mom being pregnant with me and the two of you going to an anti-war rally where the police came and used billy clubs and tear gas against you all." She'd heard the stories of her mother's friends surrounding her mother after a police man kicked her, and the way they surged in anger, pushing the police back, pelting them with mud and stones.

"It was a miracle we got her to the hospital like we did. She had blood flowing from her head and I was so scared she had gotten injured in the belly, that you had gotten injured, but after they got her cleaned up, she grabbed my hand and said, the baby kicked! The baby kicked. And we knew you were one of us right then."

Lolly nodded.

Lolly faded in and out as the election returns came in and went first one way and then the other. But by the end of the night, it seemed that Aunt Jewel and her beloved Al Gore had their victory. Lolly rose from the recliner stiffly. The whole political enterprise seemed fraught with unnecessary conflict. What was wrong with the human race, she wondered. People always needed to deny that they were just like everyone else.

"I'm going to bed," she said, draping the afghan over her shoulders and heading into the bedroom.

"Good night, dear," Aunt Jewel said and turned off the television.

As Lolly stood in her bedroom, she felt the dizzy sensation return. Something inside her head had gone haywire. She couldn't see out of one of her eyes. She dropped to her bed. Something was wrong.

Something was terribly wrong.

Thursday, November 9

Jen walked inside the small café beside Lake Ella and ordered a cappuccino. The man behind the coffee bar was someone she had known by sight for years and yet still didn't know his name.

"Thanks," she said when he handed her the big porcelain mug.

"Pretty crazy, isn't it? Not to know who the president is," the guy said. "I never heard of an election night like that."

"Yeah, and this town is turning into a zoo," Jen answered.

She took her cup of coffee outside to the deck and sat under the shade of leafy limbs of an oak tree. The smell of autumn skipped across the lake and swirled around her.

The lake was a serene silver-blue mirror. A fat white duck trailed by a line of little yellow ducks skirted along the edge of the lake.

Jen pondered her situation. She had known as soon as she stepped out of the theater building that the man and woman waiting beside the Blazer were Duke and Dina—Sonya's husband and mother. She recognized them from the photos, but she might have known them anyway. Dina looked like an older and more elegant version of her imprisoned daughter. They both looked worried as they frowned and darted their eyes about. Duke was taller than she expected, and Dina a little wider. He wore a Seminole T-shirt, trying to blend in, she assumed. Dina was dressed in a stylish pink silk dress and high heels that made her stick out in the college town where the uniform of the day usually entailed Birkenstocks and thrift-store jeans.

Jen had led them to a little concrete table beside the building. They sat down each on a little curved stone bench. Duke cleared his throat, but Dina jumped in.

"We want to thank you for getting Tomas away from my son. That son of a bitch is crazy," Dina said, apparently unaware of the implications of the name she had called her son.

"You don't have to worry. Ziggy will never get his hands on my boy again," Duke said. "That's taken care of."

Jen didn't want to hear any details. She wondered what to say to these two career criminals. Then she saw tears falling along Duke's almost handsome face.

"What is it?" she asked.

"I want my boy back, Miss. Don't you see? He's mine. He's my kid. I didn't know Ziggy was going to try to sell him. I would have killed him with my bare hands if I had known what he was doing," Duke said, leaning across the table. Jen backed away from him, gazing at those hands. But she reminded herself this was a father talking, not a violent criminal. As far as she had been able to learn Duke had never been violent or involved with violence.

"Look, you're a nice lady. I can see that," Dina said. "We're asking for your help in getting Duke's son back. If you can just tell us where they're keeping him..."

Jen stared at the two of them.

"And if you get him back, what then?" she asked. "Then suppose the two of you get busted, ripping people off, and you go to prison as well. Who is going to raise him then?"

Duke glanced at Dina and then looked at Jen. His mouth was crumpled with grief.

"I know you're gonna have a hard time believing this, but I'm off the con. I've made enough money I can go legit. I got a body shop business in Toronto. Dina here is gonna work in the office. We don't need this anymore. We don't need to lose the only family we got left."

"So, why don't you go to the state of Florida and tell them this?

Tell them you've got a legitimate business and you just want to raise your son," Jen asked.

"Are you kidding? The State of Florida has pinned every unsolved burglary in their files on us," Dina scoffed. "We go to Canada. They're not coming after us. We're not murderers, after all."

"And what about Sonya?" Jen asked. "What will she do when she gets out?"

"She'll find us," Duke said. "You know she doesn't want her baby raised by the state. I'm Tomas's father. Dina is his grandmother. No matter what else you think about us, we love that kid with all our hearts." Duke's voice cracked and he bit his lips. Dina let the tears run freely down her face.

"I don't know how I can help you," Jen said, abashed by all these tears. "I don't know what's happened to him."

"You can find out," Dina said, sharply, reaching out and clutching Jen's hands. "That's all we're asking."

Jen slowly pulled her hand away from Dina's grip.

"I don't know. Let me think about this. How can I reach you?" Again she saw the two of them look at each other. They didn't know whether or not to trust her. *Well, too bad*, she thought. They'd have to. She might just throw their information away. She might call the cops on them. She wasn't exactly sure what she would do, but they had to trust her.

Duke handed her a card with a mobile phone number on it.

"Call me, please. Please," he said. Then he stood up and with his hand on his mother-in-law's back, he gently steered her to a dark blue pickup truck. Dina looked back at her with a last begging glance.

Jen had gone home and tried to sleep on it. Now, here she was at the Black Dog Café, overlooking the lake and wondering, what in the hell to do. Lolly's friend at Social Services had said that Tomas was unadoptable. He would be transferred from one foster home to another until Sonya got out of prison and even then she might not be able to convince a judge to release the boy to her. Jen had even checked into being a foster parent herself, but was single, had no steady income and if they ever did a background check, forget it.

She took a sip of her cappuccino and stared at the water. She wished some magical sign would appear – a *deus ex machina* like they had in the old operas, Athena or some other goddess stepping out of that fountain that sprayed in the middle of the lake and created miniature rainbows in the tiny droplets. The goddess might whisper instructions to her, tell her what to do. But there was nothing. No voice whispering through the leaves of the trees, no shroud of Turin in the clouds. There were only the people making their daily rounds of the lake, a few mothers with young children, an old woman being wheeled in a wheelchair, a few puffs of cloud above and the mottled face of the moon in the sky—a daylight moon. She gazed up at it. She didn't know much about the phases of the moon. This one was nearly full but why sometimes the moon was out and visible in the middle of the day she never quite understood.

She thought about the look on Duke's face—the eyes so dark and sad, the way his jaw muscle worked anxiously under his stubble-skin. He looked as if he were being eaten from the inside. How it had surprised her—this concern of a father for his child. And for a moment that old flame of bitterness lit inside her.

The last time Jen saw her father she was eleven years old, and he had come through town with a black-haired woman who smiled hard at her and Lolly from the front seat of a yellow Cadillac. Her dad was blustery and full of lies.

"Hey, girls, come see your old man," he said, standing on the sidewalk in front of the house. Lolly had been timid, but Jen had run into his arms and engulfed herself in the thick boozy aroma of him. He wanted to take them out to the finest seafood restaurant on the coast, he said, which meant Angelo's, of course. As her father drove down highway 98 to the little seaside towns, sipping on a cold beer, Jen hung over the seat while he told of meeting John Wayne in his younger days and consulting with him on a war movie. He recounted his exploits in Vietnam—all bullshit, Jen later learned—and then began to talk about his latest business deal.

"Do you know what a merger is, girls?"

Neither of them did, but it gave him ample reason to pinch his girlfriend, Dorrie, and for her to slap his arm playfully and turn to the girls with a bestial grin. She had little flecks of lipstick on her teeth and saliva on her lips.

Jen took a sip of coffee and wished she weren't remembering this, but the whole scene replayed in her mind and there seemed to be no stop button for it.

On the way back from Angelo's, Lolly who was sitting in the backseat, got carsick and threw up her fried shrimp all over the white seat. Dorrie started screaming at their dad to pull over, which he did and then Dorrie jumped out of the car and continued to scream as if someone had let loose a poisonous snake in the car. Jen found the whole thing so funny, she peed in her pants which didn't help the condition or the smell of the car.

After their dad had cleaned up what he could of the mess and coaxed Dorrie back into the car, which belonged to her and not him, he turned to the two girls and said, "I'll call your mother to come get you." Then he handed Jen an envelope, and he and Dorrie got in the car and sped away. Jen looked in the envelope. Inside was a check written out to her mother for fifteen thousand dollars. Lolly cried for the good part of an hour before their mother's old car came trundling down the road.

Years later their mother confessed the check had bounced. They'd never gotten a dime from him.

Once, a few years ago, she had tried to track him down. An aunt claimed he was living in a retirement community in North Carolina, but when she finally found the place, they said his lease had not been renewed. They didn't say why. Just that he was gone and there was no forwarding address. Jen figured he was homeless somewhere. Or dead.

A breeze came and shook the hard brown leaves out of the oak tree and onto the deck. An acorn tumbled onto her table. And her decision came that easily. She quickly got up and, leaving her mug on the table, took the steps down to the Blazer. She'd need Lolly's help on this; she only hoped her sister was having a good day.

"How are you doing?" Jen asked, looking closely at Lolly, who was watering the potted plants on the porch.

"Oh, I had a scare the other night. My brain blinked out, but it seems to be working again," Lolly said with a shrug.

"That doesn't sound good," Jen said.

"Let's not worry about it now. Come on into my office and we'll find that info you need."

Jen followed Lolly into the bedroom at the front of the house that was now Lolly's office. This had once been Jen's bedroom when they had lived in the house as children. Now the walls were painted sage-green; sundry African masks hung over the bookcases, spilling over with old books that Lolly had collected from garage sales and antique stores.

"Honey, don't you know they gave me full access from my home computer so I can keep on working," Lolly said. "They wanted me to keep working after I die, but I refused. Okay, so let's see the report you got from Zack and see where we can go from here."

Jen sat beside her sister and watched her plug in various pass codes and begin searching through databanks. Lolly sat in an old rolling wooden chair at a desk that looked like it belonged to an elementary school teacher from the 1940s. But her computer was fast, and Lolly was a pro at getting the information Jen asked for. At one point, she had to call one of her friends to get into the right database, but pretty soon she had the address and the name of Tomas's foster parents.

"They live in Scenic Heights," Lolly said, reading the monitor. "A Presbyterian family. Got four foster kids right now. Little ones, too. Must be gluttons for punishment. Didn't you used to have a friend in high school who lived in that neighborhood?"

"Yes," Jen said and picked up a small pink satin thing that looked like a miniature pillow. "What is this?"

"It's a breast. Aunt Jewel made it for me," Lolly said with a wide grin. Jen burst out laughing. "Isn't that the sweetest thing?"

"That's so like Aunt Jewel," Jen said.

Lolly took it from her and held it in her palm.

"So what are you going to do?"

"Remember that scene where Dustin Hoffman transforms himself into Tootsie?"

"Yeah," Lolly nodded.

"Well, I'm going to do a Tootsie. I'll be back later."

"Wait a minute, sister. You're gonna need some paperwork. Hang on and I'll print you out some forms and a nice letter. Got my State of Florida letterhead right here."

"Are we doing the right thing?" Jen asked and glanced through the blinds at the flowerless azalea bushes outside.

"What do you think?" Lolly responded, as she gazed at her computer monitor.

"Yeah," Jen said. "Absolutely."

Lolly turned and winked at her.

Friday November 10

Sonya was in a light restless sleep when she felt a hand on her back and someone gently rousing her. Her eyes popped open. In the half-light that they left on in case of emergencies, she saw Panther's wide eyes and her big smile.

"Shhh," Panther whispered.

Sonya pushed the hair out of her face.

"What is it?"

"I want a kiss," Panther said in a soft voice.

Sonya buried her face in her pillow, then looked up and whispered, "You are such a fool." And yet she was glad, so glad finally for this chance at a kiss, the first real kiss of her life, the first kiss she ever truly desired. Panther's lips touched hers softly and then she ran her soft wet tongue over Sonya's lips and into her mouth.

Sonya kissed her back hungrily. She reached for her and Panther leaned in.

"I can't think of nothing but you," Panther said in her ear. "I just had to come over and wake you. Are you mad?"

Sonya shook her head, falling back in the bed, looking up at Panther, as if the sight of her was gold.

"I got to go before I get caught and sent to the box. Good night," Panther whispered again.

"Good night," Sonya whispered and placed her fingertips over Panther's mouth. Then she was gone. Sonya closed her eyes. She knew what Panther had risked, being out of bed, sneaking into Sonya's aisle. How would they endure it? She had never been in love before, had no idea that it could be like this, like there was nothing left of her, not one cell of her body that did not belong to Panther.

And then there was the guilt. How could she, a mother, have forgotten about her son? She tried to imagine him, but it was difficult. He was fading from her memory. All that was left was a giant ache. At least, he wasn't with Ziggy anymore. She had talked to Duke the day before, and he swore they would get Tomas back somehow.

She sat up in the bed and looked around. Everyone was sleeping. She looked across the dorm at Alice's bunk, remembering what Alice had said about feeling connected to her ancestors. What do you do when your ancestors are all crooks? Someone was talking in her sleep. The C.O. came in and Sonya lay back down as she made her rounds. Then all was quiet. Sonya said a prayer for her son and fell asleep.

The next morning, Sonya sat on the toilet. Her period had started, and the flow of blood was thick and fast. *Why be born a woman*, she wondered, doubled over with cramps. Finally, the pain eased somewhat. Standing she looked at the bright red stain in the toilet. Then she flushed it away. As she came out of the stall, she bumped into a large body and stepped back.

"Hey, thief. Don't you ever wonder what happened to that butcher knife?" Magna asked, leaning against the doorway, her arms across her thick chest.

"Don't threaten me, you gorilla," Sonya said.

Magna laughed, but Sonya could tell the insult stung her. Sonya pushed past her. She noticed Riley, such a pretty but such a cold woman, washing her face at one of the sinks. As Sonya washed her hands, their eyes met in the mirror. Riley's were blue and cold as stones. Sonya shivered. She hurried out of the bathroom and went into the dorm to get ready for work.

Saturday, November 11

Jen went to the theater building on campus. Her key opened the door to the dressing rooms and she went to the back of the room where the makeup class was held. There was everything she needed, except the brown contact lenses, but she had a pair of those at home. She sat down, placed a black wig over her auburn hair. Now, a little makeup putty for a longer nose. Oh, cheek implants. Boy that made a difference. Not just the face though. She started searching through the wardrobe racks and found a padded bra and hip pads. Ha, a pair of polyester slacks. Now into the prop rooms. She rifled through the glasses. The pair she found was unobtrusive. You didn't want to look like you were trying to be *incognito*.

She opened the briefcase and pulled out the fake documents that Lolly had helped her concoct with State of Florida letterhead. She had never known that Lolly could be so devious, but Lolly was all for helping Sonya's husband get the baby. Somehow they both knew it was the right thing to do. With Lolly helping her, Jen felt somewhat less like a criminal herself. This was certainly not a task that she'd turn to Zack for help. She sighed as she thought about Zack. It was difficult not to compare this relationship to the one she'd had with Daniel and before that with Lyle. How could she have stood those men, she wondered. Zack was like solder welding her back together. And, Lord, just thinking about sex with him left her weak-kneed. She shook the thoughts from her head and realized she needed to get focused.

Scenic Heights was a sweet neighborhood of ranch houses built in the 1960s and 70s. Some were L-shaped. Some were just rectangular boxes. The house where the McCall family lived was of the L-shape variety. It had a small concrete porch on the front of the house and a carport under which a dented mini-van was parked. Jen rang the doorbell. A woman with frosted hair opened the door and tilted her head questioningly at Jen.

"Mrs. McCall? I'm Katherine Hepburn with social services," Jen said, having not thought of a last name until it came spilling out of her mouth. *Stupid move*, she thought, but the woman didn't seem to notice.

"Oh, I didn't expect you till next week," Mary McCall said. "Come in. Excuse the mess. Have you come for Tomas?"

Jen's breath caught. This could be good luck, and bad as well.

"Yes, I have. We had to change the schedule."

The place didn't look too bad, Jen thought. Toys were scattered everywhere, and a Big Wheel was turned upside down on the living room floor, but the place wasn't dirty. A television played Teletubbies and an infant swung in an automatic swing and watched. A child of around three was sitting in a high chair at the table methodically smashing Cheerios into a fine sandy powder, and there in a playpen in the corner Tomas sat on his rump, stacking colored rings on a yellow plastic cone.

"Here's the release letter. Would you sign it please?" Jen said, pulling the documents from her briefcase.

The woman took the letter from Jen and read it, and then glanced at the transfer documents. She didn't seem to be suspicious. From what Jen had surmised, the whole foster system had enough holes in it to drive a tank through.

"Tomas is a sweet boy. Doesn't make a peep."

"If you'll just sign here that you are releasing the child to me, then I can take him right now."

"I'm glad to. I love babies but three little ones is too much, and we're taking care of a seven year old, too, but she's at school."

"A lot of children need homes, don't they?" Jen said.

"Yep, they do," the woman replied. "Well, let me get Tommy's diaper bag for you. He doesn't have much else. We got him a few little things, but they'll fit in the bag."

The woman walked out of the room. The infant began fussing, but Tomas merely looked for another toy to play with. Jen squatted down so she could be eye to eye with him. Of course, he wouldn't remember her. She'd only had him for maybe a half an hour. He seemed shy and avoided her gaze.

"Here ya go," the woman said, handing Jen the diaper bag. Then she reached down and scooped Tomas up and handed him also to Jen. Tomas tried to wriggle back out of her arms to the toys below, his arms anxiously waving. Jen clutched onto him, the diaper bag dangling from her shoulder. It was rather like trying to hold onto a very large, slippery fish. She pulled him up to her shoulder and quickly headed to the door.

"I'll bring your briefcase," the woman said, following behind her. They got to the rental car that Jen had picked up an hour earlier and the woman looked inside.

"Where's the car seat?"

Jen caught her breath. A car seat. She hadn't thought of a car seat. Shit. What was she going to say?

"You are supposed to have it," Jen said. "How did you get him here?"

"They didn't give me a carseat. I bought his at a garage sale."

Jen sighed impatiently. "It would be nice if the legislature would give us a little more money. How about I bring it back to you tomorrow?" Jen gazed steadily into the woman's eyes and saw how tired the woman was. She wasn't going to put up a fight.

"Well, okay. Are you new to this job?" the woman asked, setting the briefcase in the back of the car.

"Yes, I am," Jen admitted.

The woman turned and went to her mini-van where she pulled out a contraption that looked like an ejection seat from a fighter jet. "Here, I'll take Tommy."

Jenny handed Tomas to the woman and looked skeptically at the car seat. What the hell was she supposed to do with it? She placed it on the front passenger seat and tried to figure out how to strap it in while the woman bounced Tomas on her hip and said, "Bye, Tommy. Bye, bye. Be a good boy."

Finally Mrs. McCall seemed to realize that Jen had no idea what she was doing.

"Here, I better put that in for you," she said. "The turnover rate among you people is so high. No wonder so many of these children fall through the cracks. It's a crying shame," the woman said, effortlessly snapping the carseat into the back seat and facing it toward the rear of the car.

"Thank you," Jen said.

A baby inside the house began to wail and the woman turned with a wave and dashed inside. Before shutting the car door, Jen leaned over to Tomas and said, "Do you want to see Daddy?"

For the first time, the child's eyes connected with her, and then he began to look around frantically.

"Dada?" his small voice asked. "Dada? Dada! Dada!"

"I guess that answers that," Jen said. She shut the door, got in the front and pulled away from the house as quickly as she could without seeming to hurry.

She turned on the radio to the oldies station. That seemed the most appropriate music for a baby. "Buttercup" was playing. Jen sang along with her own squeaky voice, and all the while Tomas babbled in the car seat.

Monday, November 20

Lolly walked out of the examination room, through the halls and into the waiting room where Nicole was sitting, reading a magazine. It was late in the day, and all the other patients had gone. The receptionist at the front desk was on the phone with her boyfriend.

"What did they say?" Nicole asked, rising. "Is the new chemo working?"

Lolly thought about telling the truth, but she didn't want to have to deal with Nicole's grief right now.

"Honey," she said. "They couldn't tell me all that much. Some funny looking stuff on my brain scan, but that could be anything. They're gonna check again next week."

The whole thing was all so complicated to other people that she didn't have to worry about sounding too obtuse. Nicole reached into her bag and handed Lolly a card.

"What is this?"

"It's the 23rd Psalm," Nicole said. "Violet gave it to me when I left you-know-where. I thought you should have it."

"Thank you," Lolly said and hugged her. They walked out of the office into the brisk evening. There was a chill in the air and Lolly shivered.

A car rode by with football flags flying.

"I'll take you home," Lolly said as they got into her car. "But you be sure to tell those people you have to come take care of me on

Thanksgiving. Tell them cancer doesn't take a holiday if they give you any flack."

"I will. What I won't tell them is how you hardly need any care these days," Nicole said with a grin as she got in the passenger side of the car. "I cannot tell you how happy I am they let you hire me. I would hate to be stuck in that place on a football weekend. I thought they were into football in Miami, but this whole town shuts down. Ain't nothing like this. I guess I shouldn't say ain't."

"Honey, don't ever lose your roots or your language. It's what makes you an interesting writer. Now, I can guarantee you that those professors are gonna try to squeeze your beefsteak writing into a McDonald's hamburger patty, but don't you let them. You may have to go bilingual for a bit, but when you do *your* writing, you go back to your original tongue. It's poetry, honey, remember that."

"I hear ya, girl," Nicole said.

Lolly laughed. She felt easy around Nicole, and it seemed that Nicole felt easy around her, too. That was good because most of the time Lolly was too tired to be putting on an act for someone.

Lolly drove along the canopied roads to the work release center. Autumn had blossomed in Tallahassee. The oak trees stayed full of leaves and Spanish moss. They didn't have the gorgeous leaf colors that she had grown to love at college in North Carolina, but there was a crispness to the air and the energy of all those college students that made her feel happy. Lolly didn't want to think about the doctor's words that day, instead she thought about Jen handing over little Tomas to her father. Jen had called her that night and relayed the whole happy ending. Lolly was all for happy endings right about now. Even if they weren't hers.

"Lolly, don't you like football?" Nicole asked.

"Not really," Lolly said. "They didn't have football where I was an undergraduate. I think those are probably the formative years when you bond to a team."

"I loved the Hurricanes, but I think I can switch sides. I want to forget about everything that happened in Miami. That place was too big for me. Where did you go to college anyway?"

"I went to a small liberal arts school outside Asheville. And then came back home for my master's degree. Really, I just wanted to take a bunch of poetry classes, and I got into doing the workshops first with juveniles and then at the women's prison. Someday I'd like to do that fulltime."

There was a long silence as they both realized that someday might not come. Lolly changed the subject.

"You know what was cool about the college I went to? Everybody had to work. And my job was in the gardens. I loved it."

"You and my momma would get along. She's never happier than when she's got her hands deep in the dirt."

"Well, maybe I'll get a chance to meet her sometime," Lolly said.

"I doubt it," Nicole said, shaking her head wistfully. "Those people done wrote me off."

Lolly shrugged. She had a plan, but it was a secret.

As she pulled up to the two-story brick building where the work release women were housed, Lolly said, "Don't forget to tell them I need you on Thanksgiving Day, okay? That way you and Jen and I can have a little turkey feast and you don't have to be stuck here. I'll see you tomorrow."

Nicole stepped out of Lolly's car. She was so cute and tiny with such big bright eyes. Lolly waved at her. Somehow she was going to convince Nicole's parents to come join them for Thanksgiving Day. Hell, she'd pull the cancer card if she had to.

Just as she was pulling out of the driveway, a monstrous black Lincoln Navigator nearly careened into her.

"Watch it, jerk," Lolly muttered. She hated those ridiculous, ostentatious air-polluting mobile status symbols. *Why did Americans have to be so... American*, she wondered. What was so difficult about realizing that other people occupied the planet? Oh, well, she figured she had to let go of her firebrand. Why did she continue to rail against the evils of a world that would happily crumble away without her? The country didn't even have a president, but the outcome, she feared, was decided. Governor Jeb would make sure of that. How odd to be living in the most important small town in America right now and not to care anymore. Of course, she did care. But she couldn't get out there in the fray. When death sat beside you and held your hand, it didn't really matter who was the president. She was tired. She needed to keep the engine of her life running for just another week or so. After Thanksgiving she could let go. She could give in to the shadow growing inside her head.

Thursday November 23

While Aunt Jewel commiserated with Mr. and Mrs. Parks in the living room about the state of the country without a president and railed against Jeb Bush's henchwoman, Madame Secretary of State or "the Wicked Witch of the Panhandle", Lolly put the finishing touches on the sweet potato pie. The food looked good, but Lolly's appetite had withered. Even that drug the doctor had given her that made her so hungry for awhile seemed to have stopped working.

She checked the oven. Aunt Jewel had already made the turkey and dressing as well as the mashed potatoes. Nicole's mother had brought an enormous mess of green beans from her own garden. Zack made a squash casserole that he swore was the best thing this side of the Mason-Dixon line, Jen had earlier cooked the cranberries, and the rolls were on the sheet waiting to be slid into the oven at the last minute.

"Need any more help?" Zack asked.

"You can make the iced tea," Lolly said. "Then just stick it in the fridge. Jen should be back any minute with Nicole."

Brenda, who looked like an older -- but not by much -- version of Nicole, came to the doorway and said, "How 'bout I help you set the table? I know you aren't gonna treat us like guests."

"I wouldn't dream of it," Lolly said. "Here. The dishes are out, but the silverware hasn't been set." Lolly handed Brenda a handful of knives and forks.

"What a pretty pattern," Brenda said, admiring the fork handles.

"They were my mother's," Lolly said.

When Brenda took the silverware to the dining room, Lolly saw a movement at the window. She turned to face it and saw Jen's face peeking in at her. Alarmed, she quietly went out the back door and onto the deck. The day was overcast and a slight chill ran along Lolly's spine. Jen's hands were waving nervously.

"Come here," Jen said, turning quickly and walking down the back steps.

"Where? What is it? What's wrong?" Lolly asked. She followed Jen around the side of the house to the driveway. The neighbor's poodle began to yap furiously at them until Lolly finally snapped her fingers at the dog and he rushed over to lick her hand.

"She wasn't there. One of the residents said she left already. They thought she left with a man," Jen whispered.

"A man?" Lolly asked. She was dumbfounded. Surely, it couldn't be the editor of the little paper where Nicole was working part-time. He was happily married, and he didn't take that much of a personal interest in Nicole. She closed her eyes and tried to think. Where would Nicole have met a man? Something nagged at her. What was it? Then the picture zoomed into her mind. It was that car. Not a car really. A behemoth. The black Lincoln Navigator that nearly ran her down in front of the work release center. She had glimpsed the man's face through the front window. Handsome and hard-edged—a cold glance that passed through her.

"It's Antwan," she said. "She's with Antwan. If they find out, they'll send her right back to prison."

Jen and Lolly stared at each other. Lolly noticed Jen chewing on her bottom lip.

"We've got to find her," Lolly said. "Will Zack help? Or will he turn her in?"

"I think Zack's got bigger fish to fry than Nicole," Jen said.

"Okay, I'll explain to her parents that I need to go to sign her out of the center. That there's some problem there. You stay here and entertain them. Send Zack with me, okay?"

"You know where to find them, right?" Jen said.

"Not really," Lolly admitted.

"Where would you go if you'd been locked up for over two years and your rich boyfriend came and picked you up? You'd be in the nearest hotel room you could find."

"You think?"

"Duh."

"But there isn't a single hotel room available in this whole town," Lolly said. "Every reporter in the world is here with his little satellite dish."

"Oh, yeah," Jen said, hands on hips, looking down at the ground.

Lolly glanced around fretfully. Nicole's parents had to be wondering what was taking so long. Then she noticed someone walking down the street. Lolly walked to the edge of the yard and peered at the person. It was a woman in a dress and high heels. A young black woman. It was Nicole.

"Well, there she is, Jen," Lolly said. Jen came and stood beside her.

"The prodigal child," Jen said.

"Let us welcome her with open arms."

From the Journal of
Nicole Parks

There was one girl at the work release center named Francie—a pretty white girl with long blond hair and a cute little figure. She had a pretty good job, working as a receptionist for some friend of her daddy. We figured she'd be back on the streets, well taken care of, the way so many of them are. But don't you know one night they found her smoking crack in the bathroom? She was all wild looking and screaming at those people not to touch her, she was gonna sue somebody if they touched her. And you know, they touched her all right, carted her ass right over to the jail to wait for transport back to the penitentiary.

One of the other women summarized ol' Francie's plight by saying, "The girl just fell. That's all. Sometimes it happens."

Well, I fell, too. Here's how it happened. I was all dressed up and ready to go to Lolly's, lingering in the room I shared with a couple of other women when a girl named Tookie sticks her head in the door and says to me, "Your ride is here." So I sign the log and walk out into a gorgeous autumn day expecting to see Jen in her dusty old Blazer. The other girls were envious of me cause some of them didn't have work—it being a holiday—and they'd have to stay and eat turkey at the house there with one of those mean old staff members.

I was halfway down the walk to the driveway when I realized I didn't see Jen's truck. I looked around and across the street I saw him. My heart started beating 80 miles a minute. He was as debonair as ever, leaning against his black Lincoln Navigator, one of those little cigars in his mouth.

Did I stop and ask myself what I was doing? Did I remind myself of how he had disappeared from the radar while I was locked up? Did I even think for a moment of Lolly and Jen making a Thanksgiving dinner and waiting on me? No. Not only no but hell no.

I walked over and in full view of the "facility" let Antwan sweep me in his arms and kiss me, his tongue all over my mouth. Then we got into the Lincoln Navigator and started to drive. His hand rubbed my thigh as he said, "Baby cakes, I sure did miss you. Damn, you look fine. Put on a little weight tho', but we'll go knock that shit off right now." Just being in the car with him got me feeling so hot I couldn't even sit still. I wanted him bad. I wanted him like a fiend wants a rock of crack. We rode straight to the Holiday Inn, and Antwan and I strolled in there to the registration desk and asked for a room. The guy looked at us and laughed. He literally laughed.

"I don't even have a broom closet available," he said. "Where y'all been? Don't you know we got reporters from all over the world here? The fate of the only superpower in the world is hanging right here in Tallahassee, folks."

Antwan's face went hard and angry, his lips pulled in tight, but there was nothing he could do. 'Cept stick a gun in some reporter's face and make him give us their room. And he wasn't going to do that. So we got back in the Navigator and Antwan said, "Don't worry, boo. We'll go find us a nice secluded spot and you can give me that head job I been waiting for all these 27 months."

And that's when it dawned on me that he thought I was a genuine sucker in all senses of the word. And then I realized that obviously I was, or else I wouldn't be in the dang vehicle with him in the first place. And I thought back to that day in the cafeteria prison when Viola Carpenter asked me and Daffy if we had ever loved a man so much we would lay down on the railroad tracks and not get up, not even if a train was coming straight for us, if that man told us not to. And what had happened to Viola? Well, she would be spending her child-bearing years in a state prison. And if it weren't for me, she'd still be letting that man's spirit dog her to death. So who was I to save her and not save myself?

"Look, baby, I know just where we should go," I told him. "Go on down Monroe Street. I'll show you where to go."

Antwan licked his lips. He suddenly didn't look good to me anymore. I saw right through him to his heart, no bigger than a lima bean. Another face wasn't far from my mind and that was Viola's brother Junebug. He didn't have half the looks of Antwan but I imagined he was twice the man and I was tired of little boys. I directed Antwan to a gas station a half block from Lolly's house.

"Why we stopping here?" Antwan asked.

"I need to get something, lover," I said. Then I got out of the truck and I looked at him hard in the face. "But you don't need to wait for me. 'Cause this trip is over and done. And don't come back." I slammed the door of his precious SUV and walked away.

"You hit the road, you got damn bitch," Antwan yelled, and that made me feel even better because it sealed the deal. He couldn't even take rejection like a man.

So I turned around and yelled back, "Bye, bye, sissy boy."

I heard him gun his engine and squeal out of there. I was so mad at myself for having gotten in there with him, but I was proud at the same time. Had I finally gotten some smarts? Had those long months locked up with all those crazy women finally taught me the most important lesson of all—how to respect myself? Huh! And Momma and Daddy thought that sending me to college was gonna wise me up. I'd sure gotten schooled but it wasn't at college.

I walked that half block down to Lolly's house and saw her and Jen standing in the yard, looking worried. Then Lolly opened her arms wide and smiled big as the sunrise. I walked up and gave her a big hug and then over her shoulder I saw someone come out onto her porch. They opened the screen door and tears sprung to my eyes. There was my daddy standing big and tall like a mountain in the doorway and my momma looking over his shoulder at me. And at first Daddy's face was like a stiff mask like when I used to come home late but a second later it softened and he walked down the steps. I let go of Lolly and ran to him, ran like I was running for my life, letting my high heels fall off my feet and soon I had my arms wrapped around his neck and I was crying, no I was sobbing on his shirt. And in my heart I was saying, "Thank you, Jesus. Thank you, thank you, sweet Jesus."

Thursday, November 23

Sonya leaned against the concrete block wall of the rec room with Panther by her side. A couple of women were playing ping pong, others were just talking loudly the way they always did about absolutely nothing, and a few were dancing over in the corner. C.O. Barbie was on duty that day, and she didn't look too pleased to be spending her Thanksgiving Day with that crew. She had little tiny teeth and a rectangular smile on the rare occasions when she smiled at all. Right now she was carefully watching the dancers to make sure that there wasn't any touching going on. Panther's eyes cut over to Sonya and she whispered, "Meet me in the bathroom in five minutes."

Then Panther sauntered over to the ping-pong game. Alice walked in the door and waved at Sonya. She stopped at the desk to sign in and then came over.

"How's the baby?" she asked.

A wave of happiness washed over Sonya. "He's doing good, Alice. Real good. I talked to my ma this morning, and she said that her and Duke and Tomas have a house in Canada. Duke's gone legit. You know, no one, not even me, loved that baby like Duke loved him."

"He's gone legit?"

"Yeah, and still making good money. He's a contractor for real now. It makes me so happy knowing that Tomas won't grow up in the life. I mean, I never thought anything was so wrong with it, but I don't want him to end up in a place like this."

Alice nodded. She was still so kind and wise. Sonya wished she could hug her, but C.O. Barbie would throw her in the box so quick she'd have to have someone pick up her ass and deliver it. Oh, the hell with C.O. Barbie. Sonya saw Panther step into the bathroom. The bathrooms in the dorm had no privacy but this bathroom and a few others were actually closed.

"I talked to Mariposa yesterday," Alice was saying. "She says her brother is doing real good. He's got a job and everything. I think you did a real good thing."

"Thanks," Sonya said. Then she noticed Alice's friend Riley watching them. She had a momentary shiver. Something about Riley reminded her of a lizard, something about that hooded gaze of hers. Sonya thought that Riley would never really understand Alice. Alice was not a "stud"; nor was she like any of the other women. Alice was somehow above the normal needs and selfish desires that everyone else had, but she never acted superior. She was simply Alice.

"I'll talk to you later," Sonya said, and Alice glanced toward the bathroom.

Alice grinned and said, "Be careful."

Sonya felt herself blush. But C.O. Barbie was busy giving Lucille a hard time about something, and now was the time. She slipped into the bathroom quickly where Panther was waiting by the door. With one hand Panther held the door shut and the other she wrapped around Sonya's waist. The kiss was sweet and warm. This was a Thanksgiving Day Sonya would never forget. Panther caressed her breast and kissed her neck and said, "I love you."

"I love you, too," Sonya said. "We can't stay in here any longer."

"I know," Panther said. "I just need one more kiss."

But the kiss turned into something else. It was like the descent of a thick cloud, and for a moment Sonya had no idea where she was. Panther's hands slid up under Sonya's prison frock and expertly moved between her legs.

"What are you doing?" Sonya croaked.

"I'm looking for a door, baby," Panther said, her voice husky with desire. And Sonya felt every muscle give way as Panther's fingers found the slickness between her legs.

"This is what I want," Panther said.

"We'll get caught," Sonya said, not sure she even gave a damn. And then she knew she didn't give a damn because Panther's fingers were rubbing against an incredibly sweet spot just below her pubic bone and her other hand had hold of Sonya's ass and inside Sonya's brain everything else was obliterated by the rocket's red glare.

"God in heaven," she said, sliding down the wall.

Panther had finished her. Panther laughed and went to the sink.

"I hate to do this," she said and plunged her hands under the running water. "I'd like to keep you on me all day."

Sonya sighed, and Panther walked out of the bathroom. When Sonya came out, C.O. Barbie eyeballed her suspiciously but it was too late. That cat would have to catch another mouse.

"Come on, let's play ping pong," Panther said. They joined Lucille and Daffy for a game of doubles. Sonya could barely keep her knees from shaking.

"Our girl Nicole be working for Lolly," Daffy said. "Helping take care of her. Y'all know she is bad sick. Nicole wrote me last week and said she thought Lolly might die. That hurt me to my heart."

"No," Sonya said, her happy mood darkening from the news. "I thought they would cure her. I don't want Lolly to die."

"Me neither," Lucille said. "But you can want all you want. God is going to do what God wants to do. And might be God wants Lolly in heaven."

The buzzer for count rang, and C.O. Barbie stood up and announced they had to get back to their dorms, "Pronto." And Mariposa muttered, "Like she Spanish or something." Daffy collected the ping pong paddles and Sonya and Panther lingered to be the last to leave so their hands could clasp quickly while C.O. Barbie wasn't looking. But even as Panther's fingers brushed against Sonya's, Sonya felt an uneasiness, something disturbing her. She looked at the sky and there was suddenly a gathering force of dark clouds all decked out in riot gear.

She looked around. What wasn't right? Then she knew. Alice wasn't in the crowd returning to the dorm. And neither was Riley.

"Wait up," she said to Panther. "I'll be right back."

C.O. Barbie was up ahead, not even looking back to make sure everyone had left. Sonya ducked back in the rec room and hurried to the bathroom. Maybe they hadn't heard the buzzer. She pulled the door open and stepped inside. Immediately she wished she hadn't. There stood Riley in front of the second stall, her right arm bright red and a kitchen knife in her hand. Riley looked at her, with her mouth open, panting like a dog.

Sonya stared at her.

"What have you done?" Sonya asked quietly. Riley didn't answer. Her lizard eyes seemed stunned. Sonya looked down and under the last stall she could see a slumped form in prison blues.

"Alice?" she asked. Her voice came out weak and desperate.

"Get out of here," Riley screamed. And she rushed at Sonya with the knife raised high over her head. Sonya had been dodging Ziggy's attacks her whole life long, and she had learned from him how to fight dirty. A quick duck and an even quicker kick to Riley's knee. Riley fell sprawling to the floor. Sonya jumped on Riley's back, lifted her head by the strawberry blond hair and slammed it into the floor. The knife fell from Riley's grip, but she used both hands to push up and snakelike squirmed around, toppling Sonya off of her. As she fell Sonya looked over and saw Alice leaned back against the wall, her legs splayed, blood thick and dark on her shirt and arms, her eyes closed.

Sonya turned to Riley who had crawled to the corner under sink. The knife lay on the floor between them. Sonya reached for the knife as she heard the door open behind her.

"No!" someone screamed. Sonya looked up to see Panther push-ing past C.O. Barbie and at the same time a movement caught her eye. She turned in time to see Riley lunging toward her. Sonya turned and felt the knife plunge deep into Riley's chest. Riley whimpered and gagged, and blood spurted out of her mouth. She slumped to the floor beside Sonya and the two of them lay face to face as Riley gasped for air and Sonya slowly pulled her fingers off the knife

Then Sonya heard a groan and turned to see Alice's eyes flutter open.

Monday, December 2

Jen's stomach felt hollow like a drum. Lolly hadn't left the bed in two days. The Hospice nurse had been dumping morphine into her system, but now the nurse was gone and there was a quiet moment. Outside the world was a teeming, screaming cacophony what with end-of-semester parties and the never-ending presidential election and the reporters swarming around the city like locusts. It was so chaotic. You couldn't drive anywhere. Television trucks blocked streets. The enormous influx of visitors filled every restaurant and bar. She and Zack had tried to go to their favorite place the night before but there was a two-hour wait. Even the supermarket aisles were clogged with out-of-towners. Fortunately classes were almost over so that meant a good portion of the town's population would be heading out over the next week as they finished exams.

She didn't bother to knock on Lolly's door. Just entered and found Nicole cleaning up. Nicole had been staying all night and day since she got out of work release on the first of the month.

"Do you know about Sonya?" Nicole asked in a whisper.

"What?" Jen asked.

Nicole glanced down the hallway at Lolly sleeping in her big four-poster bed.

"Let's go out on the back deck," Nicole said.

Jen followed her outside. December was balmy as it so often is in North Florida. Nights were cold but during the day when the sun was out, you didn't even need a jacket.

"So what happened to Sonya? Is her son okay?"

"What son? No, Sonya killed somebody in the prison."

"What?" Jen asked and sat down heavily in the metal fan-back chair.

"Yeah, girl, this chick named Riley showed up just before I left for work release. I remember her though I only saw her a little bit. She came in, all cocky. She'd been down before, down in Broward, and she was one of those hard cases – killed some guy over money he owed her. Said she was one high-class call girl and she had the looks, but not the class. Anyway, she came in the dorm and latched on Indian from the jump. Seems they knew each other from the last time she was locked up."

"Indian? Do you mean Alice?"

"Yeah, Alice. Anyway, Daffy wrote me and told me this Riley chick was crazy. She musta been because on Thanksgiving Day she stabbed Indian with a kitchen knife – that same one that went missing last summer, I believe. Anyway, she stabs Indian and Sonya comes up on them, sees what is happening, takes the knife away from the crazy girl and then goes crazy herself and stabs Riley." Nicole's eyes were wide as she finished her story. Jen felt numb. She looked up at the clean sky and tried to absorb this news. Finally, she asked, "But why? Why would she do something so stupid?"

Nicole crossed her arms and said, "'Cause that place will make you crazy if you aren't already nuts, and most of us were already a little crazy before we went in."

"Is Alice hurt? Is she dead?" Jen asked, the enormity of the event finally becoming clear to her at the same time she asked herself how she had let herself get involved, how she had exposed herself to this level of possible pain.

"They say she's in the hospital. She's gonna be okay, I think," Nicole said.

"And the other woman is dead?"

"Yep."

"How did you hear all this?"

"From Lucille. She came to the work release center yesterday afternoon. I stopped by to sign some paperwork and get some things I had left and there she was. Then this morning, Sonya's lawyer called to talk to Lolly. I talked to him instead, said I was Lolly's assistant. Anyway, he said Sonya was going to be charged with manslaughter."

Jen shook her head and thought of Tomas. Poor Sonya. Why had she thrown her life away? Why had she taken that woman's life?

"How much more time will she get?"

"Could be anything from five to fifteen, even twenty years. But probably not that much. It sounds like Riley was dangerous. She'd already stabbed Indian. Lucille heard that Riley was planning on jumping the fence and she thought Indian was going to snitch on her."

Jen didn't say anything for a few minutes, and neither did Nicole. They sat on the deck and looked out at the white camellias that were in full bloom. Jen was grateful that Lolly had managed to plant so much white in the backyard. It was beautiful all year long.

"Let's not mention any of this to Lolly," she said.

"Any of what?"

Jen turned around and saw Lolly standing in the doorway. Her eyes looked clear and her voice was strong. Jen suddenly remember when Lolly was five years old, and how she wanted a doll that Jen was holding. She was so determined to get that doll, and finally she did.

Nicole inhaled deeply and started the story all over again.

When she was done, Lolly said, "Doesn't she have a girlfriend now, Nicole?"

"Yeah, Panther," Nicole said. "They were stone in love when I left."

"Maybe she just plans to stay there where she has love," Lolly said and pulled one of the camellias from the bush. "Maybe there's nothing left for her out here."

Wednesday, December 6

It was chilly when Lolly came out of her room. The hardwood floor felt cold on her foot. Aunt Jewel was in the kitchen washing dishes. Lolly stepped into the kitchen onto the linoleum and saw Aunt Jewel leaning over the sink, washing dishes. Aunt Jewel turned to face her and smiled.

"How come you aren't at the protest, Auntie?" Lolly asked.

"Oh, I thought I'd rather spend the morning with you," Aunt Jewel said, wiping the white curls off her face with her forearm.

Lolly leaned on her crutches and smelled the aroma of coffee. She was feeling stronger than she had in weeks. Her mind felt clear. That constant blood rushing sound was gone. Even her eyes seemed to focus better. This was it, she realized. Her own little miracle.

"I don't want to lie around here all day," Lolly said. "Let me put on my leg, and get dressed. Then let's go."

"Go?" Aunt Jewel asked, turning with a stunned look on her face. "Where we going, honey?"

"Down to the Capitol. We've got to stand by our man, Aunt Jewel." Lolly swiveled around and headed down the hallway to her room.

"Glory be!" Aunt Jewel shouted.

Lolly found her maroon sweater in the antique cabinet in the corner of her room. She slipped her stump into the soft netting at the top of her prosthetic and slid a pair of jeans on. Last she put on a pair of bright green sneakers. This is what she would have done if she hadn't gotten sick. This is who she was. She looked in the mirror at herself.

"Hello, you," she said. Her green eyes gleamed back at her. "Okay, Aunt Jewel, I'm ready," she hollered.

Aunt Jewel handed her a travel-cup filled with coffee and the two of them stepped out into the chilly morning air. The sunlight falling through the pine trees across the street promised a quick warm up of the day. They got into Aunt Jewel's pickup truck and Lolly settled back against the seat, feeling as if she might live to be a hundred. Steam rose from her coffee cup.

Christmas decorations hung from the light posts, and Lolly thought of all the Christmases of her childhood. How these cheap silver tinsel cutouts had enthralled her. They still did in a way. As they approached downtown, it was difficult to tell at first that anything was going on. Then they noticed a crowd of people crossing the street and saw that the parking places on Monroe were all taken. They turned down a street that ran along the city park, which was filled with camellias and oak trees that reminded Lolly of the absolute meaninglessness of all the political sturm and drang. She thought of a poem she'd written once, an ode to live oak trees. "Grandfathers," she'd called them. It was a rather obvious comparison of the calm and longevity of the trees with the transience of human affairs. No one had published that poem, but she liked it. What she was enjoying the most this morning was the cool functioning of her own mind, the thoughts and associations that stood up and waved at her. When was the last time she'd even thought of poetry? She couldn't remember.

"Look at this," Aunt Jewel said as they drove behind the Capitol. The plaza was thronged with people. "I wonder where Reverend Jackson is?"

"Oh, just look for the TV cameras," Lolly said with a laugh.

"All right. Where we gonna park?"

Lolly smiled and held up a card. "This will get us into a state lot and we can park in the handicapped spot." Lolly had been harangued a few times by elderly people when she'd parked in handicapped zones. She'd often been tempted to pull off her leg and hit the self-righteous complainers over the head with it.

They soon parked and trekked toward the plaza.

"You're moving good, honey," Aunt Jewel said.

"You know I always did love to walk," Lolly said. In so many ways, before the cancer came back, she had been just like everyone else. "And this is for a good cause."

"Democracy is a damn good cause," Aunt Jewel intoned.

"Why do we have this stupid electoral college?" Lolly asked.

"I don't know," Aunt Jewel answered. "You'd think if they could get rid of 'blue' laws, they could scrap that antiquated system. Of course, Jeb and his buddies are planning on stacking the electorates and then none of this'll matter anyway."

"Oh, look," Lolly said. They were still half a block away from the plaza when they saw a fresh-faced college boy in a Kappa Delta shirt holding a sign with a picture of Al Gore. The sign said, "The Gorch who stole Christmas."

Aunt Jewel jumped in his face and said, "You may be going to college but you are an idiot."

"Lady, I'm not letting Al Gore ruin this country. You people can't steal this election," he said with a sneer.

"Ruin the country? You mean by keeping our air clean and not clear cutting every forest from here to the Pacific?"

"Screw the forests. We need a good economy."

"We can have both!" Aunt Jewel shrieked. Lolly tugged on her arm and looked around. They were obviously in the middle of the Republican camp, which was keeping its distance from the main festivities.

"We better get to our side of this civil war before you get us killed," Lolly said.

Aunt Jewel muttered, "You're right. These people smell blood."

Lolly and Aunt Jewel glanced in each other's eyes. For a moment they both acknowledged the utter futility of the cause. But it was only for a moment.

They reached the plaza where it looked like a few thousand people were milling about. Many of them were Africans-Americans who had taken buses up from South Florida.

Lolly and Aunt Jewel were walking the steps of the plaza when Lolly pointed to another sign. This one had a picture of a Christmas tree and said, "George W. Bush. The dimmest bulb on the tree."

"The war of the placards," Lolly muttered. The slogans were humorous, but deceptive, she thought. A group of about six middle-aged black women, wearing bright blue sweatshirts, were clapping and singing as Lolly and Aunt Jewel passed them. Some children ran helter-skelter through the grownups. A young man wearing African beads and dreadlocks bumped into Lolly, and she lost her balance, falling back against Aunt Jewel, who helped her back up.

"I'm so sorry, miss," he said, stopping to look into her eyes. "Are you okay?"

"I'm fine," Lolly said.

"That's good to know." His smile was broad and warm. The reflection of the sun sparkled on the glass windows of the buildings.

"Lolly," someone shouted. "Over here."

She turned and saw Jeremy, wearing a tweed jacket over a sweater. He stood on the fringes of the crowd. The Gore supporters were an amorphous organism. Ex-hippies, college professors, working women, people of color and regular state workers. Lolly smiled at Jeremy. It was good to see him. Then she saw a few feet away Sue and Rusty and a large group from her office. They ought to have been at work, but they probably couldn't resist the excitement.

Sue saw her and pushed through the crowd to reach her. She threw her arms around Lolly.

"God, you look great!" she said.

"I feel great," Lolly said.

"Patricia Ireland is on the stage. Can you see her?" Sue asked.

Lolly tried to see over the heads in front of her, but it was useless. Jeremy approached, swinging his arms as he walked toward her.

"Hey, lady," he said.

Sue was siphoned off by Aunt Jewel.

"Hey," Lolly said to Jeremy. "Long time."

"I know. I'm sorry," he said, with a glance to the ground. *Oh Lord,* Lolly thought, *he feels guilty.* She wished people could see her without feeling guilt, or pity, or pain.

He reached an arm around her and kissed her on the cheek.

"I'm glad to see you," he said.

Before she could answer, a chant swelled up from their side of the plaza: "Let the votes count! Let the votes count!"

Lolly joined in, laughing as she did so. Somehow this felt slightly ridiculous, but she was enjoying the moment. Then a set of gigantic speakers began to blare out "Respect" and people were dancing and Lolly found herself clapping and singing along as if she were at a concert instead of a political protest.

When the song was over, Jesse Jackson took to the stage and decried the election "irregularities" that prevented blacks from voting in November's election, and he lambasted the Republicans for trying to obstruct a recount.

"We are gathered today in a quest for democracy. To even the playing field," Jackson's musical voice rose from the speakers. Lolly could see the dome of the old capitol building and the flags that flew there. "Our mission is one person, one vote. We want democracy by inclusion, not exclusion."

Lolly felt an odd surge of pride. The political situation looked so disastrous, but on the other hand, here they were voicing opinions and just down the street people were voicing different opinions and no one was being shot down, tanks weren't rumbling toward them. In fact, the idea of such a thing wasn't even in the realm of possibility as far as most people were concerned. She wasn't unaware of history. She knew that such freedom had not always been the case. She'd seen the

pictures of the dogs that Bull Connor sicced on Civil Rights protest-
ers. She'd heard Neil Young wail about the "four dead in O-hi-o." Her
mother had often told her about Senator McCarthy and the witch
hunts of the 1950s. And she knew there were no guarantees for the
future, but for today at this rally, they had that cherished freedom to
speak out, to be heard. And it was good. And for a moment she forgot
that she was dying.

Monday, December 11

Jen plugged the last of her grades into the computer. She hated giving grades. She didn't mind teaching, but coming up with these arbitrary standards for awarding status stuck like a spoon being shoved down her throat. So many teachers were proud of their extraordinary ability to give Ds and Fs. She'd never forget Amanda Hathaway pompously declaring that she never gave out A's. As if that made her somehow superior to those struggling students who could very well wind up far more successful than she had ever been. What did grades have to do with theater? But Jen realized she was avoiding the bigger and more personal question. Why was she teaching—as an adjunct no less? She thought about the drama production that she and Lolly had done at the prison. Now, that was a different kind of teaching entirely. It was more like equals sharing knowledge and offering guidance. And the production had been thrilling. She wouldn't mind doing that again. She leaned back in her chair and ran a hand through her thick hair. That wouldn't happen, would it? Because Lolly wouldn't be around to make it happen.

The thought saddened her. She quickly gathered up her belongings and stuffed them into her bag. She wouldn't be back 'til after the Christmas break when the new semester would start. She had a bag of Godiva chocolates in her drawer, wrapped in a nice green ribbon for the secretary. Always take care of the office workers, she believed. They were the lifeblood of any organization.

She picked up her satchel, the chocolates, and glanced around the room. Nothing she needed for a few weeks. In fact, the office was pretty barren, a temporary housing that had somehow become permanent. She shut off the light and locked the door and headed down to the main office to drop off the chocolates and say "Happy Holidays" to the chair.

"Jen, come in for a minute, please," Ralph said when she popped her head in his office. Ralph wasn't a bad guy. A little on the weak side, but he generally looked out for Jen, and so she had nothing to complain about. He had an Alfred Hitchcock lower lip and sleepy eyes, but he was unfailingly cordial, which in this often contentious environment made him the perfect administrator.

Jen was wearing a dark velour sweat suit and her hair in a ponytail since it wasn't a teaching day. She knew she didn't exactly look "professorial," but she was comfortable and probably pretty cute.

"What's up?" she asked as she came in to Ralph's spacious office.

"You still haven't finished your dissertation?" he asked.

"Mmm, no," she said.

He leaned forward. "Just out of curiosity, how badly do you want the degree?"

Jen stumbled over her words, but managed to say, "I want it."

Ralph shook his head slightly.

"I don't have any classes for you next term," he said.

"What?" Jen erupted. They were actually denying her this incredibly shitty job that she was, by all accounts, quite good at. "Who's going to teach Intro to Theater and Basic Acting?"

Ralph tapped his folded hands on the desk.

"One of Amanda's students."

Jen growled. "She finally got rid of me, didn't she?" She sat down in a wooden chair and stared over at his bookshelves. The academics had dissected, analyzed, quantified and qualified every possible aspect of drama but they could never get at its soul no matter how many words they tried to bury it with.

Ralph cleared his throat.

"Jen, you should be out there working in the field. You're wonderful on stage and your instincts as a director, from what I've seen, are very good."

"I'm a 32-year-old woman," she said dismally. "I can't live like a gypsy my whole life. I was hoping that teaching would give me some stability."

"You are the perfect age for a variety of roles," Ralph nattered on. "You can play anything from 25 to 40."

"I'll have to leave Tallahassee."

"Maybe it's time," he said. She wondered how much he knew about Lolly. "I'm saying this as your friend."

Jen stood up. No point in telling him that she had met someone who made staying in one place seem like a good idea.

"Thanks, Ralph," she said. "I guess."

He grinned and shrugged helplessly. She turned and walked out the door. The secretary had just taken a bite of one of the Godiva chocolates.

By the time she got in her truck and had pulled out of the parking lot, she realized Ralph was right. If she didn't make a move now, she'd never make one. She would not think about Zack and what this might mean for their relationship. When had a man ever given up a career for a woman? Well, there was that British king who lost his job by marrying a commoner, but he was an exception.

The first thing she had to do was call her agency in Atlanta and tell them she wanted to get back in the game fulltime. For the past few years they'd only been sending her out on local jobs, and those were few and far between. Ralph was right, she told herself again. Except for Lolly, she had no reason to stay. And the truth was that Lolly would be leaving before she did. She ached at the thought of it, but there was no hiding from it any longer. Lolly was tired of fighting, and Jen knew it was unfair to try to hold onto her.

She pulled up to Lolly's house and parked on the grass. As she came up to the porch, she saw Lolly sitting outside in the big Adirondack chair with a throw wrapped around her. Jen came onto the porch and kissed Lolly's wan cheek. It was amazing the gentleness she felt for her dying sister. A gift, she realized.

Lolly smiled and shut her eyes.

"Did you eat anything today?" Jen asked.

"Soup," Lolly said.

"Sounds good." She ran her hand over Lolly's head. Nicole came out and said, "Hey, girl."

"Hey," Jen said.

"She's doing pretty good today."

"I can see that."

They stood without speaking and looked at Lolly, who gazed up at them as if they were parents she was hoping to please.

Jen broke out of her trance and said, "I need to make some calls."

A few minutes later she was on the phone with her agent, Alana.

"Oh my Gawd, Jen. You are so perfect for this role. I can't believe your timing," she said in an almost perfect iambic rhythm. "Can you get up to Wilmington by Wednesday morning? If you can, you are a sure bet for this one, babe."

"Yeah, I guess I can," Jen said. "I hate to leave my sister though."

"Hey, are you back in the game or not? I mean it's only twenty-four hours there and back. Can't she live without you that long?" Jen didn't bother to explain.

"Tell me about the role."

"It's a mom."

"A mom?"

"Best roles for your age bracket, babe. Especially on network TV. You could be set for life. Think of the residuals," Alana was practically salivating.

"But what about... my image," Jen said, delicately.

"Babe, that stuff is ancient history. For God's sake, look at

Madonna. She puts out that sex book and still could get cast as the Virgin Mary. No one cares if you were a skin flick diva once upon a time. You are the only one that matters to."

For the second time that day, someone else seemed to know her better than she knew herself.

"So how old are her kids?" Jen asked, not wanting to be vain, but really she didn't want to be some 18-year-old's mother.

"Two teenage sons, one of them is going to be president someday."

"Sounds interesting."

"The mom is very flaky."

"I can do flaky."

Jen felt that sudden longing that she hadn't felt for a role in a long time. Was this it? Was this her golden opportunity?

"I'll be there," she said.

"Your audition will be at 11 a.m. sharp, babe," Alana said and clicked onto her other line.

Jen went back outside.

"Lolly, I've got an audition for a network television show in Wilmington. Will you be okay if I leave for a couple of days?"

Lolly pulled the throw tight around her shoulders and nodded.

"Of course, I will. I mean I would come with you but someone has to stay here and take care of Nicole," Lolly said with her characteristic grin. Nicole was sitting in the other chair, painting her fingernails.

"You sure?" Jen asked.

"Sure, I'm sure," Lolly answered. At that moment the garbage truck pulled up and as the man came running up to get the big black garbage can, he waved to Lolly. She waved back. Jen shook her head. Was there anyone the woman wasn't friends with?

Tuesday, December 12

Sonya strolled through the hallway at the County Jail. The drunks and the shoplifters and worthless-check writers watched her curiously. They were all doing county time and the sight of her in her prison dress was like a warning bell. It made them feel smug and yet somehow inferior at the same time. Sonya's insides had turned to plastic by now – plastic heart beating, plastic stomach digesting the jail food, plastic liver, plastic lungs pumping the stale jail air in and out. She barely noticed the jail inmates or heard their muttered comments. "Damn, look at old girl."

She was led into the visiting room by a young, black jail officer with a narrow waist and shiny Hollywood hair. The officer unlocked the door to the small room, ushered Sonya in and said, "You have fifteen minutes."

Jeremy Erwin sat at a table. Sonya was glad she didn't have to talk to him through a glass window. Official visits carried a certain privilege. Not that she had to worry about family visiting.

Jeremy had a grown a beard since the last time she saw him. He was a nice looking man with warm brown eyes. She sat across from him.

"I'm in trouble now, ain't I?" she said.

"Some," he said with a nod.

"How bad?"

"They want to say it's manslaughter. I'm pushing for self-defense,"

Jeremy said. "You will lose all your gain time, no matter what happens, but we may be able to beat this other charge especially since your friend Alice is still alive."

Sonya laid her head on the table. It felt like the plastic inside was melting. Alice alive. *Good girl*, she thought, *you didn't let that crazy bitch kill you.* She swallowed hard and raised her head again.

"You seen her?"

"Yeah, I took a deposition from her this morning. She gave me a letter for you."

Jeremy handed Sonya a white standard-sized enveloped from his briefcase. Sonya felt the damp streak of a tear on her face, but she didn't bother to wipe it away. Lord, she couldn't wait to get back to the compound.

Sonya lay on her bunk and opened the letter. A drunk woman about thirty years old with a tattoo of a spider web on her neck was crying on the other side of the cell. Sonya turned her back to the woman and started to read.

Dear Sonya,

I heard that you saved my life. And now they're looking to throw down another charge on you. I want you to know that my prayers and the prayers of all my family are with you. I'm still in some pain. OK – lots of pain. Riley did some damage to my guts and it's taken them three operations to get everything sewn back up again. I have to pee through a catheter and the doctors tell me I need to fart! Can you believe that?

The food here is not so bad. And they actually let my moms come in and see me. She keeps asking can she send you money or anything. I told her your people were pretty well off, but when you get out you can be sure you'll be getting a box full of baskets and beads. She does really nice bead work.

Sonya, I need to explain some things about Riley to you. Please don't think it's to make you feel bad. Just to help you understand her. She wasn't always so crazy. I know you've heard the rumors about that "major" that got transferred just before you got to the prison. Well, they're mostly true. He used to be at the joint down south. When Riley was locked up the first time, he had her locked up in the box on some bogus charge. I don't know exactly what he did to her, but when she came out it was like all the light had been sucked out of her. I know that she wasn't a killer before that happened to her. But she got out and got all those drugs in her and something changed. When she came back in, I tried to help her. But she just knew she was going to wind up in the box for something and that somebody would do to her what happened before. So that's why she wanted to escape so bad. I told her it was suicide. She didn't believe me, thought I snitched on her. Riley was like a cornered rat. I have forgiven her. It was her own fault that she wound up dead, not yours, but I still remember who she was before all this happened.

Now I guess you and me have something in common. We've both killed someone. I know the circumstances were different, but there's something that changes when you've taken a life. You will feel it for a while, and truthfully somehow it is always with you. A kind of sadness. You carry it with you. Not to say you won't go on with your life. Ten years from now when you're free and back with your family or maybe just on your own, you won't be the same person you are now. But somewhere deep in your mind you'll remember Riley. And she'll be like your long-lost sister. But you'll also remember me, I think. And you'll know you have a good friend forever. Take care of yourself. Get a good lawyer so you don't get dealt with another charge.

In Love, friendship and gratitude,

A

Sonya folded the letter and put it back in the white envelope. She then folded the envelope and stuffed it in her pocket. She thought of Alice. It was the first time she realized that Riley might have killed Alice if Sonya hadn't come in to look for them. She rubbed her hand over her arm and stared at the cinder block wall. *It was worth it*, she thought. Whatever happened. Whatever she had to live with. And for a moment she felt as if she were floating. She held her breath but then it came rushing out of her lungs and new air entered. She was breathing. She was alive. She wondered if she'd ever stopped to realize how strange and awesome a thing it was—just to breathe, just to be aware. She didn't want to disturb this moment. Her hair lay across her cheek, her body felt the scratchy blanket beneath her, and her eyes gazed into the white block wall. It seemed as if she could put her hand through the wall. But she knew she couldn't.

"Hey, you got a cigarette?" the drunk spider web woman asked her.

Sonya rolled over and stared at the woman.

"What are you staring at?" the woman asked.

"You," Sonya answered. "Just you."

"Yakowski! You got some mail," the female guard hollered from the end of the hall. Sonya stood up and went to the slot in the door; a postcard fell to the floor. She picked it up. It was a picture of the Bay of Fundi. Canada. She turned it over and saw her name and the address of the jail in Duke's blocky penmanship. Instead of a message, someone – a child – had scribbled in purple crayon. She stared at it for a long time.

Wednesday
December 13

Jen woke in a double bed to the sound of the motel fan churning the stale air. Her stomach clenched and she bolted out of bed into the small white bathroom where she heaved into the toilet bowl. Raising her head, she felt whoozy and hung onto the sink. Now, this was odd as she hadn't had a drink in weeks. It certainly wasn't a hangover. Well, she had acted under worse conditions than a little stomach virus. She rinsed out her mouth and suddenly worried that she might have food poisoning. She thought back to what she'd eaten the night before. Taco Bell. She'd never gotten sick from Taco Bell, and how much poison could a couple of bean burritos contain anyway?

The audition wasn't till 11 that morning and it was only six. Maybe she could just lie down for a couple more hours and see how she felt.

Lolly walked through the garden in her backyard. She stopped to admire the big glass sphere on the iron pedestal that Sue had given her. It reflected the thickest blue sky that Lolly had ever seen. She continued on along the path that she had lined with stones last year and admired each flower. The morning glories against the fence cupped the air. She let her fingers brush against them and then noticed something she had never seen before. There was a small arched doorway in the fence. She pushed aside the vines and examined it. A black wrought iron door handle with a thumb latch was there. She felt like that little girl in *The Secret Garden*. With a sense of delighted curiosity, she reached for the handle and pushed her thumb down on the iron latch to release the door. She gave the door a tug and opened it.

Nicole poked her head in Lolly's room. Lolly was still sleeping, the head end of the bed raised to help her breathe, but the breathing was shallow and strained. Lolly had seemed to be doing so well yesterday when Jen left, but something felt very different today. Nicole decided not to disturb her, but she would call Rebecca, the hospice nurse, and find out when she was coming. Jen's big orange cat was curled comfortably into the comforter at Lolly's feet. Nicole never really liked cats but at this moment she was glad not to be alone.

The doorbell rang. When Nicole answered it, she found Lolly's Aunt Jewel standing there, holding a couple of coffees and a bag from Dunkin' Donuts.

"I know it's not the most wholesome breakfast in the world," Aunt Jewel said, "but they got great coffee. Here, have a cup."

Nicole gratefully took the cup of coffee and the bag of donuts into the kitchen. They both had a donut and stood by the back door looking out at Lolly's backyard.

"She sure made it pretty out there," Aunt Jewel said. "Even in winter. Look at the camellia bushes."

Nicole merely nodded. Then she said, "She's not doing that good, Ms. Jewel. I don't know what to do."

"Wait, darling," Aunt Jewel said. "We just wait."

It was nine a.m. and Jen felt fine. In fact, she was hungry, which was crazy. No way that little episode was nerves. Yes, it was a huge part, an enormous opportunity to get on a network television show. It could be the break she'd been waiting for, but she just wasn't the sort of person to get that worked up over an audition. She slipped her pretty red sweater over her head and examined herself in the mirror. She fluffed her hair and moved in close to check out her makeup. Did she look like a "mom"? What did moms look like these days, anyway? Just like everybody else from what she had observed, except they were always in a hurry. Never expect a mom to just hang out at the coffee shop for a couple hours. Okay, she figured she looked the part.

Of course, it wasn't just about looking the part. It was being the part. She looked at her reflection and said out loud, "I am a mom." The words echoed in the tiny bathroom.

"Shit!" she screamed. She looked over at the toilet bowl where she'd been genuflecting a couple of hours earlier. When? When? When? Last month. No. No, not last month. Her last period had just ended the day of Lolly's benefit, which is why it had seemed safe that night . . .

"Shit," she said again, softer this time. She walked over to the bed and sank down on the twisted bundle of white sheets and flowered bedspread.

Lolly had to bend over to get through the arched doorway. On the other side was another garden. How had they gotten these blooms in the winter? There was a dogwood decked in white flowers. Oh, and Queen Anne's lace. She saw a small pond with a little stone bench beside it. She followed the path to the pond and stuck her toes in the water. It was warm. The ripples galloped across the surface, distorting the reflection of the dogwoods.

Music was playing somewhere. Guitar music. A band. Some kids from the university probably practicing. She looked around and saw a wooden building not far away. It was sort of modern looking with big glass doors and windows on the side. That must be where the band was playing.

Nicole went outside to check Lolly's birdfeeders. She knew that was important to Lolly. A cardinal flew low past her and perched in a branch beside Lolly's window. She wished Lolly would wake up. She wanted to do something, but how did you beat back death? Nicole had lost a cousin in a dumb drunk driving accident back in high school, but that had happened so quickly she never had the time to dread it. Now she felt as if she were wearing layers of fear and misery. She wished she had her mother with her, but she realized she needed to do this on her own. She had to be strong for Lolly and strong for herself.

Jen drove along the highway, pushing fifteen miles an hour past the speed limit. There was something in her head telling her to hurry. She glanced down at the cell phone and wondered, should she call him? He didn't have to be into work till later in the day. Finally, she picked it up and pushed the speed dial.

"Hullo?"

"Hey," Jen said.

"Hey, yourself. How did the audition go?" He hadn't said a word against the idea. He wasn't the type of guy to threaten or cajole. But he knew if she got the part it would be the end of them. And that's what she hadn't been able to face.

"I didn't go to the audition."

"What?"

"I skipped out of town early. I'm on my way home."

"You don't say," he said.

She thought she could detect a lighter tone in his voice. Well, that would change momentarily. No point in wasting time, let the guillotine fall and get it over with, she thought.

"There's something I need to tell you. I should wait. I shouldn't tell you on the phone, especially while I'm driving."

"Are you breaking up with me?" he asked. "Did George Clooney ask you to marry him or something?"

"No, and stop joking."

"Well, I wasn't exactly joking."

She glanced at the passing scenery. A billboard let her know that there was a Stuckey's five miles ahead.

"I'm pregnant," she said.

Utter silence. She waited.

"Damn," he said, finally.

What could she say to that?

She knew she'd be doing this on her own. If she did it.

"Damn," he repeated. "I'll have to buy another helmet, I guess. Do they make carseats for Harleys?" Jen pulled over to the side of the road and put her head on the steering wheel.

Lolly stood outside the building looking through the glass doors. Inside there seemed to be some sort of banquet. She knew she was supposed to be in there. Someone had to organize things. That was her job. Make sure everyone knew where to sit. Make sure there were plenty of vegetarian meals for the vegetarians and meat dinners for the meat eaters. And wine. Was there enough wine at the tables? People milled about. They were laughing. Lolly bent lower so she could see around a potted plant. A young woman with dark shoulder length hair kept glancing at the doors as if she were waiting for someone.

Nicole woke up from the nap that Aunt Jewel had insisted that she take. She'd been staying in Lolly's guest room since she got out of work release, waiting, she realized, waiting for her life to really begin again, waiting for Lolly to die.

She came into the hallway and glanced in Lolly's room. The nurse was checking Lolly's IV. One of Lolly's work friends, a woman named Sue, sat in the chair beside Lolly reading a book.

Nicole walked in.

"She open her eyes?" Nicole asked.

Sue looked up from her book and gave Nicole a sad smile. She shook her head. Neither of them said anything else. Nicole could hear the TV going in the living room. She had tried to call Jen's motel room but they said she'd checked out. And the cell phone message said she wasn't in service range. The doorbell rang. She heard Aunt Jewel open the door and a man's voice. Then that attorney that helped Sonya came in. He looked at Lolly, ran a hand across her cheek, and sighed.

Nicole went to the living room to see how Aunt Jewel was doing. Some politician was giving a speech, but Aunt Jewel wasn't watching. She was staring at nothing, her lips cast downward, her eyes soft. Her old hand—a soft wrinkly sack of bones—was in the air, fingers slowly waving something away.

"I think she's going," Nicole said. "Do you want to come in?"

Aunt Jewel shook her head.

"No, she wanted to be with her friends in the end. I've already said my good-byes." She stood up and turned off the TV. "Life is so short. You let me know when it's over. I'll come in then and tend to the body."

"Yes, ma'am," Nicole said as if Aunt Jewel were her own Granny Hazel. Then she heard an engine running outside. She looked out the window.

Jen's truck gasped to a stop. She had driven the last twenty miles on empty, not daring to stop. Something was urgently pushing her on. The truck's tank was now dry as the moon and it wouldn't go another foot. But she'd made it to Lolly's. She got out of the truck and hurried to the porch. She opened the door, without knocking. Aunt Jewel gazed up at her and smiled sorrowfully.

"Thank God you're back," she said.

Jen followed Nicole to Lolly's room. The nurse was there along with Sue, who was reading from the Tibetan Book of the Dead. Jeremy stood on one side of Lolly, holding her hand. Jen took Lolly's other hand. Nicole leaned over Lolly and whispered, "Lolly, Jen's here. Your sister's here."

Lolly squeezed Jen's hand and opened her eyes.

Lolly saw Jen's face. There were tears in Jen's eyes. She wondered why. Then she heard someone laugh. It took her a second to realize the laughter was her own. Jen's face was replaced by the young woman walking toward the glass doors. The woman's face began to change and her dark hair grew gray. Suddenly Lolly recognized the woman. Lolly reached for the door, and it swung open effortlessly.

From the Journal of Nicole Parks

I guess this is what you would call the epilogue of my prison memoir. After Lolly's funeral, Jen got Lolly's house and most of the money left over from the benefit. She asked around to see if people wanted it back but none of them did. She decided to start a non-profit organization for helping artists, writers and theater people put on arts programs for people in prison. She hired me to work with her writing grants and that sort of thing. So that's what we did. She married that police detective and had a little girl baby, but she continued to work in the prisons and wherever else she could. We made a documentary that won a few awards.

I went on and finished college. Six years after Lolly died, I wound up back in prison. But this time I only go in for a few hours at a time, and when I do I take a stack of poetry in there with me and some other kinds of writing and I sit around with a bunch of women who look at me like I've just brought ambrosia to their barren tables. And I think about Lolly and Jen. And you know, Sonya comes to the class, and she shows me pictures of her little boy. Her husband put all his ill-gotten gains into legal fees to get any charges against him dropped. She says he brings the boy to see her sometimes. She's still with Panther, and they're both supposed to get out next year. They say they're planning on staying together forever. It's hard to predict what will happen but I'm betting on them making it. Alice got out. I hear it's taken a long while for her to adjust. Mostly I got a new crop of 'em and they are still giving me an education.

You're probably wondering about my love life. Well, I had a few wild oats to sow, and there was a certain wide receiver who played for the university and has since gone on to the NFL who almost had me playing wifey, but I didn't want to be in his shadow. So we parted ways. And then... Mr. Junebug came back in my life. He is kind and good and spoils me rotten.

Right now, I am currently in the process of planning a most spectacular wedding. We're getting married in May, and Jen's daughter, Hope, is going to be my flower girl. I wish Lolly could be there. When she died, I kept a pair of old pink slippers that she used to wear. I wear them a lot, and I think about her nearly every day. But Daffy will be there, and so will Lucille, so I guess in a way Lolly will be there because each of us who knew her carries a little bit of Lolly with us wherever we go.

Jen has promised to make a bouquet of white flowers for me from Lolly's garden. I imagine when I toss that bouquet into the air, Lolly will be there to catch it if only for a moment before she lets it fall into someone else's hands.

About the Author

Trish MacEnulty grew up in Jacksonville, Florida. She attended the University of Miami and the University of Florida, where she received a bachelor's degree with high honors. She went on to get a master's degree and a doctorate from the creative writing program at Florida State University where she was awarded a Kingsbury Writing Fellowship and a University Dissertation Fellowship. A former addict who spent seventeen months incarcerated in a women's prison, she later developed and facilitated arts programs for inmates and at-risk youth. In addition to three other novels, a short story collection, and a memoir, she has also written an award-winning screenplay, inspired by her experiences within the justice system.

Apprentice House is the country's only campus-based, student-staffed book publishing company. Directed by professors and industry professionals, it is a nonprofit activity of the Communication Department at Loyola University Maryland.

Using state-of-the-art technology and an experiential learning model of education, Apprentice House publishes books in untraditional ways. This dual responsibility as publishers and educators creates an unprecedented collaborative environment among faculty and students, while teaching tomorrow's editors, designers, and marketers.

Outside of class, progress on book projects is carried forth by the AH Book Publishing Club, a co-curricular campus organization supported by Loyola University Maryland's Office of Student Activities.

Eclectic and provocative, Apprentice House titles intend to entertain as well as spark dialogue on a variety of topics. Financial contributions to sustain the press's work are welcomed. Contributions are tax deductible to the fullest extent allowed by the IRS.

To learn more about Apprentice House books or to obtain submission guidelines, please visit www.apprenticehouse.com.

Apprentice House
Communication Department
Loyola University Maryland
4501 N. Charles Street
Baltimore, MD 21210
Ph: 410-617-5265 • Fax: 410-617-2198
info@apprenticehouse.com • www.apprenticehouse.com

CPSIA information can be obtained at www.ICGtesting.com
Printed in the USA
LVOW11s1611050516

486865LV00009B/858/P